Ink Saves Lives When

Undead Rise

A Reverse Harem Romance

Midnight Arcanum Academy

Book 1: Ink Saves Lives when Undead Rise

Book 2: Don't Upset the Necromancer's Pet

Book 3: Sticks & Stones Make Werewolf Bones

Book 4: Beasties that Roam Can't Go Home

RAE STAPLETON

1

MIDNIGHT WITCH

Zombies and Sacrificial Slayings. That was pretty much the news headline every single day now. Like most people, I had no idea why the dead were rising, or what had caused it. All I knew was that my mother was gone and I wanted her back.

Now.

Well, technically yesterday, but now worked too.

And this was the reason for my visit to the magical coffeeshop. Well not just mine. Julep Delphine—my mother's best-friend—was by my side.

We'd been informed that this café held the entrance to the Supernatural Headquarters where the Grand Poobah of the New Orleans Supernatural Society reigned. That's right, we had a whole magical society with a council and a police force and the entrance was apparently right through this cafe. So bizarre. Even more curious was the fact that this supernatural council was headed up by my mother's sister, Aurora Batavian. I was beginning to feel like my whole life was a lie. Back before the séance and my mother's disappearance, I thought most of what Julep said was just

3

hocus pocus. I mean we live in New Orleans. Gris-gris dolls, potions and talismans are our birthright. But I didn't really believe it, not the way the Delphines did. Turns out I should have… because it was all true. Witches, magic, even necromancers are real. Crazy right?

I've learned so much in the last thirty days from Julep. She, unlike my mother is a practicing witch and so she's been teaching me the basics of magic, something I should have already been taught. But since Mama opted out of the craft to lead a normal life, I was now off to a slow start.

I glanced down at my phone, speed reading through the latest theory by another supposed expert in the field of zombies. So far, there'd been everything from a disease-causing virus to a doomsday apocalypse. Eventually, they all came to the same conclusion: Black Magic.

According to the supernatural police force, the corpses were raised by and under the control of some necromancer. I thought about the man in the cemetery, the one who'd saved me on graduation night. The shadowy lurker had seemed so dangerous at the time and yet he'd helped me. Could he have been the necromancer? Why else was he hanging out in the cemetery? Then again, we'd also been there.

And just who was this supernatural police force? Chills trickled down my back. Maybe, just maybe, this team could help me find my mother—that is if my Aunt, the Grand Poobah couldn't use her connections to do it.

As Julep and I peered through the glass of the Café, I took in the familiar vampy furniture, voodooist art, and tourists who jammed the place, loading up on cookies, scones, and pastries. I had a vision of this café once, on my birthday. I'd envisioned zombies attacking. Then it actually happen. Tension knotted the muscles between my shoulders and I studied everything with wary eyes.

Oh, how rude, you have no idea what I'm talking about and we haven't been properly introduced. I'm Evangeline Seraphina Midnight and I'm a witch. I know, it's hard to believe because just one month ago I was just your average teenage girl, getting ready to graduate high school and go to university. It's a lot to process even for me so let's back the story up so I can set the stage for you.

***

One Month Earlier

I wasn't some teenage weirdo desperate for attention and hard up for every dude's touch. I didn't wear low cut tops just to put my boobs on display in the hopes that my crush would notice me. And… I also wasn't normally into, let's call it what it is—pervy behavior.

So why the hell was I flexing and touching myself under the cafeteria's table, while staring at the hot dude across the room. It's not as if my school's muggy, fried-food-scented cafeteria was the most sensual of spaces.

Hot damn! I am a weirdo. I groaned to myself, pulling the offending limb back up, above board, and wrapping it around the energy drink in front of me. I closed my eyes as I lifted the can to my lips wishing it was Zephyr Milano instead. The bubbly sweetness hit my tongue and tingled at the back of my throat not unlike…

No, Stop it, Evangeline! I scolded, pulling myself from my naughty fantasy.

The truth is I was just doing it out of distraction, and I hated that. *Stupid Jeremiah with his bright blue eyes and cheeky grin.* He was sitting at the table across from me—which I certainly think he chose on purpose since his tongue was stuck down some freshman's throat. This time last week, it had been my throat he'd been probing which sounded kind of gross now. Anyway, he'd totally dumped me yesterday via text—such a douche move. And so, now I was ready to show him. To be honest, I'd had my eye on this other more mysterious guy, Zephyr, long before Jeremiah slipped in and distracted me. The only reason I'd even gone out with Jeremiah was to get Zephyr's attention which hadn't worked.

Zephyr was way hotter and never dated anyone.

No one really knew him all that well and yet everyone liked him.

Most likely because he was a challenge, and that made him exotic. He made me feel like there were bats in my stomach—that's right we don't do butterflies in New Orleans.

"Hey Evie!" I turned to see a grade nine student standing behind me, holding his laptop open. "Can I sit?"

"Course, Logan," I said, patting the bench next to me. Thank goodness he hadn't been there a minute earlier. I'd been tutoring Logan in science for the last year. He was better with oil pastels than a beaker, and we'd bonded over our love of art. I loved drawing tattoos and he loved drawing fantasy game creatures, eventually it morphed into him teaching me to play games which really didn't interest me but Logan didn't have a ton of friends.

"You don't have to ask permission to sit with me, you know?"

He looked at the screen where a video game with dragons and slayers was open. "Well, most seniors don't want to be seen with a freshman."

"Oh, really? Someone should tell Jeremiah that," I pointed my thumb like some transient hitchhiker at their gross display of PDA.

Logan screwed up his face in mutual disgust. "That's my neighbor. She still sleeps in Trolls pajamas."

I shook my head. Not an image I wanted in there.

"You wanna play?" he nudged the laptop just as the bell went.

"Sorry. I don't think I'm a very good slayer of beasts."

He smiled, "Well, at least your improving. You've been tutoring me for what, like a year now and I still barely passed my last science test."

"I hope that's not true," I said.

"Hey Nerd! What cha doin'? Boring Evie with one of your little geek games?" I looked up to see Barnabé Perry and his football buddy, Carter Ross leaning against the cafeteria table. "Leave him alone, Barnabé." I held up an open ketchup packet, "or I'll use you for target practice."

"I'm just kiddin', chère, you know me." Barnabé said with a grin.

Carter's girlfriend, Harper Jones leaned forward. "Hey Evie. Hey Logan. Ignore the cool kids. They're just being obnoxious."

"What else is new?" I smirked and rolled my eyes.

Barnabé affectionately swung an arm around my shoulders. "So, chère! You comin' to my party after grad?"

Barnabé was tall and slim with an Adam's apple that

sat in the middle of his throat like a golf ball. All the girls liked him because he was rich and played sports but for some strange reason, he wouldn't leave me alone.

I sucked in my cheeks and felt a pit of anxiety form in my stomach. Barnabé was fun—way too much fun if you asked his father, the mayor. They were constantly doing damage control, especially around election time. I preferred hanging out at the tattoo parlor, listening to music and drawing. And yet, I would have considered going to the party if Zephyr was gonna be there.

"Hello? Earth to Midnight." Barnabé hip checked me as he sat down on the bench.

"Oww…. sorry. I don't know," I said, closing my notebook and shoving it hastily inside my backpack. Not an easy task with Barnabé half sitting on it. "I don't know. Maybe. I have this work thing first." I stood up slinging my backpack over my shoulder.

"What? But the wicked witch shop closes at like six."

"You mean the Wicked Witchery," I clarified, referring to the occult shop downtown where I worked. "It closes at eight, but that's not the work thing I'm talking about."

Our other friend, if you could call her that, Twila Olsen approached and waved. Great. I was slowly being outnumbered by the high school douche bags. Twila, especially was a pain in my ass. Some days, I just wished she would fall out of existence.

"Oww!" Twila picked herself off the floor. "What was that?"

Carter howled with laughter. "Did you just trip over your own feet, Olsen?"

"Whatever. Anyway, Evie, you should just call in sick," Twila Olsen said, obviously having eavesdropped on our conversation.

The Wicked Witchery was owned by my mother's best-friend, Julep and her mother, Grand-mère Zoe. Twila knew this because we'd been close friends once upon a time. "You don't think Julep will notice that I'm not at home? I live in her house, remember."

"So, what's she gonna do to you? You're moving out soon, right? Heading off to the spooky Midnight plantation before university…ooohh," she replied, throwing her voice like we were sitting by some silly campfire.

I rolled my eyes. Twila was over the top. "Yeah well, I kind of like not pissing off my mother's best friend." I ran my fingers through my dark hair and then turned to go.

"You're afraid of her, aren't you?" Twila circled me, using a ruler as a wand. "Guys, Evie's afraid the old witch will hex her. Hocus pocus, skewer the worm! Boil the bats and watch Midnight squirm."

Barnabé Perry and Carter Ross roared with laughter at her stupid antics. Harper looked at me with pity.

"Knock it off, Twila," I growled. Deep breath, Midnight. High school is almost over, and then you never have to see these assholes again. "Listen, the Delphines may be eccentric, but they're also a lot of fun and anyway, lots of people practice witchcraft these days," I retorted. "This is New Orleans."

"Okay. Don't get so serious," Twila poked me in the shoulder and I was tempted to poke her back—in the eye with a knitting needle.

She suddenly held a hand over her eye.

"What's the matter, Twila?" Harper asked.

"I don't know. I'm getting a headache."

"Maybe that witch hexed you for making fun of her?" Carter suggested.

I turned my angry stare on him and he put his hands up in surrender. "Whoa! Easy, Midnight!"

"Anyway, why don't you come skip with us. We're gonna head to the cemetery?" Twila chirped as if she hadn't just earned my wrath.

"Sorry. Can't," I said. "I need to get to history class. If I'm late again, old dragon-breath is going to fail me."

"Nothing he can do now." Barnabe interjected, "The grades are in, Midnight. Loosen up."

"Yeah, still, I'd rather not tempt fate. Another year in this hell hole and I'd probably slit my wrists. See ya," I said and headed for the cafeteria doors.

2

MIDNIGHT WITCH

E vangeline, you awake?" Mama's voice rang out the following morning. "There's a pot of coffee down here fit to wake the dead."

I set aside my sketch book and flipped over on to my back, staring up at the white cypress ceiling medallion of my room. "C'mon, doll. If you're gonna hoot with the owls, you need to soar with the eagles. It's your big day." That was her way of saying if I were going to stay up late, I still had to get my butt out of bed early.

Little did she know, I'd been up for hours thanks to this weird dream I'd had about her. Ever since, my nerves wouldn't let me get back to sleep. So, I'd sketched out three Viking-style rune tattoos. I'd even drawn one in pen on the back of my hand. Of course, I'd have to scrub it off. It wouldn't exactly go with my fancy dress. Today was commencement day, the day I said goodbye to high school forever. The clock might as well have been ticking backward. Apparently, I wasn't alone—my bestie, Cricket Duvall had messaged me three times already, demanding that I ditch my plans for tonight's grad party.

"Evangeline Seraphine Midnight! Will you answer me already, child? You are giving me gray hair," Mama hollered.

Like she'd know if she had a gray hair. Mom was way too vain to miss a coloring. She was always changing her hair color and she could pull it off too—pastel pink, mermaid green. The woman's skin practically sparkled and she wouldn't even wear a one-piece, insisting it was like giving up and buying a mini-van.

"I'm up!" I croaked and planted my feet on the floor, noticing the tattoo I'd drawn on my foot was almost completely gone. I'd only drawn it yesterday after my shower. Weird that it had rubbed off already. It sort of looked like a spider web in the shape of a beetle and it was encircled by all these cool Nordic runes.

"Good." I could hear Mama's footsteps come halfway up the stairs. I stuck my head out my door in time to see her sashaying back down the stairs. The macabre fairy skeleton on the back of her thigh in full display. Mama was the queen of attitude and she always looked the part. She turned back and smiled. Her pearly whites sparkled almost as much as her skirt which was thankfully offset by the grungy black rocker tee, "See you in an hour. I have to stop by the parlor for a quick consult. Oh, and I'm dropping Julep off at the shop so it'll just be you and Grand-mèrc here."

"Yes, ma'am," I hollered back. "If you're gonna be near The Witchery, would you swing by Café du Monde?" I loved it when Mama let us eat beignets for breakfast. She was kind of a health nut so most of the time it was egg whites and sprouted bread. *Gag.*

"Yes, fine. I'll bring back some freshly-made beignets. Be dressed when I get back. I mean it, Evangeline... don't you make us late for that salon appointment!"

I started to text Cricket back but my thumb accidently brushed the Pinterest app and it opened back up to the page on ink. I was always perusing the thing for inspiration, not to mention, just biding my time until Mama would let me get another real one. Not that she'd approved of the first one. I'd sort of practiced on myself—a geometric moon goddess tattoo that I thought turned out pretty damn good—if I did say so, myself.

I scrolled through the page. Apparently, the app thought I'd like this multi-headed dog and I did. It was actually pretty similar to a few of my sketches. *The hound of Hades guards the Underworld to prevent the dead from leaving.* It would look amazing on my ribs. No way Mama would let me get it for real though. *Sigh.* I'd have to just use pen for now and maybe some clear nail polish to make it last. Julep had taught me that little trick. Of course, I'd have to hide it. For some reason Mama now objected to me even wearing my pen drawings at the parlor. I guess my artwork embarrassed her, although I didn't know why. Mama, herself was covered in ink and everyone else said my drawings were really good.

Her tattoo parlor, *Blood Magick*, was one of the best in New Orleans and I couldn't wait to follow in her footsteps. I used to be her apprentice, which meant a good portion of my day consisted of tracing and drawing. Sometimes, she let me help the other artists out, setting up and breaking down stations, and, of course, tattooing on grapefruit was a big part of my weekends. But not anymore. She sort of put me on probation after I tattooed that geometric moon goddess on my forearm. Now I worked at the occult shop downtown for Julep and Grand-mère Zoe Delphine.

"Oh, Evie… one more thing."

"Yeah…"

"There's a gift down here for you—no peeking!" I could practically see her smile as she said it.

A gift, eh? Well, now I was up for sure. I reached down and grabbed my faded blue jeans off the floor. I couldn't wait to see what she'd gotten me. My own tattoo machine, maybe? There was no harm in looking at the size of the bag, right?! If Mama really didn't want me to peek, then she wouldn't have told me, duh. Fingers crossed it was a new set of wheels!

I'd been pestering her for my granddad's shiny,

tuxedo-black '67 Chevelle since I got my license almost a year ago. She'd inherited the mean-looking muscle car with the red interior when her parents died but she refused to drive it because it reminded her of a giant coffin. Perhaps, a troublesome thought since we'd just stuck her parents in theirs. Or maybe, she just preferred two wheels to four—as in her motorcycle.

My eighteenth birthday wasn't for another month but maybe, just maybe, she'd decided to surprise me early. I threw on a bra and soft, black tee and hurried down the stairs. *Could you fit a new car in the kitchen?* No, that was ridiculous but maybe the bag held the keys! I could hardly contain my excitement at the thought.

The usual aroma of Murphy's oil soap was overpowered by the nutty scent of flavored coffee and it sharpened as I rounded the corner into the kitchen. It was still popping and crackling away. Mom must have put on a fresh pot of chicory for me. She was always doing sweet little things like that. I paused only for a moment to glare at the percolator then turned my attention to the gift bag on the island. It couldn't hurt to peek while I waited.

Then suddenly a chill ran through me.

People around here took "the shudders" seriously. Oh well, maybe this was just one of those rare cases where a chill was just a chill. Still, it made me nervous. Grand-mère

Delphine said to always listen to your gut. She said that she'd ignored hers once before and still regretted it to this day.

I could hear voices coming from the mudroom, so I crept closer—maybe they were talking about my new car.

"That reminds me." It was Julep, speaking. "This came for you the other day. Sorry."

I peeked around the corner and saw my mother frown as she shrugged on her leather jacket.

"Who's it from?" Julep asked between bites of muffin, crumbs tumbling down on to her flamboyant outfit. Julep was a little extra. Her day-to-day look varied, but you could count on her to be some sort of cross between a hippie, a street urchin and a gothic witch. The bright yellow vest reached almost to her calves and matched her oversized hoop earrings; underneath she wore a white T-shirt with a pentagram on it and under that, a long patchwork peasant skirt.

"It's my sister's handwriting."

Julep choked on her next swallow. "Oh, Briar, what does that queen bitch want with you now?"

"Oh, you know, only my first-born. She's been emailing me too."

"The hell she has. Tell Rumpelstiltskin she can suck it."

Mama chuckled.

"Seriously, what does she want with our Evie girl?" Julep replied indignantly. "Do you want me to open it or hex her?"

"No, you know my sister. Tattooing makes me unfit to stick to the gum on her high-and-mighty shoe."

"Well, they are Louboutins."

"Touché. She just doesn't want the same future for Evangeline—not that I can blame her."

"Briar, my dear, you are racking up points in Heaven talking sweet about her, and that's the blessed truth."

"Naw, I'm no saint. I—"

The kitchen door smacked shut. *Damn!* They'd left and closed the door behind them. I really wanted to hear the rest of that conversation.

"Evangeline, *bébé*? That you?"

Abandoning my plans to snoop for the moment, I walked into the back parlor and found Julep's elderly mother, Grand-mère Delphine on the sofa. Clad in mustard linen pants and a crisp white and blue printed blouse, her long silver hair pulled up into an updo, she was watching the news with a cutting board perched on her lap. The Delphines were like family to us including the cat, Bakeneko who was nestled in beside her. We'd lived with them in this Victorian Italianate for as long as I could remember. Bakeneko's glossy black fur caught the soft light in the room, and I had the overwhelming urge to stroke him. Bakeneko had that effect on me. Grand-mère said he bewitched us so we'd forget that he was a tiny psychopath who constantly left half-dead animals at our door.

"My sweet girl." She removed her glasses and wiped the thick lenses on the hem of her blouse. "What day is it?" Grand-mère Delphine was second-sighted—combine that with her age and she was more likely to scramble her days than her eggs. She still gave readings at the Witchery though, so I took that as a good sign. Everyone from thrill-seeking tourists to experienced practitioners came looking for candles, occult books, voodoo dolls, and psychic readings from her.

"It's graduation day, Grand-mère." I reached down to give her a hug good morning and a shudder slipped loose.

Grand-mère looked at me, concerned, and drawled, "Someone's walkin' on your grave."

"Nah, don't be silly, Grand-mère."

She pursed her lips. "Shudders. I don't like it."

"It was nothing. I'm just cold," I said, eyeing the ginger and herbs on the cutting board.

"It's impossible to be cold in Louisiana, girl."

"What exactly are you doing anyway?" I asked, changing the subject.

"Peddling my drugs… what's it look like, sugar?"

I snorted. Mama always joked that Grand-mère was

the Tinkerbell of Voodoo Kingpins, selling batches of fairy dusted herbs to the neighbors.

"It looks like you're makin' gris-gris bags for the Witchery."

"That I am. That I am. We got some brides comin' in this weekend looking for some party favors." She chopped some more and then carefully packed up the completed pouches. "You all set for the big day then?"

I nodded, "Yep, excited to graduate and even more excited to work at the parlor this summer. I'm hoping Mama will let me come back." I shuddered again.

"Hmph…something's not right," Grand-mère said, shaking her head. "Just not right." She pulled a safety pin out of a box on the table and then took a tiny black bag that smelled like anise and pinned it inside my tank top above my heart.

"Oh please, Grand-mère. I am so not in the mood for love these days."

"It ain't for love."

Feeling uneasy, I looked at the old woman as the phone rang. "Then what is it for?"

"Protection," she said grimly, "from evil."

Grand-mère was superstitious to say the least, so I nodded and left the pin in place. When she got these thoughts in her head, she'd do and hang all sorts of crazy things. One time I took a doll out of my drawer that she'd placed there and she about had a stroke. Since then, we all agreed it was better to leave her special charms in place.

As I headed back toward the doorway to grab the phone it stopped ringing and she said, "You were on the other side, you know? The waterfall. You were knock-knock-knocking on heaven's door." She started to sing an old rock tune that Mama always played. Randomly breaking out in song was just one of the old woman's kooky quirks. She stopped suddenly, growing agitated. "Well, answer me, child! You experienced astral projection, didn't you?" Grand-mère let go of the knife, her long fingers clickety-clacked against the cutting board.

"I had a dream, is all. You're reading my mind," I replied. Grand-mère often talked nonsense but she was correct that I'd had a dream about a jungle waterfall.

"Nope. Nope. Nope. It was real. You went to the place between worlds. The veil. The border. The other realm. It has so many names," Grand-mère said, her voice wavering as she spoke.

Suddenly the anchorman caught Grand-mère's and my attention with the words *missing dead*. She fumbled for the remote and turned up the volume.

"The New Orleans Police Department is asking for the public's help solving a grave robbing incident that happened Friday night. If anyone has any information about the incident, please call crime stoppers—"

"It's a sick, sick world. Isn't it *bébé?*" Grand-mère said, turning the volume back down.

I nodded, trying to ignore how the story made me feel. I turned to go but she reached out and grabbed my wrist. "Evie, you shouldn't be able to go to the waterfall. Only the dead should be traveling the astral plane."

"Why?"

"Because Evangeline, don't you understand that you're faking your death when you go there. You're removing your soul like it's some sort of soiled coat. There are so many reasons why this is dangerous. For one thing you're leaving your body just hanging out—unprotected. Secondly, you never know who's gonna hitchhike home with you. Ghosts— the bad ones—they wait for their chance. Don't be a fool, girl. They are restless, and they will wait for the hell hounds to look away, and then they run! They run for that golden waterfall and they follow you back to Earth. You're like a key that opens the door for them. No more explorations over there. Only the dead belong there, okay?"

"But… but that doesn't make any sense. It must have been a dream. I saw Mama there." I glanced back to see her scratching her head. "You said that place is not for the living, did you not? Well, Mama's not dead." *Oh, my goodness.* I paused in my thought. Grand-mère appeared to be thinking as well. Was it a premonition? "Does that mean my mother is going to die?"

"You certain it was her?"

"Yes."

She grimaced. "Let's hope not."

I nodded, swallowed and hurried back into the kitchen. That had not been a very reassuring answer. Grand-mère had begun mumbling, "what's she getting herself into now," and her eyes had gone white like she was having a vision. It was always best to leave her be when she went into a trance so I left the room. I grabbed an apple out of the fruit bowl on the counter and a paring knife from the drawer.

Might as well eat something while I teased myself with the pretty, pink-striped bag. I carved off a piece of apple and popped it into my mouth. That big red bow was just begging to be untied. Before I knew it, I'd set the knife down and was carefully moving the tissue paper aside. Inside was a wooden box. I unclipped the clasp and let out a sigh. Now this didn't look like a tattoo machine or a set of car keys.

It was a silk bag.

Carefully, I removed the object from the bag and laid it on the table.

A mirror?

What good was a mirror that was all black? I picked

the knife back up and sliced off another hunk of apple, carelessly slicing my thumb in the process. *Owww!* I dropped the knife with a thud and stuck my thumb in my mouth like a giant baby.

Suddenly the room was spinning. When I looked down, I noticed I was dripping blood onto the mirror but before I could wipe it away, my vision went squirrelly. I could see the kitchen around me but something else was coming into focus as well, almost as if the two spaces were partially transparent and layered over one another. I could see my feet now but the shoes, they weren't mine. Distantly, I heard Grand-mère's voice from the other room, but my eyelids had fallen closed.

When I opened them, the coppery smell of blood hit me like I'd just stepped inside a morgue, but this was no morgue. It was a coffee shop.

3

THE FIERY TEMPERED BEAST

P olice cars strobed the city's street with blue and red lights. Baudoin Remoussin, looked over at the alpha boss, Demas Batavian—a scholarly professor by day, a guard dog by night and the brains of their team. Neither of them spoke although it was obvious what they were thinking. Radio silence from the New Orleans Police Department (NOPD) wasn't unheard of but it didn't usually warrant the presence of their tracking unit unless supernatural citizens were involved. Words like vampire hive, werewolf pack, faerie attack and zombie uprising were an automatic rollout for the Society's special attack dog unit.

Bodhi looked out the window and then looked back over at the professor. The man was so tall that his head almost touched the roof of the jeep.

"Where are the uniforms, and why aren't they answering?" Bodhi felt a tingle of fear grip his body. There was something apocalyptic in the air.

The professor rolled down his window and sniffed. "You smell that?"

Bodhi didn't have wolf senses like Demas but he'd

caught the hint of decay as well. It was coming from two different directions. The building in front of them and the café down the street. "Definitely zombies, boss. It's got to be him."

"It could be vamps," Eleutian Dupre III suggested, always seeing the glass half full.

"No, vamps are better at hiding the smell. Right, Zephyr?" Bodhi looked back at their young vampire team mate who laughed good-naturedly at the jab. After serving alongside each other in Hell's guard unit, the small group of friends could get away with that kind of ribbing.

Bodhi and Demas were first to exit, followed by Eleutian, Colten and Zephyr. They checked the two police cars in front of them and found them empty.

They say opposites attract, or at least work well together, and that was true for this motley crew of five. The former hounds of hell, disgraced and booted from the underworld for allowing a powerful necromancer to escape, were now back in their human form living topside, tasked to protect humanity by hunting down the supernatural monsters of the world until and unless they could correct their mistake. Then, just maybe then… they would be reinstated. They were only missing one team member, Grimm. Even thinking of him, hurt Bodhi's heart. In hell, they'd been one and now it was like there was a piece missing. He was either dead or he'd betrayed them which made him as good as dead. Bodhi felt his inner dragon start to rage. He tamped it down and forced himself to focus. Demas had warned him not to run that hot in public. The last thing the council needed was people panicking over a fucking dragon in the city.

"It looks like they chased them in here." Bodhi pointed to the building directly in front of them.

Colten Ryu, a no-nonsense ginger-haired gargoyle with broad shoulders and shit-ton of pent up aggression must have smelled the decay too, his posture stiffened. He was quite possibly the toughest of them all, a street savvy ex-assassin, always ready to pounce, with great reflexes and a high pain tolerance. Bodhi could attest to the pain high tolerance especially since he'd watched his psychotic brothers torture him. They'd chained him in a dungeon and forced him to fight in their underground clubs. Bodhi had been the one to free him and they'd went on the run. Guarding hell's gate had been a breeze for Bodhi compared to growing up in the shadow of the mafia.

"Do you want me and the high school hunk to flush them out?"

Zephyr, the youngest of the unit gave Colten an elbow to the ribs. Being a vampire, he'd been just fast enough to get it in. Despite his fast reflexes and sharp teeth, he rarely needed to resort to violence to get his way, his café-au-lait coloring, washboard abs and vampiric allure made him an asset in the art of seduction. Which is why he'd been the one to go undercover at the local high school. They'd caught a whiff of Grimm there though it hadn't panned out.

Bodhi adjusted his weapon, "We go in. We have to assume that the officers are hurt. You and Zephyr take the lead, we'll be right behind you."

Colten and Zephyr had just entered the building when a scream sounded, high and piteous, from the alley down the street.

"Lou!" Demas called to the blond-haired mage who preferred arcing magic to blazing guns and wielding knives. "Back the men up—"

"Yes, Sir." Eleutian nodded, obeying his Alpha's command. After all, he was a good ole southern boy who did as he was told—mostly.

Demas turned to Bodhi, but he didn't have to say anything, Bodhi was already charging toward the café. There was another scream and the two men ran faster. Somehow Bodhi knew the undead would be in the same direction as the scream.

***

MIDNIGHT WITCH

Zombies! Monsters!" a woman screamed.

"They're coming!" screamed another.

My heart shot into my throat, and shocked cries rippled through the café. *Calm down, Evangeline.* I told myself. *You're just dreaming again.* Lately, all sorts of weird things had begun happening to me. Not just the dreams or the astral projection as Grand-mère had called it, but also when I'd thought of something, it happened. I wasn't one hundred percent sure if I was some sort of telekinetic freak or just ready for the psych ward.

I took in the details of the coffee shop's interior—a mix of aged wood, red velvet, and large pieces of strategically placed voodooist art.

I yanked my earbuds out to listen, momentarily wondering when I'd even put in earbuds? The woman sounded nearby—perhaps one street over.

"The dead have come back to life! Zombies!"

The café around me was suddenly filled with nervous chatter.

Zombies? Roaming the streets of New Orleans? How absurd.

The woman shrieked again, and I saw her from where I stood inside the internet café, running from the direction of the park, her face white and eyes huge. Following her were in fact the walking dead.

The corpse closest to her was skeletally thin, a gaunt pale hand reached out as it moved in halting steps, and stumbled to a stop like a drunk at last call. Its skull gleamed where chunks of skin and hair were missing. I felt chills as it rotated toward the café. Its sockets were empty, and yet somehow it sensed us. There were others, each in varying stages of decomposition, and they also slowed and turned to face the café.

The second corpse chasing the woman staggered closer, more coordinated with a certain grace, like a marionette. It wasn't quite as decomposed so likely it was more recently deceased. Whatever the reason, it was unfortunate for the woman running. When at last the zombie was only three feet away, it lunged, both hands outstretched.

The scruffy boy beside me lost it. His shrill voice was barely audible in the panicked crowds. "Get out—move!"

But I couldn't. Baristas and customers alike pushed and heaved to look out the glass front.

My breathing turned shallow. Adrenaline bubbled inside me as I closed my laptop and backed up against the wall. A business man's elbow jabbed into my ribs, and I almost dropped my computer.

I took a fortifying breath and shoved off the wall,

aiming for the STAFF-ONLY entrance. Once I reached the door, I pushed through another and slammed it shut behind me. My muscles shook and I had to lean against the door, but I was safe. I could ride out the storm here. The kitchen had led outside. I scanned the tiny alley.

Long moments passed. The screams and pelting footsteps outside didn't fade. This could be a long wait, but at least I was protected from the stampede.

A cell phone pinged loudly from my pocket and I snatched it out. It was a mass emergency alert: "Walking Dead Seen Escaping Holt Cemetery. Take Cover."

The date was wrong.

Hell, come to think of it, the cell phone was all wrong. I pushed it back into my pocket. This had to be a joke. A bad dream, maybe? Thanks to the news story about the grave robber.

And that was when I noticed the smell. My hands froze around my laptop. I lifted my gaze with deliberate caution and met the decomposing irises of a corpse at the entrance of the alley.

I shrieked and clambered backward, trying desperately to get back inside the café but the door only opened from the inside. Why had I come outside? What the hell had I been thinking?

I felt for my shoulder, a bag rested there. I opened it

and rifled blindly through the contents. A wallet, water bottle and car keys. Nothing to defend myself with.

Shit! Shit! Shit!

Panic gripped me, and I fought to maintain control, but it was no use. I was just a girl. How the hell was I supposed to fight off the fucking walking dead. Whimpers burst from my mouth as I flipped back around to face it. I lifted the laptop deciding my only hope was to bash it in the skull when I noticed that its arm was fully extended, but not in a menacing way. It was trying to give me something, but it was having trouble because its fingers were so stiff. My legs wobbled, and I pushed shakily forward taking a sheet of paper from its hand.

"Thank you," I whispered, unsure of what to say to a corpse that had not only spared my life but given me stationery. *Did they make greeting cards for that?*

In a slow, convulsive move it turned and shambled away.

Seconds passed and still I could not seem to breathe. Why hadn't it hurt me?

I unfolded the paper until the words were clear.

My breath hitched as I read it: *Sorry, I disappeared. Be home as soon as it's safe.*

And that was all it said, except for *Love Mama* scrawled at the bottom. When I flipped it around, it was blank aside from some dirt and a stationery crest that I didn't recognize.

Even though the zombie had moved on, the stink lingered, so perhaps there were more waiting outside the alley. I was trapped—

I heard a loud bang like a gun shot and then a wooden bolt flew through the air—not far from my head.

My heart jolted, and my whole body jumped with it. What the devil was that?

The vision slammed into me along with a realization. I wasn't really here. I could see parts of the kitchen around me again. I parted my lips to say something, but what could I say?

"Hey!" A darkly handsome man with bad-boy looks and skin that I could have sworn shimmered like scales shouted at me. He had a tattoo on his forearm, the multi-headed guard dog I'd seen on my phone. He pointed his gun at me while the man behind him aimed some sort modified crossbow. I had to be dreaming.

"Who are you?" he shouted again. "Are you the one controlling these things?"

Three more of his men appeared in a blur behind him. My mind grasped to make sense of what was happening. *They could see me?*

Suddenly, the men were wiped from my view, along

with the alley outside the coffee shop.

My heartbeat galloped faster than the headless horseman on Halloween.

I was back in the kitchen.

Holy shit!

Mama was right to have warned me. I never should have peeked in that present. I grasped the counter for support.

Mama! Oh, Goddess, Mama!

No. Settle down, Evangeline. The paper wasn't meant for me. My mother was with Julep, but that made no sense.

Kicking myself for not looking in a mirror, I suddenly wondered whose life I'd just glimpsed.

As if reading my thoughts, Grand-mère strolled into the room, "Up to no good, huh?"

I looked up. Still in shock. She smiled at me, now completely lucid and headed for the coffee pot. It was strange how fast her behavior changed, like a pendulum—Mama called it her cognitive function and said it was declining because Grand-mère was getting older. Julep said it was a side effect to being a seer. I quickly shoved the mirror back in the giftbag. She whistled to herself as she filled two mugs and I looked around the kitchen. Anchoring myself once again, I let my eyes focus on all the knick-knacks that the Delphines had collected over the years. Both Julep and Grand-mère hoarded

35

tacky souvenirs—the uglier the better.

I was so lost in thought, I jumped when Grand-mère pushed a cup towards me and said, "Drink up. It looks like you need it."

I pulled the mug towards me and took a sip.

"What's with the zombie gaze?"

I coughed, almost spitting out my coffee. "Zombie – "That had a caught me off guard.

"You look stunned, child," Grand-mère interrupted. "What happened?"

I took another sip before replying, "I-I don't know. I guess I'm just nervous about giving a speech today. My cell phone's alarm went off and I remembered that Mama would be back soon. Anyway," I cradled my mug and hurried for the doorway. "Thank you for this, but I really should get ready. I have a hair appointment to get to."

"Evangeline Seraphine Midnight!" she yelled.

Too late. My feet were already padding up the stairs.

4

MIDNIGHT WITCH

The roar of applause filled my ears as I delivered the final line. I'd done my best to overcome my nerves, delivering an inspirational valedictorian speech without picturing anyone naked, worried that I'd magically strip them in the process. I'd only had a little trouble when my eyes had landed on my least favorite history teacher.

The sound of the Principal clearing his throat reminded me to join my fellow students so that the academic procession could make their exit. I'd barely managed to walk off the stage before I was drenched in sweat. These robes were overkill. Wait, don't think about the word 'kill'. *Ugh. I was so hot.* That led to thoughts of fire. The other students didn't seem to notice that I was mentally melting down. They were all too caught up in getting out of the gym and celebrating.

"So, tonight we *fais do-do*?" Barnabé Perry said, cocking an eyebrow from beside me.

"Yeah. You comin' to the Perrys tonight, Midnight?" Carter echoed, leaning forward from Barnabé's other side.

"I promise to offer you a little *lagniappe*." Barnabé said with a grin as he elbowed me in the boob.

Harper turned back from the row in front of us and whispered, "And by that, he means booze and drugs."

"What else is new?" I smirked and rolled my eyes.

Barnabé affectionately swung an arm around my shoulders. "Stop worryin', *chère*! You worry too much. It'll be fun, I promise."

"Yeah, I don't know. I promised I'd help out at one of the Delphine's séances tonight. I guess the family who hired them, the Badeauxes are friends of Mama's or something, so they requested our presence."

"Councilman Badeaux? He's friends with my dad. They're into hoo-doo?"

"Yeah, I guess his wife is really into the occult."

"Cool, but it's graduation and you deserve to celebrate."

"I'll maybe come out after the séance. Text me later."

"Promise to come?"

"Oh, you and Cricket…you guys never give up! Let's just get through this ceremony first," I said, wishing the teachers would hurry up and exit so that we could. "Do I really look all right?" I asked, fixing my hair.

"Sweet as honey," he replied automatically.

"You're not even looking at me."

He smiled that big old Howdy-Doody grin and turned up the southern boy accent. "Oh, yes, darlin', I am. I am always lookin' at you."

Soon, the students were starting to move row by row. Unfortunately, I'd reached my boiling point. Like for real, I'd started to imagine smoke rising from a garbage can. It was time for air. With the way my week was going, I'd set the high school's gym a blaze.

There was a flutter of voices behind me as I butted into the aisle out of turn and raced outside of the auditorium.

Mama found me a couple minutes later by the fountain. She strutted up like she owned the place. Nothing new there. "Oh Lordy, there you are. You gave me an awful fright. What's wrong, sugar? Why'd you run?"

I jerked up from my forward bend. I couldn't bring myself to tell her the truth. "Sorry, Mama." I offered her a small smile. "Overwhelm… you know, with the crowd and the heat and the thought of leaving you and everything."

Mama wrapped an arm around my back and I gasped. Her grip was tight but comforting. She was always surprising people with her strength. "Oh, honey, I understand. I remember what it was like, but you'll meet new friends and you'll still have us. Anyway, we have the whole summer before you move into your dorm. And we're gonna have a blast at the Midnight Estate. Your aunt has gotten the guest house all fixed up and ready for us, and eventually we'll move into the mansion."

My lips pursed at the mention of my grandparent's antebellum mansion on the Mississippi River. I'd hardly known them. I'd seen pictures of them as well as of the Plantation that was just thirty minutes outside of New Orleans. Both looked terrifying. The mansion was the kind of place you imagined draped in Spanish moss. You know the type: plenty of white columns with the bones of ghostly soldiers poking through the makeshift graveyard out back, alligators prowling the nearby swamp. Although as far as I knew the plantation had none of those things. My grandparents simply hadn't approved of my mother's choices and so we hadn't spent much time with them. At least they hadn't disowned her like the rest of the family. They'd been uptight socialites, the kind who threw big lavish parties. We weren't their glass of bubbly, as Mama liked to put it. We had seen my aunt on occasion, although not for a long time. Her and Mama had had some sort of falling out that they'd only just squashed. From what I could remember, she was tall and thin. An image of Nicole Kidman flashed in my mind, only with slightly darker hair.

When my grandparents passed last year, Mama inherited the estate but we'd yet to visit. She was too busy pretending they hadn't died. I think she lived with a lot of regret, not that she'd talk about any of it. Aside from saying that Aunt Aurora took care of it all so she didn't have to.

"What's the matter, honey? You curled your nose up like you smelled rot." Her comment reminded me of this morning's zombie incident once again. I toyed with the idea of telling her that I'd snooped and found that magical mirror, but chickened out.

"It's nothing Mama. I just don't remember your parents all that well. And from what I remember of Aunt Aurora—she played with me like a doll."

Mama laughed, "Oh yes, I remember that... until she grew bored that is. She stuck bows in your hair and you'd rip 'em right out, just as soon as her back was turned, and those shorts." She laughed so hard tears came to her eyes. I couldn't help but laugh too, "you remember, *mon ange*, you'd wear the shorts under those frilly skirts she bought you then you'd strip the skirts straight off after dinner and run outside to play in the trees. I just laughed and laughed."

"Hey, there you two are," Julep said, coming outside to join us. She'd changed into a mauve swing dress which was tame for her taste and she'd pulled her dark wavy hair back with a beaded scarf that had most likely come from Grand-mère's closet. "You missed the most hilarious wardrobe malfunction. Remember that history teacher, the one with the bad breath who always picked on you?"

I groaned. "Tell me his pants didn't fall down."

"What? How did you know? That man was always right good at embarrassin' you. Nice to see the tables turned, that's for damn sure. I took a picture." She laughed and held up her phone. "Speaking of which, let's get a few more so we can go to dinner."

I bobbed my head like the teeter-totter I felt like I was on today.

Mama and Julep exchanged a look when Mama's phone buzzed. "It's her," Mama grumbled, typing away. "She wants us to attend."

"Her, who?" I asked.

They both ignored me.

"No," Julep shook her head. "This is your daughter's big day. Tell that highfalutin' snob she'd best be waitin' until our girl is out of her cap and gown."

"Who, Mama?"

"Oh, just a client, dear."

Julep continued to grimace, "Ain't nobody need her bossy ass around—pardon my language—plus, you need to have that talk with Evie first."

"What talk?"

Mama gave Julep a dirty look as she turned to me. Something was definitely up, "It's nothing darling, we'll save it for later, okay?"

My stomach rumbled with nervous energy. Had they noticed my kooky behavior, after all?

"Come on, snuggle together, now," Julep said with a wave of her hand.

For a moment, holding onto my mom with a big grin on my face as Julep clicked away, everything was perfect. All the weirdness faded away.

"Oh, shoot. I forgot my purse inside. You didn't grab it, did ya, Julep?" Mama asked.

"No, I thought you took it with you. My mother is still in there, anyway. I should help her out. We'll be right back, honey," Julep said, taking off inside after Mama.

I sat down on the side of the fountain to wait. Unfortunately, I started thinking about how out of control I felt lately. Boom! I exploded into tears and the water fountain right next to me did the same.

A chunk of the concrete flew through the air just as a guy walked by, and at first it looked like it would miss him, but at the last moment, the boy disappeared underneath it.

"Help!" I screamed.

The guy had been hit - I was sure of it - he'd been hit - he was surely dead.

"Did you see that?" I asked, frantically looking around for Mama and Julep. I fully expecting to see a dead body, but the boy was standing right in front of me, dusting off his pants. He was whole and unhurt.

"You should be dead," I whispered.

"Excuse me?" he asked, a quizzical smile on his face.

I was a little taken aback - I recognized him. The tanned skin, short black hair and dark brown eyes that held small flecks of yellow. It was my crush, Zephyr Milano.

Maybe I was dreaming. Maybe I just thought I'd seen him get hit with the debris. That had to be it. I was just tired.

"I haven't seen you around school lately," I blurted awkwardly.

"That would be because I don't actually go there anymore. I graduated last year, although I was helping one of the teachers for a bit this semester."

I licked my lips and nodded. When had my mouth gone so dry? It's not like he was some super tall model or something. Why was I drooling over him like this? But oh, that mouth. That sculpted mouth that made my knees weak with something entirely different than nervousness. And that night-dark hair—my fingers itched to weave themselves into its softness. That lithe, flat-muscled body, and that chest. I stared at his chest. I couldn't take it anymore before I knew what I was doing, I reached out and placed my right hand on his pectoral muscle. Yep, it felt just as good as it looked. He glanced down and smiled. Okay, so it was definitely just my imagination. He had totally not been hit by the fountain. Holy shit. What was I doing? "Sorry." I pulled my hand back before I began caressing him, "I like your shirt. It's soft." Oh, damn that sounded so stupid.

"It is soft," his grin widened, "my pants are soft too."

Ahh! Was this guy for real? What a cheesy line and I was still totally into him. He smelled like testosterone. He smelled like everything I ever hoped a guy would smell like and I just wanted to rub myself all over him.

"Your different," he said, squinting and looking me over like I was under a microscope. "There's something… about you."

He leaned in and I suddenly felt afraid that he might see the real me.

I shook my head, though I knew he was right. Even when I was little, I knew I wasn't like everyone else."

"I'm normal," I blurted out the words like a damned fool. *What was wrong with me?*

He laughed. "I'm just headed over there," he explained, motioning to the café next door. "You wanna come? We were obviously fated to run into each other today."

"I'd love to," I blushed. There was something about this guy that just made me want to rip my clothes off, "But I have this whole graduating thing to do."

"Right. You're a busy, absolutely normal girl. I get it.

Go on then, break my heart."

Oh hell, he was flirting with me. "Thanks, anyway."

"If you change your mind, I'll be there," Zephyr said, smiling and showing his bright white, even teeth. "I'm buying."

Before I could respond, Mama, Julep and Grand-mère materialized at my side.

"Is everyone okay?" Julep asked, her eyes wide. Car sirens were going off in all directions from fallen debris and I realized only now that I was dripping wet.

Zephyr waved as I turned my head to look back. "See you around, Midnight," he said, pulling up the collar on his jean jacket and walking in the opposite direction.

I shook my head. The buzzing in my ears subsided the further away he got. That boy did something to my senses.

Julep frowned and stared off in the distance at him, then she nudged Mama.

"Earth to Evie!" Mama said, tugging my arm. *Why was everyone always saying that to me?*

Julep waved us on to her Jeep—Mama's motorcycle wasn't exactly practical for our family outings.

"Sorry about having to get in your vehicle wet...the fountain was a mistake," I blurted when we finally reached the Grand Cherokee.

Mama gave me a puzzled look as she climbed into the backseat with me. "What do you mean a mistake? It's not like you made it explode."

"Actually, that's exactly what happened. I made that fountain explode. It's been a heck of a day." I paused for a minute to take a deep breath, "Don't be mad, okay?"

"Evie… just spit it out."

I sighed, feeling rather dejected. "Fine. It started when I opened your present. I know, I know you told me not to…" I rushed to explain, "but I did and it made me travel into someone's else's body in the future or something!"

"What do you mean the present made you travel into a body? You hit somebody?"

"No. Like astral projection or whatever."

"I have no idea what you're talking about. Your present is right here in my purse," she said and removed a small box that jingled suspiciously like keys, "and as you can see, it's still sealed."

"But you said it was downstairs…"

"It was downstairs."

"What about the striped bag with the bow?"

"Oh, that present wasn't from Briar, *bébé*," Grandmère chimed in. "That one was from me."

"What did you give her, Zoe?" Mama asked, suspiciously.

"What? She wasn't meant to open it until you'd talked to her."

"Why don't we discuss this at dinner," Julep said, turning back to give Mama a look I didn't understand. "Evie, which restaurant would you like to go to? It's your special day."

"I can't go to a restaurant like this." I retorted indignantly. "I'm wet."

"Well, we can stop so you can change."

"No, we won't have time. Besides what I have to tell you all is crazy."

Mama lifted one eyebrow, a quirk I tried to mimic but couldn't. "An exploding fountain, huh? What are you a terrorist now?"

No, just a time and space travelling nutball. I thought to myself. Taking a deep breath, I decided to go for it. "Whenever I think something lately, it happens."

"Oh sweet goddess, your stupid sister was right." Julep whispered.

Mama bit her lip but said nothing.

"I'm a freak of nature." I continued.

"Let me guess. You thought about the fountain exploding?" Mama asked, gently.

"Actually, I felt like I was exploding… with emotion. But that is what happens lately."

For a moment, they all just stared at me, then they exchanged a look.

"Oh, honey. You're not a freak, I promise," my mom wiped a finger underneath my eye. "You are special though. It's a family trait."

"A family trait? Things like this happen to us because we're Midnights?"

Mama paused as if she were going to explain but then decided against it. "We're magical, honey and unfortunately, magic isn't something we can just rip out of our hair like a bow." She leaned forward, "Take us home, Julep. We'll order pizza and Evie can changed before the séance. We'll celebrate this weekend instead."

***

THE HORNY TEENAGE VAMP

Zephyr watched the girl from school walk away. She ran her fingers through her hair as she moved and his dick throbbed like a cartoon character's thumb after a good accidental nailing. That was the second time this week, he'd contemplated stealing a way with her to a bathroom or a broom closet so he could bury himself so deep inside, he'd need a map to find his way out. There was just something about her but he couldn't put his finger on it. He'd seen her at least five times before—always staring at him. Like she wanted to devour him right back. And he was totally game but he also knew she might just be a regular high school girl and if that was the case then it wasn't right. He didn't like taking advantage of innocents. They were powerless to resist his lure. Now Supernatural beings on the other hand, he had no problem with. They knew what he was and what they were getting into. But he didn't know if she was one or not. She seemed magical and yet not.

"Milano?"

Zephyr closed his eyes, ignoring his stony-faced partner, Colten Ryu. He didn't want to face reality. Didn't want to talk about the fucking necromancing nightmare or the walking dead. Thinking about Evangeline Midnight just felt too good.

"Dude. What the fuck?"

"What?" Zephyr said, opening his eyes at last.

"We gotta go! Team meeting, remember? Bodhi will set your ball hairs on fire if we're late again. Or are you too busy falling in love?" Colten traced his fingers down Zephyr's stomach, mimicking Evangeline's moves. Then batted his eyes soulfully.

"Jealous much?" Zephyr shot back. "And anyway, you'd make an ugly chick."

"How dare you! I'm beautiful." Colten pretended to preen and then attempted to punch Zephyr playfully in the gut but Zephyr saw it coming and spun out of the way.

"Too slow. Time to go."

And they marched across the road to the cafe. Zephyr's mood growing heavier with every step away from the pretty girl.

5

MIDNIGHT WITCH

E veryone just loves the macabre, don't they?" Julep's client, Jilaiya Badeaux said as she dramatically closed the velvet drapes, thrusting the parlor—where Mama and the Delphines were setting up for the séance—into near darkness. She spoke so fast and curled her tongue so often that it took me a minute to catch up to what she was saying. When I didn't answer, she turned and laughed. "Am I speaking too fast? I was raised in India and although I've lived here for many years, I tend to revert to what's comfortable."

I smiled. "It's okay."

"I'll try to slow down."

"Do you miss your home?"

"You mean India?" she asked, linking her arm around mine like we were school girl friends.

I nodded.

"Not really. I'm happy here. My daughter, Pepper on the other hand, well, she loves it there. Come now, let me show you my collection of Madhubani paintings before we get this séance started and maybe we'll stumble upon her. She's just your age, you know." She tugged me to the left and we started up the marble staircase.

"She lives here?" I asked.

"Actually, she lives in India most of the time with her grandmother, but she's visiting for the summer or she's supposed to be. I'm sure it won't be long before she finds an excuse to leave us. I'm afraid we don't get on all that well," she said as we reached the top of the stairs.

The Badeaux's home was large and sterile like a museum. There was lots of white marble and stone columns. Her private sitting room, on the hand was warm and inviting. Strung over the furniture like blankets were silk saris and pashmina shaws, and on the table was an assortment of exotic tea. The floors were covered in Oriental rugs and the windows draped with thick, scarlet drapes.

"You're surprised?" she asked, as I walked to the fireplace where a small, cozy fire burned.

"Well, yes. It's very different from the rest of the house."

"You think of it as a house," Jilaiya said with a chuckle. "It's more like a giant mausoleum, or so Pepper complains. Speaking of which, let me go check her suite."

While Jilaiya went to look for Pepper, I wandered the room examining her paintings, and handcrafted puppets, I ended up before a shelf admiring a hair accessory, I'd seen Julep wear in photos. She'd told me once that it represented the third eye and gave her the ability to control emotions.

"Do you like that?" Jilaiya asked. I hadn't even heard her enter the room.

Smiling, I turned toward her and nodded.

"That's called a maang tikka." She picked it up and laid it against my forehead. "It looks beautiful on you. It used to be traditional bridal wear in India but the vintage appeal has made it main stream these days. Too bad we didn't meet sooner, it would have been perfect for your graduation ceremony today."

I smiled, politely and took the clip from her hands, admiring it before placing it back on the shelf. "Did you give Julep something like this once?"

"I did." Jilaiya moved to my side, and motioned me to a pair of rose-colored armchairs beside the fireplace. "Please, sit. Katherine will be right in with champagne."

"Oh, thank you but I'm underage."

"What?" Jilaiya insisted. "Poppycock! It's only champagne. We must celebrate your graduation!"

As we crossed to the seats, I noticed a collection of portraits over the fireplace. One was of her, one was of her husband, Councilman Louis Badeaux, and one was of another couple with a baby. A dark-haired man and a light-haired woman.

"Who is that woman?" I asked, dropping into a chair as she eased into the other. Something about her reminded me of Grand-mère Delphine. Bone structure, perhaps.

For a moment her shoulders seemed to droop, and when she didn't reply, I worried I'd committed a faux pas. But finally she spoke, "That's Louis's older brother, and that is his family with him. She gave me a sad smile. "They've all passed on now—an accident. Sarah was like a sister to me— my closest friend in all the world. But… she's gone. Sad really, they're all gone. They're the reason I'm holding this get-together."

"Oh, I'm sorry for your loss."

"Don't be. We all lose the people we love at some point or another. That's life, but I would like to talk to them one last time."

Right then, a gray-haired woman in black and white bustled into the parlor with a tray of champagne. The crystal flutes rattled, as she walked.

Jilaiya removed one from the woman's tray and extended it toward me, her face lined with annoyance. "Please accept my apology for Katherine's nerves. Anything to do with the occult scares her."

"That's all right." I smiled reassuringly at Katherine. "The occult is supposed to be scary, but there's nothing to worry about. The Delphines are professionals."

Jilaiya nodded in agreement and motioned for me to take the glass. "Now tell me about yourself? What are your hobbies?"

"I like to draw."

"You do? An artist, just like your mother! Will you tattoo like her, then?"

I nodded. "I hope one day, yes! May I ask why you requested my mother and I come. I mean, it's so nice to be included but how do you know her and our family?"

Her lips quirked up happily. "I think that's a question best saved for your mother, dear, but I promise"—she tilted almost conspiratorially toward me—"I'll see that she tells you."

I fidgeted with my hands.

"Now, let's cheers to a fun night, shall we?" she clinked her flute against mine and tipped her glass back finishing the whole thing.

When I'd done the same, she pulled me to my feet. "It's almost time for the charades to begin."

When we returned downstairs, the sofa and armchairs in the parlor had been pushed to the walls. Everyone was seated around an enormous oval table at the center of the room and munching on cheese and bread.

Shadows billowed from the candles, and the Ouija

board shone under their light. The candles I knew were meant to attract the spirits, but the way they flickered across everyone's faces was unnerving, even to me. I couldn't imagine how the maid, Katherine felt. She stood in the corner vibrating softly in what I assumed was fear.

Jilaiya took her seat near her husband at the head of the table beside Julep; Pepper Badeaux beside her father; followed by Grand-mère, Mama and me. There was one empty chair which I guess was meant for our ghostly guest.

"Tonight, we shall commune with the other side in an attempt to conjure our loved ones," Julep stood in front of her seat as she spoke in a low voice, her head held high. "In order to do this you must take the hand of the person next to you."

"Ooooohhh, the ghosts are coming."

"Pepper! Knock it off!" Jilaiya scolded.

"Let us begin," Julep continued ignoring the girl's mockery, "we shall share energies and chant together in order to call forth the spirits of our loved ones." She lowered herself gracefully into her chair and extended her arms by example. "We will begin with Gabe Badeaux."

A wave of nods and whispers moved around the table.

Julep lowered her eyelids. "Gabe Badeaux, I am here with your brother, Louis and his wife Jilaiya. They call to you on the other side of the great waterfall. Commune with us, Gabe, and move among us."

The guests and I repeated her words for several minutes and waited, our eyes closed. Next, she tried his wife, Sarah.

Several silent moments passed, and then Julep led everyone in another chant. On the third round of chanting, Jilaiya decided we would move on, and try the Ouija board.

"Gabe!" Julep called once again, her face a mask of professionalism. "Are you there?"

Nothing happened once again. I felt bad for Julep. This séance was a bust. Perhaps, she needed a little help. I gave the planchette a little nudge—forcing it onto the "yes."

"Have you a message?" Julep gasped, excitedly.

Someone else forced the planchette over to the "no," and everyone twittered. Suddenly, the planchette shook and flew out of our hands, landing on the floor.

"Quickly, take up hands once again," Julep said. "Ghosts don't like interference." She looked at me when she said it. *Busted.*

Mama's hand was sweaty, but I held it, squeezing it to convey my fear.

A heavy, hollow bang rose from beneath the floor and with it came the smell of soil. *What the hell was going on?* In the course of a week, it felt like everything I knew was being challenged.

Thump! Another bang from below, and my whole body flinched.

"Gabe!" Julep exclaimed, her eyes enormous and filled with shock. "Is that you? Bang once for no and twice for yes."

Thump, thump!

Joy broke through Jilaiya's lips. "Gabe! You've come back." Her eyes sparkled under the candlelight with tears. "Is Sarah with you? Have you reunited with your son?"

The tension ratcheted as the room grew colder, and the thumps more insistent. Then the lamps began to rattle as if even they were scared. Someone let out a whimper from the corner and scurried from the room. Katherine, maybe?

Mama glanced over her shoulder to where the maid had been and then shifted uncomfortably. The wine and water glasses had all joined in now too like a symphony coming together.

Vapor suddenly puffed from my mouth and I wasn't the only one. Eyes darted around the table, but none of us dared to break the chain. *What would happen?* Would it leave us vulnerable or would it stop this charade?

Thump!

More banging!

"Oh, Gabe! Louis and I have missed you, Sarah and

Mel too." Jilaiya's smile gleamed in the candles' glow. "Julep, please invite him into our realm already. I'm sure Louis would like to see his brother."

"No, Jilaiya," Mama said, interrupting. She freed her hand from my grasp. "I don't think that's a good idea. Something's not right."

Jilaiya blinked at us, I knew it was because of the candlelight but her eyes were like empty holes.

Pepper pushed to her feet. "I'm frightened!"

"Pepper, sit down and hush," Jilaiya shouted over her.

Thump, thump! The whole room vibrated now. It was unsettling to say the least.

"Gabe," Jilaiya called, "know that you are welcome in this house."

Pepper shook violently. She really was terrified.

"Mama!" I shrieked. "Let's go!"

Julep clasped her hands to her chest. "You are welcome to move among us."

"Enough!" Mama yelled in a voice that was strangled with fear.

The smell of rot and grave dirt intensified along with Pepper's whimpers.

The spirit had joined us.

Mama lunged forward and grabbed a candle. She lifted the flame high and scanned the room. "You're not welcome here. Go back!" she waved the flame this way and that in search of the spirit's location. "Go back!"

And then I saw it, crouched beside the door, an unnatural clot of black in the darkness—shapeless, sentient, and waiting. I was paralyzed as if time had frozen. Even the flames of the candles stood still.

Until it moved. Then my breath returned with such force that I crumpled back onto my seat. The darkness elongated into the rough shape of a man, but thinner and taller, with arms that stretched to the floor. I forced my body to move, my nerves refueled by terror. I picked up a candle and brandished it toward the evil, and the flame almost sputtered out.

"Leave," Grand-mère rasped. "You're not welcome here."

The shape undulated forward—reminding me of the New Orleans' Shadow Man– the top-hat wearing voodoo villain from that silly children's movie. But this was no silly trickster shadow.

And it was moving toward Mama and me.

Pepper screamed and fainted though neither of her parents noticed.

I gritted my teeth, the impulse to run away was strong but I couldn't break the circle.

"Brother!" Louis screeched.

"Gabe, oh Gabe!" Jilaiya moved forward, but Grand-mère bowed over the table and seized her by the arm.

"No! Everyone stay back." She held her back.

"You must leave!" I followed Mama's move and shoved the candle forward. The spirit paused. "Go back!" For a moment I thought I was victorious. Then the spirit rushed at me in a furious streak of black, and the cold consumed me. I tried to step back but it was too late. It was the coldest thing I'd ever felt—maybe because we lived in Louisiana where the temperature never got below forty, but the closest I could come to describe it would be to say ice has formed on the inside of my bones. Was the spirit entering me? I grabbed for my goddess tattoo with my free hand to gather power and strength and the feeling disappeared.

I turned to see where the shadow had fled to and realized it was only a matter of feet away from my mother, a shadow of death hanging motionless.

Then, faster than my mind could process, it was gone. Poofed from existence like the men from my vision earlier.

Julep and Mama were both collapsed in a dead faint. Pepper was awake again and sobbing in her father's arms. Jilaiya, on the other hand sat limp in her seat, draped across the table with her eyes closed.

6

MIDNIGHT WITCH

Cricket gave my hair an admonishing yank as she dragged the straighter down it, curving her wrist as she did so.

"Oww. Easy, Cricket. I'm attached to that."

"Sorry, babe. Your hair is waging war on me, and I can't allow it to best me. You know how it is. Gotta show it who's boss," she said, and tossed her own perfectly styled blonde locks over her shoulder. She'd spotted me as soon as I entered the party after the botched séance and hauled me into the Perry's humongous bathroom. Apparently, I looked as rough as I felt. Not that I could share any of what had just happened with my friends. Who would believe me? I was having trouble believing me, and I could still feel the demon ghost—malevolent spirit, or whatever it was as it went through me, leaving behind its icy tingle.

"Did you see that dress on Harper?" said Twila— bitchy as usual. She'd unfortunately followed us in here, chirping away and swaying to the music that drifted in from the other room. "She must have lubed up before squeezing it on and those cutouts. My God, what's she going to wear next? A tube top?"

"Two band aids," said Cricket smoothing down her tasteful one-shouldered eyelet dress.

"She should have spent more time on that frizzy head of hers." Twila added in a low voice, reapplying her bright-pink lipstick. "Speaking of which, I can't believe you brought your straightener to the grad party. It's like you knew Evie would arrive late and need styling."

"Huh?" I murmured absently, hearing my name. I tended to tune out when Twila bad mouthed people.

"What is with you lately, girl?" said Twila. "You are always daydreaming."

"Oh, sorry," I said flatly. Under Cricket's expert fingers, my hair was becoming a work of art, a soft mass of dark and twisted waves.

"There." Cricket put the last pin in my hair. "All fixed up. Let's go dance."

"What? And ruin this masterpiece? Hell, no. I'm taking a selfie and sitting in the corner for the rest of the night."

"Very funny," she said, and yanked me out of the bathroom. "I need an excuse to torture you with a touch up session later."

"So, you got your eye on anybody tonight, Evie?"

Twila asked smoothly as we headed outside into the kaleidoscope of color and activity that was the Perry's backyard.

I shook my head, secretly holding out hope that Zephyr would show up.

"If you're done with Barnabé, can I have him?"

I snorted. "Twila, you do whatever you want. Barnabé and I are just friends."

A whistle that sounded more like a cat call cut me off. I looked over to a group of guys who were eying us up like we were hot dogs at a stadium. Speak of the devil. We were instantly mobbed by Barnabé and his crew. In the dizzying whirl of bodies, I kept searching for one dark head. Sadly, I didn't see it.

Instead the guy next to me was breathing heavily, smelling of punch, Axe body spray and breath mints. I ignored him in the hopes that he would go away. Twila was already out on the dance floor, shimmering under the lights. But nowhere did I see Zephyr—and why would I? He'd told me he didn't go to our school anymore. I shouldn't be surprised that he didn't attend high school parties.

Ugh, one more whiff of that body spray and I was going to be sick. I grabbed Cricket's wrist and we hit the dance floor which had been cleverly constructed over the pool. It was time to force myself to have fun.

I threw myself into the whirl of color and music. I danced with everyone, laughing too loudly, and I even flirted back with Barnabé because let's face it, he was closest. His friends were around us, a shouting, laughing crowd. The mayor and his chaperones had disappeared and someone poured something from brown paper bags into everyone's punch.

Jokes flew back and forth, and I laughed even when they didn't make sense. Barnabé's arm circled my waist, and I just laughed harder. The girls were getting shrill, the boys rowdy.

"I've got an idea," Barnabé suddenly announced to the group, pulling me tight to him. "Let's go someplace more fun."

Somebody shouted, "Like where? Your dad's liquor cabinet?"

Barnabé was grinning, a big, boozy, reckless grin. "No, I mean spooky. Like the cemetery."

Barnabé's date was still standing outside the circle." Barnabé, that's crazy," she said, her voice high and thin. "I won't go there."

"Great, then, you stay here." Barnabé fished keys out of his pocket and waved them at the rest of the crowd. "Who isn't a huge chicken?" he said.

"Hey, I'm up for it," said Carter, and there was a

chorus of approval.

"Me, too," I said, clear and defiant. "Hell, I'd already seen the dead twice today." I smiled up at Barnabé, and he practically swung me off my feet.

Next thing I knew I was standing outside the cemetery watching Carter as he scaled the gates of St. Roch, and opened it from the other side.

We wandered for a good ten minutes before pausing. Harper, was having trouble keeping up in her skyhigh stilettos—not quite so practical out here. I was thankful I'd worn flats. Barnabé unzipped his backpack and pulled out a six-pack. "Let the real party begin." He offered me a beer, but I shook my head. My head was foggy enough. I was beginning to wonder if someone had slipped me a party drug earlier.

"Why don't we go inside that thing?" Harper said, pointing to the empty hole of the church doorway.

Barnabé wound his arms around me, clasping me to him backwards. I looked over to see Carter and Harper in much the same position, except that Harper, eyes shut, was looking as if she enjoyed him grinding his pelvis into her.

Most of the others had dispersed. I had no idea where they'd gone but I wanted to follow suit.

"I thought Cricket was coming. She's my ride home tonight."

"Don't worry. I'll make sure you get home."

I looked up at the moon. It looked supernatural, huge and red, hovering just above the horizon like a giant pumpkin. It reminded me of the zombies and the séance and I suddenly regretted coming out at all.

Won't your parents be upset that you left your own party?" I hedged. "I think we should go back."

There was a pause in the rubbing. Then Barnabé sighed and said, "Sure, babe." He looked at Carter and Harper. "What about you two?"

Carter grinned. "We'll just stay here a while." Harper giggled, her eyes still shut.

"This way, Barnabé said, tugging me. "I know a shortcut." And the next moment, he was leading me deeper inside the graveyard. "I just want to show you something first, honest, it's on the way. Look, there, you see that? That's my great granddad," He pointed to a creepy statue by a mausoleum.

The bright moonlight cast strange shadows, and there were pools of impenetrable darkness everywhere. I couldn't contain my shivering as a bat circled overhead.

"Poor baby, that dress is sexy as hell but it's not very practical, now, is it." He wrapped his arms tight around me and squeezed when I tried to push him away.

"Barnabé, I want to go; I want to go right now …"

"Sure, babe, we'll go," he said, but he didn't move.

"Barnabé, let go," I said. His arms around me had merely been annoying, restricting, before but now with a sense of shock I felt his hands groping for bare skin.

Never in my life had I been in a situation like this, far away from any help. I attempted to stomp his foot, but he evaded me. "Barnabé, take your hands off me."

"C'mon, Evangeline, my little ice queen. Hey, that rhymes." He started laughing hysterically at his own joke while I remained stoic. "Oh, I'm just joking. What's gotten into you? Here, let me warm you up…"

"Barnabé, let go," I choked out. I tried to wrench myself away from him. Barnabé stumbled, and then his full weight was on me, crushing me into the tangle of ivy and weeds on the ground. I spoke desperately. "I'll kill you, Barnabé. I mean it. Get off me."

He giggled. "You are so cute when you're stern." Then I felt his mouth hot and wet on my face. I was still pinned beneath him, and his sloppy kisses were moving down my throat. I heard cloth tear.

"Oops," Barnabé mumbled. "Sorry 'bout that."

I twisted my head, and my mouth met Barnabé's hand, clumsily caressing my cheek. I bit it, sinking my teeth into the fleshy palm. I bit hard, tasting blood, hearing Barnabé's agonized yowl. The hand jerked away.

"Hey! I said I was sorry!" Barnabé looked aggrievedly at his maimed hand. Then his face darkened, and he clenched the hand into a fist.

This is it, I thought with nightmare calmness. He's going to knock me out. I braced myself for the blow.

Then something moved. *Oh no, not a zombie.* Helplessly, I watched as the shape in the darkness moved out of the shadows and toward us. It seemed almost as if the darkness itself had come to life and was coalescing as I watched, taking on form – human form, the form of a young man.

"Get off her now."

The voice was scary.

Before he had a chance to do anything else, Barnabé was thrown from me. Knocked unconscious from the look of it.

I rolled to the side, gasping, one hand clutching my torn dress.

My relief was so sudden and complete that it was painful. I let the breath out that I'd been holding and looked up.

An ordinary guy stood over me, smiling faintly, as if amused by my reaction.

Well… perhaps not quite ordinary. He was a total babe. His face was pale in the moonlight, but I could see that his features were clearly defined and nearly perfect under a shock of dark hair. Those cheekbones were a sculptor's dream. And he'd been almost invisible because he was wearing black: soft black boots, black jeans, black sweater, and leather jacket.

He was still smiling faintly.

"Who are you?" I demanded. When he didn't answer, I stepped back. "Were you following us?"

"Well, that's a strange thank you, but to answer your question, no, I just like the cemeteries," he said. His voice was soft, cultured, but I could still hear the amusement and I found it disconcerting.

"I have two other friends out here," I said accusingly.

He raised his eyebrows and smiled. "I don't know if I'd call them friends, considering that they weren't helping you."

"Well, regardless, they should be coming any moment now," I said in the bravest voice I could manage.

"You're scared of me," he said gravely. "Even though I just saved you."

"I am not!" I snapped. I felt foolish in front of him somehow, like a child being humored by an older, cool kid. "I was just startled," I continued. "Which is hardly surprising, what with you lurking in the dark like that. It's not exactly normal."

"Interesting what you consider normal. I mean, what's a one-sided dry hump among friends, right?" he was still laughing at me; I could tell by his eyes. He had taken a step closer, and I could see that those eyes were unusual. As if you could look deeper and deeper until you fell into them.

I realized I was staring. Why wasn't he leaving? I wanted to get out of here. I moved away, putting a tombstone between us.

He was just standing there, unmoving, watching me. Why didn't he say something?

"Were you visiting someone—a lost loved one?"

I knew I should be grateful but he was still gazing at me, those dark eyes fixed on me in a way that made me more and more... hot. Why was I hot? I swallowed.

With his eyes on my lips, he murmured, "Oh, yes."

"What?" Could he hear my thoughts? My cheeks and throat were flushing, burning with blood. I felt so light-headed. If only he'd stop looking at me...

"Yes, I came here looking for someone," he repeated, no louder than before. Then, in one step he moved toward me.

I couldn't breathe. He was standing so close. Close enough to touch. I could smell a faint hint of cologne and the leather of his jacket. And his eyes still held mine – I could not look away from them. They were like no eyes I had ever seen, such a light blue that they practically glowed, and yet the pupils dilated like a predatory animal. They filled my vision as he leaned toward me, bending his head down to mine. I felt my own eyes half close, losing focus. I felt my head tilt back, my lips part.

No! Just in time I whipped my head to the side. I felt as if I'd just pulled myself back from the edge of a precipice. What am I doing? I thought in shock. I was about to let him kiss me. A total stranger, someone I met only a few minutes ago.

I swallowed. My nostrils flared as I breathed hard. I tried to keep my voice steady and dignified.

"I should be going now," I said. "I hope you find whoever it is you're looking for."

He was looking at me oddly, with an expression I couldn't understand. It was a mixture of annoyance and grudging respect — and something else. Something hot and fierce and protective that frightened me in a different way.

He waited until I started to walk away to respond, "I'm definitely close."

When I turned, I could see nothing in the darkness. Nothing but an owl.

7

MIDNIGHT WITCH

I t was too quiet. I stopped sketching and stared at the exposed brick of the kitchen wall, listening. The air conditioner whirred and there was the faint hum from the dishwasher, but there should have been noise from upstairs. A quick glance at the coffee maker confirmed that it was almost three in the afternoon. I'd had a doozy of a hangover this morning so I'd sheepishly rolled out of bed not that long ago.

Mom should have been awake by now. And even if she'd gone into work, she should have been back already. She never worked past two on the weekend.

I swiveled on her barstool, legs dangling, as I considered checking the driveway for her Kawasaki. Then I heard the distinctive creak of the floorboard in the hall, followed seconds later by the far-off squeak of the upstairs bedroom door. Huh? She must be home. I gritted my teeth and turned back to my sketchbook. I couldn't even remember a time when Mama had slept this late. That séance must have really exhausted her, either that or she went out after I left for the grad party. The lights had all been out when I got home and I just assumed everyone was fast asleep. Part of me wanted to go and bug her for sleeping in, but the other part of me didn't want to look her in the eyes after last night. I wasn't ready to tell her about Barnabé and the cemetery and yet I knew she'd guess that something was wrong as soon as she saw me. She could read me like an ice cream menu and she had those memorized—her one indulgence in life.

When I heard the side door five minutes later, I let out a small sigh of relief that I hadn't realized I was holding.

"I'm back," Julep called as she stepped inside the kitchen and plunked down two brown bags dotted with grease stains. "Hope you're hungry." She tossed her hair out of her eyes and put her hands on her hips. "Where's Mama and Briar?"

The aromas of shrimp po' boys and French fries filled the kitchen. "I don't know? I just got up about an hour ago. I figured they were with you," I said, squirming. "I did hear movement upstairs a few minutes ago." I reached around my sketchbook for a French fry so hot I could barely touch it. "Did you guys go out last night after the séance or something."

The floorboards at the top of the stairs groaned. Julep looked at me. "No? I was at work. You guys were all asleep

75

when I left, or so I assumed." Julep held up her hands. "Maybe I should go check on them." Her tone softened. "I was a little worried when we got home. The séance was a bit of a clusterfuck, and to be honest your mother seemed off. She actually went straight to bed—like when does she go to bed before the witching hour?"

Another noise from upstairs caught our attention. "Briar? Mama?" Julep called.

We paused, listening for her rapid descent—My mother always came down the stairs fast, whereas Grandmère was slow and steady, but it was absolutely quiet.

Julep raised her eyebrows at me. "That's weird. I can understand my mother ignoring us. She's partially deaf, but why isn't Briar answering."

I hopped off my stool and walked over to the staircase. Bakeneko, weaved figure eights between my ankles and I bent down to pet his silky black fur. "Were you sleeping in Mama's room?" Bakeneko just stared at me with ice blue eyes and flicked his tail. "Mama?"

"Evangeline? Is that you dear?" Grand-mère said, shuffling into view. She began to descend the stairs.

"Is Mama up there?"

"Heck no. She's been gone since early this morning."

"Early this morning?" Julep repeated, coming to join us. "What do you mean?"

"I had a nightmare and thought I heard the front door, so I got up and peeked inside to check on everyone. You and Evie were sound asleep but Briar's bed was made."

"Why didn't you wake us?" Julep demanded.

"What do you mean, honey?" Grand-mère retorted. "Why would I wake you? I just assumed Briar had somewhere to be. What's going on? Is everything okay?"

"I don't know. I've got a bad feeling inside," Julep said, and we all shuddered.

8

MIDNIGHT WITCH

One Month Later

And now that you're all caught up. It's time to get back to enlisting the help of my estranged Aunt Aurora of the New Orleans Supernatural Society's help in order to save my mother from this necromancer, or whatever doomsday apocalypse was happening in the world.

As Julep and I peered through the glass of the Café, I took in the familiar vampy furniture, voodooist art, and tourists who jammed the place, loading up on cookies, scones, and pastries. This was the café I'd envisioned when the zombies attacked. Tension knotted the muscles between my shoulders and I studied everything with wary eyes.

We pushed open the bright red door and walked through the charming little coffee shop, entering an elevator under the back stairs, that led down to the Society Headquarters. Julep trailed after me through the long, dark hallway that led to my aunt's office, where my courage abandoned me.

"So, this is all really happening? A secret magical society, wow," I muttered to Julep as we came to the door.

"You're not going to get hysterical on me, are you?" she gripped my shoulders to ground me, her layered braided wrist bands that were spelled with protections and charms jingled as she did. "We don't have to see your aunt. We can look for your Mama on our own, fo' true." Julep seemed to hold my aunt in contempt, for what, I wasn't sure.

"I appreciate that, really, but that hasn't worked so far." Julep and I had tried scrying with crystals and a map to no end. "The sooner I do this, the sooner we can find Mama."

Julep nodded and wiped away a tear. "Aurora does have connections." She sucked her teeth and cupped my cheeks between her palms. "Let's do this."

I paused as Julep opened my aunt's door reassuring myself that I would find her, no matter what. If this didn't work, I'd contact that supernatural police force I'd read about. The one, the city council had pulled together to hunt monsters. See if they could help me find Mama.

Aurora was on the phone, but waved a cheery hello in our direction, then motioned for us to come in. She was not quite what I remembered—certainly not Nicole Kidman as I'd pictured. Although she was regal in her business suit and definitely the antithesis of my mother, who was slightly shorter with bright hair, curves and too many tattoos to count.

A minute later, she hung up the phone and greeted me. "Evangeline, dear. How nice to see you." She shocked me by coming around the desk and gathering me in her arms. "I'm so glad we didn't lose you too."

We broke apart, and I started to sit down in one of the open seats.

"Oh, don't sit just yet, dear."

She reached across her desk and pressed a button on the intercom. "Is the car here?"

"Yes, Madam Batavian. It's waiting."

"Perfect. Tell the driver we'll be right there, and let Demas know. Please, follow me," she said, as she pressed a button under her desk, opening the doors behind her.

"Where are we going?"

"To my car, dear? It's right this way."

"I thought we were having a lunch meeting."

"We are. We'll eat on the way. Is that okay?

I looked at Julep and we both nodded and followed Aurora down a hallway to a parking garage where a stretch limo was waiting. Her driver opened the door for us and Aunt Aurora motioned for Julep and I to enter first. The limo was some sort of magical anomaly like the underground parking garage, or it had to be, at least in my opinion. No regular car—limo or no—was this big. I mean, there was a dining table between us.

Her assistant appeared with menus, as if we were at a drive-thru and took our orders. Part of me wondered if she had a kitchen down here, or if she too wielded magic of some sort.

A moment later she returned with our drinks and three bowls of crawfish etouffee—similar to gumbo, and the limo began to move. I cradled my soda and cleared my throat. "So, have you heard from Mama?"

She hesitated, "No. I'm looking but there's been no sign of her."

"However, it's been a month and we need to discuss your living arrangements. Your mother and I had plans for you this summer."

I couldn't help but raise my eyebrows at the comment. "Since when did my mother make plans with you about my life."

"Since you turned eighteen and came into your powers, but that's beside the point. You know she inherited our parents' home, right?"

"Sure. The decrepit old mansion on the Mississippi."

"The estate," she said with emphasis, "has been in the family for hundreds of years: the house, the grounds, and the gatekeeper's guest house. There is also a trust that is entailed to the property."

"Okay. What does this have to do with me?"

Aurora sipped her tea. "The plantation belonged to Daddy's family. Both the property and the entailment must be passed on to blood relatives. Since I was the result of an indiscretion on Maman's part, the estate went to my half-sister Briar."

"And you're not bitter about that at all, now are ya?" Julep quipped.

"Don't be silly. I loved Briar—rebellion and all. Of course, not everyone felt that way. The Badeaux side of the family tree were a little more than miffed. They felt that your mother should have to forfeit her rights as heir to the estate."

"Badeaux? You mean Jilaiya?" I asked, picking at my nail polish—a nervous habit Mama hated. "Why would they have a say in my mother's life?"

"Why, because we're related. Jilaiya Badeaux is the daughter of Odeo Midnight. Your great-uncle."

I looked to Julep. "Did you know this?"

Julep sheepishly nodded her head. "Your mother was going to tell you at dinner before we went to the séance but then that explosion happened with the fountain and, as you know, our conversation focused more on your magical talents and what you'd been experiencing."

My stomach churned.

"Why did they feel she should forfeit her rights as

heir?"

Aurora paused. She looked thrown by my question

"It was because your mother gave up her magic," Julep answered for her.

"Anyway," Aurora went on, "Daddy was a huge believer in family and he refused to disown your mother as the rest of the family did."

I didn't want to be disloyal to Mama but I was often angry with her now, not only for seemingly disappearing from my life when I needed her most, but for the fact that she had chosen to turn her back on who she was—denying me my own magical upbringing.

We paused for the next few minutes to slurp and chew our lunch in silence.

After Julep had finished, she said, "So, *chère*. Quit beatin' 'round the bush. You goin' to try to take the house from Evangeline now that Briar's MIA, or what?"

Aurora opened up the large leather purse she carried and pulled out a file. "No! How could you insinuate such a thing, Julep Delphine? Get this straight in that squirrely head of yours, you might not see fit to like me, and that's fine, but know that I love my sister and her girl just as much as you do." She took a deep breath and turned to me, smoothing back her hair. "I apologize for my outburst. This is the deed to the house and that's where were going right now."

"To the plantation?" I questioned.

"I thought you'd want to see it in person. With Briar missing, the Badeauxes could come sniffing around. I wanted to make sure you had it. You are Briar's heir and, therefore, it's yours. Your mother intended for you to live there this summer anyway." I snatched at it and flipped it open.

Inside was the deed, along with a photo of a dirt-smudged little girl holding a furry little weasel—a real one. I stared at the photo taken in front of the manor.

"What are these?"

"Those are some old photos that my father kept. He cherished his visits with you."

"What is that I'm holding?"

Julep took one of the pictures from me, "That was your mom's pet for years but he ran away."

"What is he—a weasel?"

"No, I believe he was a black-footed ferret. Very rare in the world of polecats—they're almost extinct. Your Mama loved him so."

I picked up the other photographs—they were of a massive Greek-Revival mansion. It had two dozen columns that brooded against a backdrop of mighty oaks and Spanish moss. I looked through each of the photos, studying the different angles.

This was mine now. It felt unreal, like something out

of a movie.

"I really am sorry, my dear. I wish I'd tried harder to spend time with you and your mother. I was really looking forward to spending more time with the both of you."

The back of my eyes burned, but I had to stop shedding tears. I'd done that for almost four weeks straight now. Snapping the file shut, I forced myself to think.

"There's something else you need to know." Aurora said, "Nobody has been inside since Daddy died. Well, I've been to the guest house but not the actual mansion. Gran won't let anyone in."

I was about to ask her about Gran when I accidently touched the corner of the photo. It burned and I pulled my hand away.

"Are you okay?"

I nodded and stared at the offending image. The house had changed ever so slightly right before my eyes. It now looked like a puzzle that was out of sync. I rubbed my eyes and the picture righted itself.

Huh? I looked up at her and raised an eyebrow. "What do you mean, Gran won't let anybody in?"

Aurora let out a soft laugh. "I don't know how else to say it. It's a strange place. You would have to experience it to believe it."

"N'awlins is a witchy place, Evie. You know this,"

Julep said.

Aurora nodded her agreement. "Yes, it's intensely magical with more portals than anywhere else in the world."

"Portals to where?"

"Why to anywhere and everywhere. Anyway, there isn't a portal now, at least not a functioning one," Aurora clarified. "It's broken, and the house has a mind of its own."

I grinned. "You're punking me?"

"'Fraid not. Growing up there was interesting, to say the least. For one thing it's haunted by my grandmother. We all called her Gran. She's got quite the sense of humor, and a temper—always blowing bulbs and shattering windows. For another, there are apparently faeries and secret spell rooms. This, according to one of my friends growing up—a seven-year-old girl who got lost in here and claimed a faerie tried to pull her through a magical mirror. Now, I'm not calling her a liar but no faeries ever played with me." Aurora said, sounding rather bitter.

I looked down at the photo, drawn there like a magnet. Large, proud and oddly shadowed, the house looked like something out of a vampire movie. I thought I could see a ghostly image peeking out of one of the windows just as we came to a stop.

The motorized partition lowered and the driver turned back to us, "We're here Madam. Shall I pull in?"

"Yes, please. Hold onto your gumbo, ladies. This drive can get a little bumpy."

A moment later, and two near spills. The driver opened the door and we all climbed out, stretching our legs.

The place was just as I'd imagined, dirty and spooky but for all its haunted house charm, the dilapidated mansion really was gorgeous. Set back in the woods away from the road, its long gravel drive was lined by old, gnarled southern live oaks, some drooping with Spanish moss.

"Wow." It was all I could think to say.

Aunt Aurora took my hand and squeezed, "I know. It's breathtaking right? The Midnights built it. You might say we were architecturally charmed."

"Charmed?" I questioned.

"Yes, they built it with magic. I think that's why it's connected to Gran." She paused for a moment, "The thing is, Evangeline, your mother could be lost in there."

"What?"

She mentioned coming out here to check on the place since we were going to be moving in."

"When? Is that where she went that morning after my graduation?"

"I don't know for sure, dear. She told me that the morning of your graduation. Anyway, it's just one of the theories I'm working on."

"I don't understand. Why haven't you gone and checked."

"Oh honey, I have. I can't get in."

"Huh? You don't have a key. Well, how do you expect me to get in?"

She gave me a funny look and for a moment it felt like she was about to reveal some big secret of the universe. "There are things your mother was supposed to tell you about—"

"Aurora…" Julep interrupted her.

I looked from Julep to Aurora and back again. There seemed to be some secret conversation happening.

"Cut the bullshit, guys. What's going on? There's something you're not telling me."

They stared a couple seconds longer then Aunt Aurora cleared her throat, "I don't know, Evangeline. I don't know if it's mere glitch in the magical build, or what?"

"The magical build or a glitch in the matrix, who knows?"

"You're losing me."

"All you need to know for now is that Gran' haunts the place and she controls the house. She won't let me inside." She handed me a skeleton key. "I'm hoping she might accept you, since you are the heiress to the mansion now."

She handed me a skeleton key.

I palmed it, feeling the teeth tingle against my skin. "So, this is the key," I said slowly.

"Yes, if she accepts you then we can look for your mother.

Before she could say another word, I ran for the door.

"Wait, Evangeline. It's dangerous." I could hear both of the women shouting at me but I forged on. I didn't care how dangerous it was if it meant saving my mother.

I climbed the steps at a breakneck need and almost did just that when I tripped. Thankfully, the door was right there. I stuck the key in and turned—well tried to turn. There was absolutely no give.

I turned around, placing my hands on my hips as Aurora made it first to the front porch. Julep wasn't long behind her but they were both wheezing.

"Evangeline, you silly girl!"

"No, you're silly. You must have given me the wrong key; this one doesn't fit."

I swiped away the tear that slipped out and nodded. What if Gran wouldn't let me in either.

"Now never you fret," Julep said, wrapping her arms around me. "We'll get in there one way or another."

Aurora too, came to comfort me, dragging me back

down the steps to the car. "The thing is dear; you're going to have to try again. I told you Gran is fussy—she won't let just anyone in and you may have scared her, attacking like that. You can try again, okay?"

I nodded my head in defeat and we walked back to the limo.

"And, now that that's been covered, we only need to discuss two things. First, your presence in society. Now that you are eighteen and about to take your rightful place as mistress of the estate, you will need to attend the society functions."

"Oh, no. Absolutely no way," Julep spat through gritted teeth, "Her mama hated that shit and you know it."

"Yes," Aunt Aurora said, giving as good as she got, "and we all know how that worked out for her." She blanched when she looked at me. "I apologize, sweet girl. That was insensitive." She inhaled deeply and dabbed at her eyes with a tissue. "It was one of my father's stipulations— that whomever owned the estate would make the social rounds. That's why Briar refused to take ownership. The truth is, Briar planned to sign the house over to you, Evangeline. She thought maybe you wouldn't be as opposed to the idea of society as she was. Now, there is a charity ball coming up—Until Midnight; it has always been an important one to our family and I hoped you would come with me."

I nodded my acceptance. Aunt Aurora was right. Mama and Julep might have had a problem with swanky parties but I sure as hell didn't. Getting all dolled up like a princess sounded like a blast.

"Now, secondly, we have the problem of how best to protect and educate you." She'd barely said the words when another vehicle pulled up the drive. A tall and handsome young man in a charcoal-gray suit that was molded to his body—all six feet and change of it—stepped from the sports car and positioned himself at her right shoulder. His car screamed playboy; his glasses screamed scholar but the tattoo that crept out of the collar of his shirt screamed savage. "Julep, I understand you've begun educating my niece and, while that's most appreciated, I would like Professor Demas Batavian to take over."

The tall, dark drink of water examined me with a critical eye, his body language impeccably polite. "Hello, Evangeline. It's nice to meet you."

Julep clenched her fingers where they rested on my shoulders in response to the tension thrumming in the air. "This is your step-son, isn't?"

"It is," Aurora answered, "although that's not why I've asked him to tutor her."

Mama had mentioned Aurora's step-son—the pet or the bookworm, as she called him, but she really hadn't done him justice. His chestnut brown hair was styled and gelled. He had blue eyes and full lips that tilted down at their corners, shielding his perfect smile—a masterpiece of orthodontics. Apparently, Aunt Aurora's pet bookworm had grown tall, really tall and strong, and—oh my goodness—handsome. Did I mention handsome? He had this energy about him—I could just tell he was the sort of intense, quiet sexy that took a woman by surprise when he let loose.

"He is a highly regarded professor at the Arcanum Academy for the Supernatural and he also has a top-secret position with our supernatural police unit which I'm not at liberty to discuss with you."

I took a deep breath, realizing I was still staring at him. Not to mention, my nether regions were tingling. "It's nice to meet you."

"Anyway," Aurora rose in a fluid motion. "Your mother and I discussed your training and while we disagreed on many things, we both agreed to your attending the Arcanum Academy in September."

"You mean, Tulane University."

Aurora glanced from her step-son to Julep and then swallowed, "Right, well, the thing is, dear—I'm not sure if your mother had time to touch on this with you but—you're not just going to any old university. The place we planned to send you is a magical campus—an extension of the

Ink Saves Lives When Undead Rise

University. It's called the Arcanum Academy for the Supernatural and as I said, Demas is actually a professor there. Now, we're still hoping to send you to the New York campus in the Fall, but there are wide gaps in your education. Therefore, the plan is for him to tutor you at the New Orleans location until you're up to speed." She walked around the desk and placed her hand on mine. "Don't worry. He's quite brilliant, you'll find. Takes after his late father in so many ways." She turned back to him, "So, when can you be packed?"

"Packed?" I interrupted, glancing between my aunt and the professor. "What are you talking about?"

"Well, you're moving here to the Midnight Estate, aren't you? Demas will need to accompany you, of course," she announced. "As I said, this place can be dangerous."

"I can protect myself," I said, pushing up my sleeves. "Julep has trained me. Just look at my tattoos?"

"You expect to protect yourself with a tattoo?" Aurora questioned.

"Yes, that's the whole point of them. They are defensive tools."

"How so?" Aurora reached out to touch the zippo lighter I'd drawn on my arm.

I jerked away from her fingers. "You don't want to touch that."

"Why not?" she gave me a narrow look. "I hardly think you're gonna hurt me with a little candle lighter."

"That one will burn you to the bone, and it will keep burning until eventually it consumes your entire body." I tilted my own forearm to look down at it. "It's kind of a magic wildfire, I guess. Trust me, it's a nasty way to die."

"How does it not burn you or anything else it touches?"

I tapped my purse to the tattooed rune on my skin. "I told you, it's a defensive spell, so it lies inert when something neutral touches it."

"You consider me your enemy?"

"No. I'm not sure what the spell would do if you came in contact with it. It's best we don't find out."

She cocked her head, "A defensive spell…hmm? I like it. You aren't worried about it melting off if you sweat or go swimming?"

"I used a liquid bandage made of polymer or sometimes nail polish. They both do the trick. They won't come off for a couple of days unless I scratch or peel them off or take them off with nail polish remover."

"Nail polish remover. Crafty." Demas smiled.

"Well, I'm glad to see you're not defenseless, niece. But the zombie attacks have increased in the city and the condition remains. Do you want the estate or not? Julep, of course, is also welcome to join you."

"I don't know," I hesitated.

She anchored one hand on her hip. "Don't be stubborn, dear. You will need all the protection you can get. I don't know if you've noticed but there is an army of undead terrorizing the city."

I looked at Julep who shrugged. "She has a point and for the record your mom was considering all of this."

Aurora nodded. "If you don't like that solution, you may stay with me in my home. Either way, you will attend the academy during the day. Tutoring begins Monday and you have two weeks to get yourself packed and adjusted to the idea of the plantation."

"Demas," Aunt Aurora lowered her voice. "You can have as many men as you want but you must keep her safe. We don't want her taken like her mother."

"Taken? I thought you said Mama got lost in the house. You think someone took her?"

"I'm sorry. Slip of the tongue, dear. That was one of the other theories I was working on. With all of these undead attacks, I'm just erring on the side of caution. Anyway, I need to go with Demas. I'm afraid this necromancer business has the whole city in a dither. My driver will take you home." She hugged me one last time, "Until the Midnight Ball."

9

MIDNIGHT WITCH

Watching the bustling crowds, bright lights and conflicting music of Bourbon street. I adjusted the bracelets Julep had charmed for me, feeling the magic as it tingled against the tattoos on my skin. I'd agreed to a secret outing with Pepper Badeaux from the séance to pump her for information. I'd learned so much from Aunt Aurora and Julep today but I couldn't help feeling like there was more to the story.

Pepper—well, the whole Badeaux family was apparently related—cousins on the Midnight side. I could hardly believe it. I'd questioned Julep on the limo ride back from the Midnight Estate but she'd refused to say more about it. Not just that, she wanted me to stay away from my new relatives, hence the need for stealth. Since Pepper was from India, she wanted to see the town so she'd arranged some silly tour for us. Not like I needed a tour guide to see the place I'd been raised in but whatever got me answers. Despite what my aunt had said about the dangers, I wasn't about to be coddled. That might have been how she did things but that was just not how my mother had raised me.

Besides, I'd worn white chucks that were good enough to sprint in, just in case one of those decomposing freaks showed up.

Waiting along with me as part of the haunted historic tour was a group of frat boys, all blonde, over six feet, and virtually indistinguishable from each other; a hipster couple in consciously geeky eyeglasses; a sporty, trim Canadian couple; and four women on the flip side of forty, clad in leggings and oversized T-shirts.

"*Laissez les bons temps rouler*," one of the women declared in a New York accent as thick as a slice of Sicilian pie.

"Evening, y'all. Please form a line," the tour guide responded as she popped open a parasol and poured on the Southern charm.

I looked around for Pepper but she was nowhere in sight. Maybe she'd gotten lost. I quickly punched in a text to let her know it was starting. Then jammed the phone back in my bag, cutting my hand on a pair of small manicure scissors. I really needed to stop dropping them in there, loose like that.

"I'll be your guide through haunted downtown N'awlins. Feel free to ask any questions you might have but do please stay with our group. Vampires and zombies tend to prey on the stragglers." The crowd gasped on cue, and she giggled like a child on chocolate. "I'm only kiddin'." Her face went stone-cold serious. "Or am I?"

The frat boys snickered. "This is gonna be better than that airboat ride."

"Uh-huh. I love Cajun Country," The New Yorker said.

"Hells yeah," the one in the middle responded. "The gators were cool but I'm totes stoked. Did you hear there was another attack last night? Some tourist was chewed to bits after wandering through the graveyard."

The tour guide cleared her throat while the girl in glasses began to chew her brightly patterned nails. "I told you this was a bad idea."

"It'll be fine. They're just teasing and besides we're not going into some graveyard," her hipster boyfriend soothed.

"It's like that show Walking Dead," the frat boy went on.

"Oh, it is not." The New Yorker retorted. "We're hardly in the middle of an apocalypse, bucko! If we were, I sure as hell wouldn't be paying for a ghost tour, am I right?"

Her lady friends cheered her on with some, hell yeahs!

"Well, maybe we're in the early stages of it— judgement day. Or maybe it's like that show True Blood where the whole place is just full of supernatural beings and the humans are only now starting to find out."

"Okay, that's quite enough. How about you let me do the scarin'?" the guide chided, and then carried on with her spiel, reminding us—namely, the frat boys—of the local liquor laws. "This is the Ludovic House,"

"Bloodsucker Mansion." One of the boys yelled out.

The crowd shifted, studying the massive house with its red-gabled roof. I attempted to listen, trying to picture the family she talked about, but found myself distracted by the eerily charming architecture of the place. Supernatural energy flowed all around it and all around here for that matter. New Orleans was a hot bed, really.

Before I knew it, the group was moving. I spun back around, chastising myself, and smacked into a wall of big… sexy hunk.

"Well, hello there?" he whispered.

"Oh my. Sorry about that."

His silver gaze swept over me, and I could have sworn lingered on my throat. "I'm Lézare Ludovic."

"Nice to meet you," I replied. "Are you with this tour group?"

"No. I'm afraid I live here. This is my home."

"Bloodsucker mansion?" The words slipped out before I could stop myself.

The man laughed at me. Well, I guess he wasn't really a man. More of a vampire. My first. Vampire. Wow. Julep had said they existed but I'd never met one before. He sounded like he'd just stepped out of the Carpathian Mountains, and holy, moly Julep was right about the intoxicating pheromones. Even his boots looked sexy enough to lick.

I flattened my spine against the warming metal of the gate behind me, and peered around him, doing my best to focus on anything but him. Hadn't that been what Julep recommended. Occupy the mind. The group and tour guide were now moving ahead like a locomotive picking up steam, without even the tiniest concern for my safety. *Thanks a lot, Susan!* I wasn't sure if that was actually the guide's name or not—probably not—but I'd seen a meme recently and it seemed to fit. She was definitely getting a two-star drive-by online. Okay, maybe a three star—I wasn't that mean. Wait— what if he'd glamoured her to forget me. *Fine*, I told my conscience, I won't give her a bad review.

"Are you looking for someone?" A smile tugged at the corner of his mouth, and his canines sharpened.

"My cousin."

"But you're alone." He lowered his head and lifted my hand to his mouth. The tip of his nose trailing my knuckles. Then his lips moved against my skin, the warmth of his exhale puffing against my palm. "What's a beautiful, intelligent girl like you doing out all alone anyway? Don't you know there are monsters roaming the city, and you smell so delicious. "Which court are you from?"

I shifted away. "I have no idea what you're talking about."

"Alright. Let's discuss something else. Are you a member of the council?" he asked, running his index finger down the side of my neck. Goosebumps prickled along my arms, and the hairs on the back of my neck stood up.

"The Supernatural Council, you mean? My aunt—" Catching the slip-up, I clamped my hand over my mouth. Why was I blabbing?

The vampire snorted with laughter. "Your secrets safe with me."

I sighed, realizing it was futile to fight his charm. "Who's your aunt?"

"Aurora Batavian."

"Wow, the head of the society. You're practically royalty then," he mused. "Forgive me for saying so, but you don't seem much like her."

"Why? Because I'm not rich and glamorous like some movie star?"

"Noooo. Because you're not stuck-up."

"Oh. Yes, well, Mama was not the conformist type. She traded in her Bentley and trust fund for a motorcycle and a tattoo parlor."

"Oh, a rebel, huh? He chuckled. "I like her already,

and your mama doesn't mind that you're not following in her bootsteps."

I shook my head. "Apparently not. Aunt Aurora says this was what she wanted for me. I can't confirm. She went missing a month ago." My words might as well have been soaked in butter, they just slid out of my mouth.

"I'm sorry to hear that. One of the victims of the zombie uprising, then?"

"We don't know. I hope not. You're a vampire, right?"

"Beautiful, funny and sharp."

"Like your fangs."

Ludovic canted his head to one side. "Are they showing? My apologies. It seems you're bleeding."

I looked down at my palm and remembered I'd cut myself on my scissors. "I should go." Ludovic stood his ground, even when I pushed on him. "Please move. I have a tour to, uh, catch up with."

Unruffled, he let me pass. "Okay. See you around…Evangeline."

My chucks slapped the sidewalk as I took off at breakneck speed eager to catch up to my group. I was about a block away when I realized he'd called me by my first name.

No time to dwell!

I'd lost the group.

I paused to check my phone to see if Pepper had responded and came under the radar of several fraternity-type dudes. Apparently catcalling women was still a thing. *Yuck!*

One of them—a cocky ballcap wearing jock from the looks of his jersey stumbled forward. He was clearly drunk, from the way he did the side-step shuffle, that or he was playing a game of imaginary hop scotch with his bros. "Hey baby, you look tired." He looked down at his crotch. Need a ride?"

Placing my hands on my hips, I snarled. "Sorry, but your bike's not big enough. Maybe try taking the training wheels off first." I turned to walk away but sensed he was following me. The hairs on the back of my neck prickled. Or maybe that was my imagination running wild.

Out of the corner of my eye, I saw a different man—this was one far more threatening, and this seemed strange even to me, but it looked as if he was juggling tiny orbs of light. Turning my head for a closer look, I saw he leaned against a motorcycle across the street. He had blonde hair, tanned skin and he wore a suit of all things. While I'd been trained in the last month to spot and identify other supernatural beings, I couldn't place his heritage. I sensed something supernatural and yet not. Whatever he was, he wasn't just your average human and he was staring right at me.

Was I wearing a please accost me sign tonight?

As I rounded the corner, I spotted an alley. Perfect! I'd duck in here and call Pepper. See where the hell she was at and then maybe call an uber. I hated to admit it but maybe Julep had been right. I walked until I was hidden by a dumpster and pulled out a phone. The hairs on my neck tingled, the further I went, the worse it got and that's when I realized why. There was a baby fox coming toward me. What the hell was a wild animal doing in the city? Wait! Were foxes dangerous? It didn't seem to be afraid of people at all. It was coming right up to me. Its ears were round—too round to be a fox. Oh, it was a ferret—like the one in the picture. Apparently, they were more common than Julep thought.

"Hey, there, fella," I called to it.

It didn't move.

Crossing my arms, I moved closer and squatted.

Oh my gosh, it had huge, whitish-blue eyes, practically supernatural in color. I decided I wasn't going to let it get any closer so I turned and started to hurry away and bumped right into one of the frat boys. Shit! He grabbed my arm and pulled me into his chest, the stench of liquor strong on his breath.

"Let go, asshole!"

"Kind of young to have a mouth like that, or are ya a big girl tonight? I wouldn't mind seeing those big girl panties."

I couldn't help but roll my eyes. After everything I'd been through lately, I was in no mood to deal with his toxic bullshit.

"If I were you, I'd let go of my arm."

"And what are you gonna do about it, sweet cheeks?"

What would I do? I decided I wouldn't need any magical intervention to deal with him. He could barely stand. I lifted my knee and connected with his crotch.

I left him hunched over, babying the family jewels and moved past him. But apparently, one of his buddy's decided to defend his honor. He ran up behind me and pushed me so hard, I hit the brick wall to my left. When I straightened up, I could feel something wet running past my eyes. Slightly disoriented, I pulled my hand back, and looked at it.

That was definitely blood.

Oh, this guy was asking for it but before I could give him his dose of retribution, he pressed his mouth to mine. Hot, metallic breath nauseated me and I decided that would be his downfall. I kissed him back, weaving a spell in my mind as I did.

The drunk's fingers released me like I'd burned him. Then he collapsed to the ground and began convulsing.

One of his buddies shouted at me and I realized

quickly that I was alone down a dark alley and outnumbered.

And that's when the ferret attacked.

It went absolutely nuts and before I knew the guys had taken off back down the alley.

The ferret lay on the ground though. It wasn't moving.

I hurried to its side and knelt down. Carefully, I patted the creature and found it's belly covered in blood— one of them must have been carrying a knife.

"Don't leave me, my little hero. I could use a friend like you. I'm going to try to heal you, okay." I'd seen Julep do it. How hard could it be? Digging into my bag, I pulled out my pen and began to draw on my skin. I needed power if this was going to work. I drew the same symbols I'd seen Julep draw. They glowed and shimmered in the moonlight. The moment I finished, I could see the wound more clearly, as if it were a ripped shirt with loose threads.

I dropped the pen back into my satchel and pressed tight to the gaping wound, reciting a healing spell the whole time. Ignoring the warm and sticky blood that oozed underneath. Nothing happened aside from my fingers tingling. I went on gut instinct and picked up the loose threads of magic. Slowly, I began to weave them, eventually tying them off into a knot.

I felt the animal's life force teeter. I took out a pair of

scissors from my manicure kit and pricked one of my fingertips then I ran a makeup brush over the blood and used it to paint the wound.

When I pulled the brush away from the ferret, its belly was scarred but the wound was closed. The adorable face turned up to me, its large, bright eyes blinking mildly. I looked around at the empty alley, then back down at the animal. Sighing, it put its front claws on me and climbed up onto my lap.

"Welcome back. Thanks for saving my ass," I whispered.

I inspected the tattoos I'd drawn on with the pen. They were gone. I'd used all of the magic up. Thank goodness I'd had just enough.

"All right, little dude," I said to the ferret. "Let's hit up one of these bars and get some grub. Magic makes me hungry." I picked it up gently. As I did, it climbed up my torso and wrapped itself around my neck. The last thing I needed was an exotic pet when I was beginning school in the Fall—unless, of course, he was meant to be my familiar. Every good witch had one, didn't they?

As I stepped out of the alley, the ferret started making noise, a cross between a growl and a whine. I put him in my satchel and placed a cloaking spell over him as fast as I could so that he would appear invisible to the average person.

Perhaps I'd have to head back to Julep's. So much for a wild night on the town.

Bitching under my breath for not staying in tonight, I backed up, and turned and strode rapidly toward the other end of the alley.

And that's when I ran into yet another scary looking man. This is why you don't go down strange city alleys. I was trapped... again.

"Bind yourself to me." Something whispered inside my head.

I stopped, flabbergasted. Had I just imagined that the animal spoke. No, of course not. I was losing it. I scanned the alley—it split in two directions.

"I know you!" The dark-haired man in front of me said. His eyes matched his wavy dark hair and yet I could see a fire lit from within them. He strode forward, but instead of running away, I walked toward him, caught like a moth to the flame. His eyes, predator-sharp, searched my face as he invaded my personal space, and crowded me against the brick wall.

"Hand him over."

"Come again?"

"Bo," someone else spoke from behind him. I looked and saw it was the blonde motorcycle dude I'd seen earlier. He was frowning as he placed a large hand on his friend's shoulder.

And that's when it dawned on me. This was the man from my vision outside the cafe. He shrugged angrily at his friend's hold.

"Back off, Lou." The man in black was breathing hard, still staring at me. I couldn't stop watching his lips.

The ferret snarled and snapped, biting at our attacker's shirt. Behind us, a crowd had gathered in the alley.

"Bo, let her go." The strength in the man's voice finally broke through.

Almost imperceptibly, the man in black listened and stepped away.

Shaken at my own impulses, I moved past him and found my face two feet from the buttons and collar of a navy-blue shirt. I angled my head slowly up and met Lou's honey-brown eyes.

"Eleutian Dupre III," he said with a bow. "At your service."

I opened and closed my mouth. My composure was thrown at how unlike charming this man was—the opposite of his dark-haired friend.

Eleutian opened his hands in a graceful apology. "Please forgive Mr. Remoussin. The man is used to getting what he wants. Women are just often drawn to him—you know how it is with the strong and mysterious types," he chuckled, "anyway, I'm afraid he's in a bit of a horn-tossing mood." He cleared his throat and looked decidedly uncomfortable. "The truth is, we just need your furry little friend there and we'll be on our way."

I looked down at the eyes peeking out of my bag. I'd forgotten he was even in there.

"He's your pet?" I questioned.

"Well, no," Eleutian answered honestly.

"This ferret saved me earlier and he got hurt in the process. I'm taking him home to take care of him."

"No, you're not." Bo growled.

I looked from the rude brute to his friend. "Did he just growl at me."

Elutian shook his head. "Ignore him."

"Right. Well, if he's not yours then he's mine now so I'm leaving. Please get out of my way."

Bo snorted.

I felt my eyes widen. What was with this guy?

"Aw right, darlin, have it your way," Eleutian replied, "but that's not a ferret."

"And I'm not your darling," I uttered. I glanced down at the adorable face tucked under my arm. Huge, bright eyes blinked up at me. Bo's attention shifted down to the creature I held.

"Oh, give me a break, Grimm!" The man grunted.

Out of the corner of my eye, I saw Eleutian's fingers clench on his friend's shoulder, and suddenly there was another man approaching.

The third man said in a conciliatory tone, "People are gathering. Let's go inside and sit down. Miss, you'll have to forgive my friends. I'm Zephyr and we're goin' inside. Would ya care to join?"

"Zephyr!" It was the hot boy I'd practically molested outside of Commencement.

"Evie! What are you doing here?"

Oh, dear, was it getting hot out here? I suddenly had the urge to remove my leather jacket. I shook my head, trying to think straight. Actually, every one of them was the type of big, bold and beautiful who could put a woman flat on her back with just one look—not that those dreamy, good looks worked on me, but I'd have to be careful. I'd seen enough of those slow-talking men with smooth ways and that velvet Southern drawl fool Mama.

I cleared my throat. "Being accosted by your friends, I guess."

"How did you find the psychopomp?" he asked.

The psychowhat?

Bo watched me now, his dark eyes cold and assessing. He had an utterly beautiful, completely mesmerizing face that was ruined by the edge of malice in his expression.

111

"Psychopomp. You know, creatures who escort newly deceased souls to the afterlife."

"Am I dead or something?" I asked.

"Hell no, you're alive," Zephyr answered. "Your heartbeat's been going off like a drum for ten minutes now. That's what attracted me."

"You're a vampire?" I asked. That made so much sense. No wonder I lost all sanity whenever he was near.

"Kinda," he replied and put an arm around me. I didn't stop him. "Come inside and we'll explain."

10

THE FIERY TEMPERED BEAST

Pulsing music spilled out onto the sidewalk as they approached the bar. Bodhi let Zephyr and Eleutian move ahead, the girl between them and watched as heads turned. It wasn't unusual for the team to garner looks—they were large, athletic-looking men and two of the three of them present tonight over six feet—but he had a feeling that it was Evangeline, the small dark-haired girl whose bright blue eyes had everyone's head turning. For someone who walked nervously, picking at her chipped black nail polish, she sure had a very powerful aura. Not that she was that small for a female, but she appeared so next to the men in his unit.

They walked forward, but their progress was interrupted by a bouncer holding up a big meaty paw "IDs!" he barked.

Bodhi watched as the girl shakily retrieved a driver's license with someone else's name - but her own picture - on its laminated surface. She bit her lip.

The bouncer waved her ID under an infrared machine, which didn't beep. He paused, frowning, and held her ID up for inspection, giving her a doubtful look.

Bodhi watched her take a pen out of her purse and draw something on her hand. She was trying to project a calm she didn't feel, her heart beating fast underneath her thin top.

A moment later, the bouncer slid the ID under the machine again and shook his head. "This isn't right," he muttered.

Shit. Bodhi hadn't even thought about the girl being underage.

He watched her rub the place on her hand where she'd just sketched, and the ink disappeared.

Suddenly the bouncer looked up, startled, almost as if he'd heard her. It felt as though time had stopped. Then, just like that, he returned her card and waved them forward.

Bodhi drew in a deep breath, filtering out the other scents in the bar to bring her feminine scent into his lungs. There was something different about her. She was supernatural, but that's all he could grasp. She held a significant amount of dark power and she made his cock stand on end—that was for sure.

With the psychopomp in her bag, she followed Zephyr to the bar's upstairs balcony overlooking Bourbon Street. She gave Bodhi one brief, sour glance before choosing a seat to his right.

He completed his study of the girl while Eleutian and

Zephyr took the bench across from them, and then he turned his attention to Grimm. It was strange to see the demon in animal form and stranger still not to hear his constant barrage of sarcastic jokes.

In a low voice, Zephyr said, "I'll go keep watch downstairs."

"Oh no. I don't think so." Evangeline crossed her arms, "If you leave, I leave."

Eleutian leaned forward and tugged Zephyr down. "He's not leaving, don't worry. I guarantee it."

For a moment Bodhi just stared at her. Her long, black, hair was pulled back in a ponytail letting her honey-toned face take the front stage. Her youthful skin was sprinkled with freckles; her lips were plush and pink but, unlike the vision, she now looked a little more gaunt. Even her breasts, which had been full and heavy before, were smaller. This girl had been through something in the last month—then again with the dead waking up and attacking the city, who hadn't?

"Text Colten," Bodhi said at last to Zephyr. "Tell him he's on solo guard duty."

As they talked, the pretty blue-haired waitress walked up to their table, carrying a tray. She looked at Bodhi first, "Lookin' good, handsome," and then the rest of the gang "What can I bring y'all? Drinks and supper?"

Bodhi smiled, "Yes, Paulette, please."

Eleutian took Paulette's hand and kissed it, "and might I add that you are lookin' lovely tonight."

Paulette gave him a look, and then her face broke into a smile that beamed all the way to the state line. "Aw, boy." She waved her hand at him. "You try that sugar on someone who might be fool enough to lap it up."

He cocked his head and grinned. "You got someone in mind?"

Bodhi waved Paulette back, "Bring us each a Vieux Carré and the evening's special."

"Actually, I'll take a peach-flavored iced tea," Evangeline corrected.

"Will do, sugar." The server slipped away.

"Now, ugh, Ms. Midnight, is it?" Eleutian asked and she nodded, "We don't mean to be hasty. We just really don't have the time. Someone's stirrin' up the gumbo 'round here. In case you've been livin' under a rock, the city is under attack. We need to speak to Grimm to figure out how to fix things."

"Who are you guys?"

"We're a special unit. We track monsters. We used to guard the gates to the underworld."

"Is this the underworld?"

Eleutian chuckled. "Might as well be for all the devils

runnin' about."

Bodhi gave him a tired look. "This is not the time for your jokes, Lou. The gate was compromised. We're now hunting down the man who broke through and all who followed him?"

"And who's that?"

"Trust me. You don't want to know," Bodhi said quietly. "That's why you should give Grimm over to us. You don't want to get tangled up in this."

"What does Grimm have to do with it?"

"He's part of our team. Or he was. We all have our roles. As Eleutian mentioned earlier, he guides the souls. He very well could have been the one who helped the man escape. It had to be someone on our team and it wasn't us and Grimm went missing about the same time."

Grimm sniffed the air like he was offended by the comment, or maybe just hungry.

"Why can't you just capture this man and re-imprison him if you're supernatural hunters?"

"Trackers and oh, what a clever idea. Why didn't we think of that?" Bodhi said, dryly.

Eleutian gave him a side glance. "Because… he's a very powerful necromancer. He can control others and he's had help coming into this realm. Not to mention he's always causing distractions. Basically, he keeps us chasing our tails."

Zephyr spoke up, "What he means is, we're strongest as a group, but the constant zombie attacks spread us thin. We usually have one more man with us for special missions—the Alpha, but he's busy tonight at Headquarters trying to formulate a plan with the council."

"Which is why," Eleutian chimed in, "we need to get back to work trackin' down a roamin' pack of dead before more of them rise from the tomb and ruin a verra fine evenin'."

Evangeline compressed those luscious lips of hers, and rubbed at her forehead, moving some of the tendrils that had come loose from her ponytail back off her face.

Much to Bodhi's surprise, she had a goose egg hidden away. "What happened there?"

Evangeline's slender black eyebrows rose as she felt at the bump. Then in a tight voice, she said, "Oh, that. Yeah, my night hasn't been great. Some guy and his buddies harassed me right before I ran into you guys in the alley? Grimm attacked them and got his belly sliced open for his trouble." She looked from Bodhi to Zephyr to Eleutian.

His belly was ripped open?!" Zephyr murmured. "It looks perfectly normal."

Her mouth quirked. "I healed him."

"What did the man look like who hurt you?" Eleutian asked. "I'll just go have a chat with him and his boys about manners and such."

The girl smiled. She had a really pretty smile. It brightened her whole face. "Don't worry about it. Grimm and I took care of him and his friends. I'm not helpless, you know." She pulled up her sleeve and showed off some fine-looking ink.

"Well, I'll be damned—" Eleutian reached out but she pulled away before he could touch her. He hesitated and caught her gaze, "I'm sorry, ma'am. That was rude of me. It's just I can feel the power risin' from it."

"It's okay. I just don't want to hurt you."

"Nice. So, who's the artist?"

Evangeline nodded, "Me."

Eleutian nodded. "Really, where did you learn to spell magic into tattoos?" he tilted his head back and forth to get a better look.

"My guardian, Julep, is a witch. She runs an occult shop and works with spells. My mom owned a tattoo shop. It gave me an idea. But I'm new to magic so it's all kind of an experiment."

"What does that one do?"

"Knocks you into next week." She held up her other fist. "This one will drive you batty."

Well, if it was anything like her ass, Bodhi thought she just might be telling the truth. "Which one makes you body jump?" Bodhi blurted out the words in more of an accusatory manner than he meant to.

"Huh?"

"Sorry, it's just outside the café. You took over someone else's body. We saw you."

A flush brightened her cheeks. "That wasn't a tattoo. I was scrying—well, I didn't know it at the time but that's what I was doing. You know, sort of like gazing into a crystal ball. I'd never done it before. As a matter of fact, I hadn't even learned I was magical yet. I guess I experienced astral projection. I still don't really know. What were you doing there?"

"We were called in to back up the police department. The zombies were attacking and the police got trapped inside a different building. I was following the trail of undead when I saw the teenager, you'd momentarily commandeered." His eyes narrowed. "Which brings me to my next question, are you always so voyeuristic, or was yesterday special?"

"No," she said emphatically. "Absolutely not." She paused to swallow. "Wait a minute. Did you say yesterday?" she looked confused. "I had that vision a month ago—before graduation." Before my mother took off.

Bodhi leaned back and crossed his arms. His black shirt strained at the collar, revealing the strong, corded muscles of his throat. He regarded her closely. "Really? Are you sure you're not working with the necromancer?"

11

MIDNIGHT WITCH

T he necromancer? You mean the one in the news?" Our conversation was interrupted as the waitress walked up with a tray of food and drinks. Bodhi nodded.

"You're fighting the necromancer?" I asked once she'd walked away.

Bodhi nodded again. "Well, there hasn't been much fighting, but we're trying. We're what you call trackers. We hunt down monsters for a living. And unfortunately, it's been more of an ass kicking so far."

"You hunt monsters? You're the Monster Squad," I said aloud, it was all starting to make sense.

Suddenly the bowl of shrimp gumbo in front of me smelled appetizing, and I thought I might be able to eat at the same table with the three males after all.

I offered Grimm a piece of the shrimp.

"You never answered my question," Bodhi said.

"No, I'm not working with any necromancer; I'm simply the student of a witch, but to be honest, I wanted to seek you out. My mother is missing."

Bodhi raised an eyebrow and gestured for me to continue, so I described everything that had happened. I rambled, backtracked, and fought off tears, but soon information about the corpse, the note, the séance, and the spirit had all poured out of me. Throughout the speech, Zephyr and Bodhi shot concerned glances back and forth.

When I had finished, Zephyr's lips compressed with distaste. "You held a séance?"

I nodded hesitantly.

Zephyr ignored me and turned to give Bodhi an ominous look.

Bodhi rubbed his hand over his head and leaned against the table. "We can't take on some run-of-the-mill haunting—we're here to stop a necromancer."

"But I don't just have a haunting! I have a missing mother and—"

"And... we don't have the time for a missing persons case. I'm sorry."

"Well, what am I supposed to do now then, huh?"

"For one thing, you could try the NOPD—they handle missing persons. For another, don't mess around with the dead or the other side or anything you don't understand. Séances invite ghosts. If you don't want ghosts then—and I know this is going to sound radical—don't host séances."

I could feel my face redden—like ripe tomato red.

Zephyr intervened, plying me with sweetness. "Evie, we really do have our hands full right now otherwise we would. But this necromancer, well... he's not just raising and freeing corpses from the mausoleums. He's killing men and women first in a ritualistic fashion—mutilating the eyes, ears, and tongues and then raising them."

Eleutian picked up the story, "Everyday folks—even open-minded ones from New Orleans are nervous as cats at a day spa. We've got the mayor and the paranormal society breathing down our necks. They can handle one or two of them walking dead—just blow the heads off—but a necromancer who's torturing, killing and then reanimating? Not too many people around here are comfortable sleeping with a serial killer of that proportion on the loose.

"And so, if the spirit you awoke is not directly threatening you, then we really have much bigger fish to fry, starting with your pal Grimm over there," Bodhi said.

"No threat?!!" I straightened. "What about Mama? What if this is connected? What if the necromancer has her? She went missing right after that séance—right before the rising. Maybe we were the ones who raised the necromancer. Have you considered that?"

Bodhi scoffed. "Do you even understand what that would take? Nobody accidently raises a necromancer."

"Well, so then maybe it wasn't us, but this spirit could

be helping him," My voice came out loud and a few heads turned. I lowered my voice once again. "I know it was evil—it touched me!"

"Evangeline." Bodhi stood stiff and straight; his jaw clenched. "There are many spirits free in New Orleans. Hauntings happen all the time, and most are harmless. Your Mama probably got spooked and ran off. Our job is to track monsters—not mothers."

"Besides," Zephyr inserted, his lips pressed into a grim line, "I hate to be the one to tell you but if the necromancer and his or her zombies have her, she's probably dead."

My stomach flipped. It punched the breath from my lungs.

I nodded, unable to speak. Zephyr's words repeated over and over in my head. Probably dead herself. Mama. Dead. No—I couldn't believe it. It was too soon to give up.

While Bodhi remained stoic, Zephyr began to eat like a growing eighteen-year old boy despite being part vampire. Meanwhile, Eleutian said, "Can't your family help you? Where's your father?"

"Dead," I told him as I slipped a piece of the table's bread to Grimm. "He died before I was born. I just graduated, learned I was supernatural, and now according to you guys, I've been orphaned all in a week."

Bodhi paused, "We don't mean to sound cold. We really are sorry to hear about your troubles."

The way he said it actually sounded sincere—for once. Clearing my throat, I said in a husky voice, "Yeah, well, saying sorry doesn't find Mama, now does it?"

Ladling the rest of the shrimp onto the bread plate I exclaimed, "Anyway, I have a big day ahead of me tomorrow. I'm starting summer school and so I think it's time we go our separate ways."

Grimm had finished eating and hopped back up. I looked into his bright eyes and said softly, "Grimm, you wanna go with your squad, or stay with me?"

He didn't answer me in words. Instead, he curled into my arms.

"Looks like you got your answer, boys. Happy monster hunting."

12

MIDNIGHT WITCH

The little hairs on the back of my neck stood with foreboding. Someone was watching me. I could feel it. One. Two. Three. I rolled over and sprung from my bed, ready to fight.

It was a man—a very naked man!

"What are you doing here?" I screeched, suddenly recognizing him as the man who'd saved me from Barnabé's affections in the cemetery.

"Relax, Evangeline. It's me." He said and transformed back into the furry little ferret who'd been curled at the end of my bed just last night. I'd forgotten all about him.

"Morning beautiful," he said, from inside my head.

"What? How?" I huffed, scrambling away.

"I apologize. No one's ever communicated with you this way—"

"No!" I shouted. The Monster Squad had been right about him. "And I'm not a morning person so if I'd known you could talk, I wouldn't have let you sleep here. I like coffee before I talk to my demon animal pets—like any normal person."

He skittered back to the other side of the room and, before my very eyes, shifted once again into a man.

He stood with his head tilted back slightly, his eyes full of strange colors as he admired my skimpy pajamas. I stood up and tugged at the tank top which might as well have been a crop top, unfortunately, that only made my boobs pop out the top. Not that it mattered, Mr. Horny Ex-Ferret's gaze still lingered over my legs.

"There. Is that better? I'm no longer an animal."

I snapped my fingers to snag his attention and said, "Aren't you?! Why do your eyes still look like that?"

He gave me a side smirk. "I'm standing here naked and you comment on my eyes? How rude."

"Oh, you're right. Sorry! Nice junk." I pulled a blanket from the bed and tossed it at him. "Now please, put it away before Julep or Grand-mère come in. Old ladies aren't as harmless as you think."

He laughed suddenly, and my heart jerked and began pounding hard. Goodness he was beautiful. Handsome was too bland a word. He reminded me of someone.

"Fine," he said, relaxing, looking around my bedroom. Then he turned back and lifted the blanket. "You're such a bore," he added casually. He took his time wrapping the blanket around his waist, clearly, not shy, and I could see why. That body was something else.

"Harrumph..." I cleared my throat. "So, the eyes? What's up with them? You look rapey and not just because you're naked in my room. Although, that too..." I said, and motioned my finger in a giant circle at his... ahem... bits and parts.

"The spiritual energy makes my eyes do this."

"Does it make your brows arch like that too? Or are you just impersonating Jack Nicholson."

"Jack who?"

"Oh, right... you're not from here... umm...let's go with the devil."

Grimm chuckled, "Naw. I got it. I was just toying with you. Who doesn't know Jackie boy? Anyway, the brows are all me, sweetheart." As he stepped closer, I noticed a tattoo of a raven peeking out from beneath his muscled arm, on his ribs. I'd seen it before. "Who did that?"

"What? This old thing?" His spooky eyes never leaving my face, he lowered his arm. "You recognize it?"

I didn't answer. I couldn't. Any words I wanted to say were trapped in my throat. "How did you get here... wait... where did this body come from? Was it yours? Did you murder one of my mother's clients?"

His nose wrinkled up. "Slow down. I don't know which question to answer first. Of course this body is mine! What are you thinking, that I stole some poor, devilishly handsome, completely ripped person's corpse?"

"Well, healthy body image aside, how else does one get a body?"

"It's . . . it's like a phase change in science," Grimm said. "You know how water can go from ice to gas, etc. Well, think of it as the process of condensation. On the spirit side I was a gas. Then as I stepped through the waterfall into the earthly side, I became water and eventually ice."

"And that's why your eyes make me feel like I'm staring into one of those trippy tube toys?"

"Do you mean a kaleidoscope?"

"Yes."

He ogled me. "It's pretty standard for anyone whose natural form is raw energy, but it goes away. It happens when I use my magic."

"So, everyone from the other side has rainbow eyes when they use magic."

"Oh, hell no, that's my signature look. Everyone is a little different—some white, some blue, some yellow, some are even red. The glowing is the common denominator."

I grunted, in understanding. It made sense. "Wait a minute! I recognize that. Why are you wearing one of my mother's tattoos?"

I reached out and ran my fingers over the black patterned wing along his rib. It wasn't just any old raven. It had a series of ruins inside of it. I'd always loved that tattoo. "Have you seen her? Did she give that to you recently?"

"No, it's old. It's like an invisibility cloak—it binds me to my master and hides me from the hell hounds. How do you know she designed it?"

"I've seen it on the wall of artwork in her tattoo parlor? What are hellhounds?"

"The guardians—you know, the Professor and Captain Brutey-pants and their team of merry men," Grimm drawled, as if that was the most obvious answer in the world. "The ones who keep guard of the gates. They keep the humans out and the monsters in. When a necromancer calls something over, they have to hide it from these guardians— these hell hounds—right away. This tattoo hides me."

"Whoa! Back up! Necromancer—I'm confused."

"Am I speaking hellcat here?" he snorted like I was some sort of simpleton who should be well-versed in the knowledge of all things occult.

"Are you suggesting my mother is a necromancer."

The muscles in his jaw twitched like he was trying not to laugh at me. "If she's the one who gave me this tattoo then yeah."

I leaned forward. "You're crazy. I don't believe you. You're some sort of trickster demon. So, where is she? I need to talk to her."

He twisted his face away. "How should I know?"

"Well, you said that tattoo connects you to your master, right?" I threw my hands up in the air. "Has anyone ever told you how infuriating you are."

"No. It's so hard to believe, isn't it? But to answer your question, I can't sense Briar."

I fidgeted. "Does that mean she's dead?"

Grimm actually looked sincere for a moment. "I hope not."

For some reason, this only confused me more. "Why haven't I seen you before? When was the last time you saw her?"

Grimm flinched as if I'd slapped him, but his eyes stayed close. "Eleven years ago. She sent me back to Hell when she stopped using magic. Since demons aren't allowed here, I was punished—forced to work as a psychopomp and so I've been guiding spirits whenever they pass."

"So why are you back here now? Are you here to guide me home?"

"Yes."

"Really? I'm going to die."

"No. Psych! I mean, I don't know. That would be cruel twist of fate though, huh." I narrowed my eyes and he went on, "In all seriousness, somebody freed me from the Underworld. They pulled me here and then they tried to use me as a locator, I guess."

"To find her?"

"Maybe? I'm sorry I can't answer your questions. I think my memory was tampered with… which is weird because only my master or someone of their blood should be able to do that. Unless, you did it, did you?"

"No, and you're no help at all." Shrugging it off, I wandered down the stairs and out onto the front porch. I felt like my head was going to explode when my phone's calendar alarm went off, "Shit. I'm late for class!"

13

MIDNIGHT WITCH

I hurried along the campus path until I came to the designated meeting place where Demas or Professor Batavian—I wasn't entirely sure what I was supposed to call him—awaited me. He wore dove-gray slacks that molded to his backside and a fitted white button-down shirt with the cuffs rolled halfway up his forearms. The edges of a tattoo curled down his forearm in startling contrast to his bookish appearance. Hot for teacher anyone?

"Good morning, Ms. Midnight. I trust you had a good weekend."

I smiled and nodded, deciding not to tell him about my new pet just yet.

"My office is this way." He indicated the clock tower behind him, and as he turned and pulled open a door that I didn't even know existed, magic pulsed and glowed. "Well, are you coming?"

I exhaled through my parted lips. "A portal? Will it hurt?"

He shook his head, "I don't think so. How else did you think we'd get to the academy? It's not in this realm."

"Is this the only portal?" I asked following him through the pulsing array of colors that led into a wood-paneled corridor.

"Oh, no. There are many others on campus, but we'll use this one for the summer."

Surprisingly, there were a number of other kids walking the halls—all dressed in a similar uniform. I tilted my head back, taking in the high, arched ceilings and almost bumped into a group of rainbow-haired girls. They whispered and giggled—their eyes moving from me to the professor.

"Knock it off, girls. You don't want to be late again for your Mastering Glamour class," the professor chided.

"Like we need a class in that," the tallest of the girls shot back.

I glanced up at the professor who just shook his head.

A fatigued-looking man with pencil shavings on his sweater and tape on the bridge of his glasses greeted us in the hallway. His scholarly corduroy appearance was underwhelming and yet my senses vibrated with a supernatural awareness. When he spotted Professor Batavian, he grinned from ear to ear, allowing the tips of his fangs to be seen. *Well, that explained it.*

"Good morning, Demas. May I steal a moment of your time this morning?"

"Of course, William, let me just get my student settled

and reading." He turned to me, "Evangeline Midnight, this is Professor Van Rogue."

The man nodded in an unassuming manner and still I bumped into Professor Batavian in an effort to get away—like a child with a stranger in a park.

"Sorry about that. Are you okay? I forget that you haven't grown up around this," Professor Batavian said once we'd entered the classroom. He rested his hands on my shoulders, a soothing presence at my back.

"No worries. If I'd grown up around it, I probably wouldn't need you though."

He laughed, "Touché. But just so you're not surprised in the future, you will encounter all types of supernatural students and teachers here—werewolves, witches, faeries and vampires to name a few. Most teachers don't flash the fur or the fangs like that though. We usually have more control than the students. I'm not sure what's going on with William today—he must be ill."

"Can I ask a question: why are there so many students here in the summertime? Do semesters run longer here?"

"Yes, and no. Many of our students live here full time. It's sort of like a boarding school for the supernatural, so students have the option of taking classes year-round."

"Why would anyone choose to take classes year-round?" I covered my mouth right after I said it. "Sorry, that slipped."

The professor laughed. "No, it's a good point. Some kids don't get along at home. The Fae for example can be a ruthless bunch. It's a court driven society so if you're not among the elite then it can be a tough place to survive. Not to mention there are four rival courts and to say there is drama is an understatement."

"And that's what those girls were—the ones with the rainbow-colored hair and the shimmery skin?"

He nodded.

Mama would have fit right in with them. The thought made me sad and I was once again reminded why I needed to study hard and learn as much about magic as humanly possible. So that I could find her.

"Of course, year-round training is also beneficial," the professor added, pulling me out of internal thoughts. "It fast-tracks students and allows them to graduate earlier. It also never hurt the resume," he finished with a wink.

After unlocking the glass bookcase, the professor removed his crossbody bag and paid a visit to a nearby bookshelf, returning with a hefty, albeit dusty volume that he placed in front of me. He pulled a rag from his drawer and gave it a wipe. "Sorry about that. It's been awhile since I taught Mage basics."

I was immediately hit with the acidic, vinegary smell

of old leather as I flipped the tome open.

"What do you teach now?" I asked.

"Mostly Advanced Transformations. Anyway, let's begin with Chapter One: Basics of Sigil Magic. This should be a review of materials covered by Ms. Delphine. I'll just pop next door while you're looking things over."

Sigils are symbols used in magic. The term usually refers to a type of pictorial signature symbolic to the magician's desired outcome.

When he returned, he leaned against his desk, "Based on the tattoos you showed me when we met the last time, I'm going to assume you're somewhat familiar."

I nodded my head.

"Great. So, give me four ways to activate them?"

"Burning, tearing, skin work and visualization."

"Excellent, and I think I know but what is your preference, Ms. Midnight?" The way he drawled my name out was so sexy.

"Skin work, of course and please call me Evie," I replied, my eyes lingering on his tattoo. I tilted my head to see if I could get a better look. Was it wrong that I wanted to undo the buttons of that stuffy, uptight shirt of his to see if there were more? My head snapped back at the sound of him clearing his throat. *Shit, did I just drool?*

"Mine too, Evie." He replied, with a smile that made me wonder if he'd just read my mind.

"These little drawings are not only effective as weapons on the body as you've discovered. They are also the key to defending the home," he explained. I blushed and kept my eyes away from his. I needed to focus on the work. I never had this problem when Julep taught me. Boys were distracting. "They create invisible barriers to keep your enemies out. Let's begin by drawing four basic defensive sigils."

I pulled out my pencil case and the lovely new grimoire I'd received for my birthday—handmade by Julep—and drew my first sigil, a long, thin and basic geometric combo of three circles representing the moon goddess Hecate and in the largest one I drew her protective animal spirit, the multi-headed dog. Inside the images I worked in various runes for strength and power. Then I picked up my blue pencil crayon and began to sketch the watercolor effect.

"It's perfect. So, where did you learn to work the symbols into the shapes like that? Do you mind?" he asked, taking my sketch book from me. He flipped a few pages through.

"These are ingenious. You've worked runes into every single facet of the drawings. Runes within runes and yet they're all so simple and elegant."

"Thank you." The glint in the professor's eyes sparked my curiosity.

"I know you've tattooed on yourself but have you tried tattooing any of these?"

"On other people, no." I looked down sheepishly at my arm and pulled up my sleeve. "Mama wouldn't let me use the machines after that. She made me cover up my arm." I teetered between shame and anger at the memory. "This tattoo is the reason I was no longer allowed to assist in the shop."

Professor Batavian smoothed his hand across the page while looking at me, like he might absorb the information through his fingertips. "This was your first attempt at tattooing and it came out like that. I can feel the power that hums from it. I think your mother was scared of something or someone seeing this."

I swallowed. This was a lot to take in. "For the last two years, I thought Mama wouldn't let me tattoo because I wasn't good enough. You're telling me this symbol is too good."

"Exactly. Ink Magic is obviously your power. Your mother must have known that, and if she was trying to hide you then maybe she was worried that you would draw attention to yourself. You know, get a reputation as the new Ink Mage of New Orleans. Someone would eventually take notice. Not to mention, what would happen or come to life had you experimented on anyone else."

"Come to life? Shit! I really am a freak of nature, aren't I?"

"No." He reached across the table and covered my hand with his. "You're supernatural. Now, let's keep going. You have three more to do and then you can take a break."

"Yes, but could we work on something else?"

"What did you have in mind?"

"The portals, other realms... ghosts. I'm just wondering how it all works."

"Ahh," The professor said, adjusting his dark frames as he walked back to his bookshelf. "You want to talk about quantum physics, then? Are you sure? That's not a topic most people willingly embark on."

"Well, I'm just thinking about what Aunt Aurora said. If I'm going to get into the house then I'm going to need to understand it. Not to mention Gran since she apparently runs the place.

"Right. Well, let's get started. Prepare for a brain cramp."

Two hours of physics, history and demonology had me rolling my shoulders to stave off the neck pain. I was badly in need of fuel.

"Is there a coffee shop on campus?"

"There is. Just down the hall past admissions. If you hit the dining hall then you've gone too far. They have excellent lattes and you'll need it. I'm expecting your next instructor to be here by the time you get back."

"Next instructor?"

"Yes, defensive training. You'll need to know how to fight. We can't always rely on magic, now can we?"

"I guess not. So, you're not a fighter?"

Professor Batavian smiled. "I can hold my own but no, it's not my expertise. You'll have a few different instructors. Colten is an expert in martial arts. He'll be here when you get back."

Colten. That name sounded familiar but I wasn't sure why.

"Next week we'll add in the arcane arts."

"The arcane arts?"

"Yes, conjuration, illusion, destruction, and baking. Which reminds me, don't eat any of the enchanting edibles."

"Enchanting edibles?" I questioned.

"It's a baked goods line available in the coffee shop. They're magically enhanced by our very own sugar mage. Trust me, it's not what you want right before combat class."

14

MIDNIGHT WITCH

When I returned from my coffee run twenty minutes later, I came face to face with the sexiest ginger I'd ever laid eyes on—like Benny from Dazed and Confused, if Benny were a tatted-up UFC champion in army fatigues. His steely blue-gray eyes—seemingly bottomless, cold and intense—added an air of danger to him even more so than his powerful frame. He was almost as tall as the professor, but he was much more solid with the shoulders of a linebacker. I inhaled the smell of his testosterone. Deeply.

"You're late!" he said.

"I am?"

Based on the broad grin stretching his cheeks, I was guessing he knew how damned intimidating he looked.

"I'm sorry. You must be Colten. I'm Evangeline Midnight." I smiled introducing myself, but my voice cracked, making me cringe. I held out my hand for him to shake, and when he grasped it in his massive mitt, I had to suppress an icy shiver of fear.

"Nice to meet you, Midnight," he said in a voice that

was a strange cross between a soft southern lilt and a Bostonian accent. A sexy smile lifted one corner of his full lips as if he were aware of the enigma. My body flushed. *What the hell is happening to me?* I'm like a dog in heat, lately.

"I know what you're thinking," he said in a low, gravelly voice.

Highly Unlikely.

"You're afraid to get physical with me?" As he spoke, he slid his hand confidently around my waist and took a step forward, forcing me to step back through the open classroom door. He kept pushing until I bumped and planted my backside against the professor's desk.

Quite the opposite. My mind raced. "Huh?" I asked, having totally missed whatever he'd just said to me. Smooth. Evangeline. Real smooth.

His throaty chuckle vibrated through my body as he leaned closer and brushed his lips against my ear. The muscles along my spine quivered as a surge of adrenaline rushed through me. He lifted my bag from my shoulder and threw it aside. Then he took my coffee from my hand. "Prepare yourself to fight me off."

"Umm… like right now. Already?"

I threw up a hand against his muscular chest. "I need a second."

"A second?" he threw back his head and laughed.

"You can't ask for a second, darlin', not when you're under attack."

He kept me in place with his groin and strong legs while he cracked his knuckles. "Go ahead. Push me off you then."

Faster than I could let out a squeak, Colten had me pinned flat against the desk, and I had no idea what to do aside from squirming under his bulk. "Come on now, Ms. Midnight," he cajoled. "It's like you want me to undress you or something."

Oh, how I did.

"Bring your knee up. Do your worst, girl."

"Sorry," I wheezed, wiggling and gyrating until I could get my knee up between us. "I'm trying."

"You're turned on, aren't you? I know I am. Part of you likes me, right here on top, doesn't it?"

I blushed, but I still didn't move, not even a tick. "I don't know why you're doing this. How is this helping?"

He suddenly got serious. "You really want to know why? There are many supernatural creatures that will seduce you. They want you off your game. They want inside those panties. You have to learn to fight them even when you're turned on." He cut his eyes to my blouse and undid the buttons. "Or shall I do you right here and now? I certainly don't mind tasting a ripe little peach like yourself." His

145

tongue trailed over my chest and down to my nipple.

Desperate and confused, I decided on the offensive. I grabbed a handful of his soft red hair and pulled his face to mine, sticking my tongue down his throat. I kissed him for a good, hard ten seconds, then I forced my knee into his groin just enough for him to ease up off me.

Momentarily stunned that I had actually pushed him away, I kicked out hard with my right foot and hit him square in the solar plexus. Oxygen exploded from his lungs, and he doubled over. More afraid of what he would do to me now I scrambled away, putting the desk between us. The clock tower rang out in the distance, and my head swam.

"I'm sorry. I don't know what came over me."

Wild laughter poured from his throat as he clapped his hands. "The will to survive came over you. You don't apologize, Evangeline, for kicking someone's ass."

"I'm sorry, I'm having trouble hearing over the thundering of my heart, but did you just say not to apologize. You're not mad?"

"Mad?" he sat in the instructor's chair and placed his feet up on the desk, folding one foot atop the other. "Hell, no, Midnight. Hard as hell, but not mad."

I let a smile slip. I liked this guy.

"I'm here to show you how to fight with no mercy. There's no such thing as a clean fight. Vampires will use their

sex appeal, strength, their age, and their skills against you."
He got to his feet and walked back around the desk, "So will
necromancers. You gotta learn to do what it takes to
survive." He gripped my shoulders until I winced. "Whatever
it takes, you understand?"

His voice was like sandpaper, deep and gritty and part
of me wanted to be back under him.

"Did you hear me, Midnight?"

He snapped his fingers and it drew me up short.

I readied my fists and bent my knees. "I do. Want to
go again?"

He smiled, "Does a dog lick its backside?"

15

MIDNIGHT WITCH

After going three rounds with my new instructor before facing off against other first-year students in the gymnasium while Coach Ryu gave tactical pointers, I was a little tuckered out, but a promise was a promise, and so here I was ready for my high class function.

Aunt Aurora looked around the ballroom and then eyed my outfit with disdain—a silver-and-pink tutu ballgown, sparkly pumps and a black leather jacket. "Come Evangeline, let us meet our guests." She snapped her fingers at the doormen, "but first perhaps, you could lose the biker jacket."

I shrugged the coat from my shoulders and smiled, "Of course. I thought it was more a Buffy-the-Vampire-Slayer meets Cinderella thing, but whatever turns that frown upside down, Auntie."

She smiled and handed my coat off to one of the gentlemen in a pinched gesture as if it had fleas, "Now, tell me whom you don't know."

"Telling you who I know would be faster. No one."

As Aunt Aurora introduced me to various members of the party, I kept my eyes open and my senses alert. Where was the professor tonight?

Aunt Aurora buzzed about the place, looking like a cover model in her black ball gown and high-heeled Louboutins. I managed to escape her after a bit and fled to an empty corridor, staying close to the wall. No wonder Mama hated these things. The people were incredibly boring. All they did was gossip about one another.

Ms. Midnight" The man—scratch that—the vampire, Ludovic, the one from the ghost tour waved to me as he approached. Two creepy pale dudes flanked him just a few paces behind.

"Well, hello, there. You travel with an entourage?" I asked, wishing suddenly that I hadn't taken off to such an isolated place.

He turned and signaled the creepy bodyguards to disappear. When he turned back to me, I felt his gaze linger on my cleavage. Or was that my neck he was lusting after. I suddenly longed to have my leather jacket back.

"You knew my name before, and you glamoured me. Are you going to tell me it's a coincidence that we ran into one another again?" I took a step back.

"No. I figured a Midnight would be at the Midnight Ball," he said. "But I didn't glamour you the other night."

"Then why did it feel like my brain was on Molly?"

Ludovic chuckled, "You mean, a sex drug? My

apologies. That was an accident. Your blood caught me off-guard and released my pheromones, and you were the one who bumped into me."

"So, if I hadn't touched you then, I wouldn't have felt like that."

"Exactly."

"Thanks for clarifying. So, how can I help you?"

"I'd like to have a drink."

"Of me?"

He cleared his throat. "Not unless you insist. No, I mean I'd like to have a drink with you?"

His fingertips toyed with his champagne glass, and he released a contented sigh as he set it down.

"You look good by the way."

I smirked. "…to the last drop?"

"I just can't win with you, can I? Good as in beautiful."

"I was testing you."

"Did I pass?"

"You did."

"Excellent, then may I have this dance?"

I hesitated. Part of me wanted to go into the ballroom with him so we'd be surrounded by people but the other part knew he could charm anyone so it really didn't matter. "I don't think that's a good idea. We both know what happens when you touch me."

"Right? The terrible, awful orgasm." He smirked. "Well, unless you're bleeding, we should be fine,"

"Really?"

"With your permission, I'll prove it to you." I nodded and he reached out and held my hand, pulling me down the hall to the main ballroom. "Kiss me." He ordered.

"You know, I feel like you need to attend a class on toxic masculinity." I dropped his hand.

He snickered. "See? I was only proving my point to you. You have freewill."

"You sexually assaulted me to prove I have freewill? My, my, you are such a charming thing, aren't you?"

"Well, when you put it that way. Listen…I'm sorry. I didn't know how else to show you."

"Mmm-hmm."

"So, may I have this dance?" he asked flatly, not waiting for an answer before he pulled me into his arms. His black eyes glittered in the candlelight.

"Was that a question?"

"Not really," Ludovic countered, spinning me away from his body and then back in, closer this time.

Ludovic raked his gaze over me, assessing. "How old are you?"

"Don't you know you never ask a woman her age.

How old are you?"

"Thirty-two," he admitted.

"Hundred?"

A belly laugh escaped his lips. "You are a genuine delight. Not to mention a valuable asset, Evangeline—"

"I'm going to stop you right there, Lézare. An asset implies ownership and I can't be owned, my fangy friend."

"Oh, yes. I'm being toxic again. You're a modern woman. My bad. Will you have dinner with me tomorrow?"

"I'm sorry. I can't."

"How about the following day then? I'll pick you up and take you out for lunch." He cut his eyes my way.

I bit my lip, teetering on the idea. "You're relentless."

"It's a vampire thing. Time is on our side."

"Okay. As long as you promise not to poke me with anything sharp—well, anything at all, really." I paused for a moment. "No assault of any sort. Got it?"

"Got it." He raised his right arm and covered the nail of his pinky with his thumb, holding the three middle fingers of his hand upward like he was some sort of a boyscout.

"Okay, lower your hand there, Junior. Nobody's buying it."

He laughed. "I still make you nervous, huh?"

"As a long-tailed cat in a room full of rocking chairs. You're a stranger. And a vampire."

The music ended and I pulled away. "Anyway, thank you for the lovely dance, but I see my aunt glaring, probably because you just saluted me on a dancefloor. Not to mention, I'm sure there are several more pompous bores she needs me to smile stupidly at."

He grinned. "Fair enough. Until we meet again."

I turned and walked away, almost immediately bumping into someone.

"Evangeline! There you are. I've been looking for you."

"Pepper!" I said, to the familiar brunette. "What happened to you the other night? You didn't show and you haven't replied to any of my texts."

"I know. I know. I'm sorry. I lost my phone enroute and then I was late to the designated spot because I was looking for it. It still hasn't turned up. I should probably just go get a new one. Anyway," she said, straightening her gown. "I knew you'd be here. Here," she said and handed me a glass of champagne.

"I've already had a glass and I don't drink," I said, nervously looking over my shoulder to see if Ludovic was still lingering.

"Are you okay?" Pepper asked.

"I made a new friend, and I don't know how I feel about him."

Pepper smirked. "The man I saw you dancing with?"

I nodded. "He's a vampire."

"Hmm…" Her lips compressed, and she tapped a finger against her bottom lip. "I don't know much about them. You'll have to ask Julep or Grand-mère Delphine about it… they're the occult experts, right?"

"Apparently. So, we're family? That's crazy, huh?"

She nodded.

"I didn't know before."

"Me either. I was an infant when my grandparents cut ties with your mother. And I've lived in India with my Nani's family for most of my life so I'm quite out of the loop on just about everything," Pepper continued.

"How did you find out?"

"My mother cried a lot after the séance. Apparently, our mothers were best friends at one time, and seeing her and Evangeline brought up all kinds of emotional baggage. Mom sided with the family after Briar was disowned," she said, picking her manicured fingernails. "To my knowledge, she never saw or spoke to your mother again but…"

"She regretted her decision," I finished for her.

"Yes. That's why she held the séance." Her manicured fingers twisted into knots at her waist. "Anyway, I was hoping that we might be friends."

Just then Aurora came up and snarled. "What are you

doing here?"

"Auntie," I cajoled. "She's a Midnight too, is she not?"

Aurora looked chastened. A look I suspected she'd never given before. "Well, yes but they've never come to this event. Where's your mother?"

"I don't really know," Pepper began. "I came on my own hoping to run into Evangeline. I heard about your mother's..." Pepper paused, her hand twitching at her side.

"Disappearance?" I cocked an eyebrow at her. "Does your mother have any ideas on what might have happened to her?"

Just then Jilaiya appeared in the doorway. She curled her finger at her daughter, motioning for her to come along.

"I'm sorry." Pepper backed toward the foyer. "I should go. I'll see you later, Evangeline."

16

THE FIERY TEMPERED BEAST

Bodhi's cell phone chimed for the third time as he parked on the road outside Evangeline's place. Van Rogue's team wanted an update on Grimm and they were relentless. He quickly fired off his coordinates and then called Eleutian to check in.

"Evenin' Bodhi. How's surveillance going? I hope you're not enjoyin' spyin' on that pretty young thang too much."

"No, just enough to be a normal red-blooded man I suppose."

"Oh, but you're not just a man. Keep that fire in check, would ya, Puff?"

"Puff?"

"Yeah, you know, as in Puff-the-magic-dragon."

"Call me that again, wizard boy and no amount of light magic will keep your insides from sizzling."

Eleutian chuckled. "Oh fine. So sorry to offend. Is Grimm still with her?"

"Yep, the little cretin is up to something."

"I wonder why he's sticking with her?" Eleutian asked. Bodhi heard him take a swig of something.

"Are you at the bar?"

"You bet. This Vieux Carré is delicious and I'm about to go bang the waitress."

Bodhi scrubbed a hand through his hair. "Which one?"

"Does it matter? I figured we'd could all use a little release."

Bodhi rolled his eyes and laughed, "True but I see right through you. You don't remember her name."

"Guilty as charged, but truth be told, I don't think she knows mine either," Eleutian replied.

"Touché. Anyway, what did you mean, you wonder why Grimm's sticking with our girl. Wouldn't you? I'm just shocked he didn't shift back... if only to say something snarky to me."

"Oh, hell yeah," Eleutian laughed, "It must have been eating him alive to keep his yap shut."

Bodhi smirked. "She's gonna be in for a surprise when that pet of hers who's all curled up on the end of her bed finally grows to the size of a full-grown man."

"Well, then again, she might not mind at all. The ladies do love him."

"I know. It's fucking annoying. Anyway, Van Rogue's been up my ass. Call him, would ya? And get on with our next mission." Bodhi waited until Eleutian hung up. Then he

157

turned his attention back to the raven-haired beauty off in the distance. She'd gone home after the high society function. He'd assumed it was going to be a quiet night and then, low and behold, he'd watched her climb from her bedroom window. Gone was the sparkly pink skirt replaced with jeans.

Where are you going now? She was either really brave or really stupid.

The darkness allowed him to stare and he couldn't help but think how beautiful she was. Evangeline Midnight was far more than a witch but what was she?

His gut had sensed Fae magic in the alley but she didn't have any of their physical characteristics and there didn't appear to be any glamour.

Several yards from the car, she swung around to confront him. "I don't like being followed. What are you doing here?"

He smiled to himself. She had good instincts for a kid.

He rolled down his window. "The team and I were worried about you after our meeting last night. I thought I'd better check in. Grimm is going to get you killed."

She laughed, far too calm for a girl so young and the wind picked up the sound, carrying it across the open space. She turned her face to him, and her eyes sparkled in the moonlight.

He felt a flash of white-hot anger and snapped in a low tone. "You don't get it. If Grimm escaped, they're going to come for him. Melinoe wanders the earth with his train of zombies, and he doesn't just let his prisoners go."

"Is that right?"

He opened his door and stood to face her. "He's toying with all of us, trying to wear us down and force us into a trap. Without thinking, he reached out for her cheek and turned her face toward him. "Give Grimm over to us. It is the safest thing for you to do."

Evangeline listened for a moment as if she were really considering his logic, then she shook her head. "I wish I could help you out, but once again he's not mine to give."

17

MIDNIGHT WITCH

When his fingers stroked the side of my face, he might as well have licked my inner thigh for the heat that roared to life down there. He had dark brooding eyes that obviously matched his dark soul—quite literally since he was from the Underworld and all. And that's what I needed to remember. He was a member of some supernatural hell hound unit that had screwed up and got demoted, and now they were on a mission to redeem themselves and rid the world of this zombie problem. He was interested in doing his job and he was seducing me into handing over the psychopomp as bait.

"Anyway, I need to go. I'm meeting my friends at the club."

"Which one?"

I gave him a quizzical look. "Metropolitan. Why, you want to come to the big fais-do-do?"

He frowned.

"Good night."

The night was getting on and I'd promised friends, namely Cricket that I'd meet them. It was Cricket's favorite new hang-out. I wasn't overly fond of it, but once again, a promise was a promise. As I turned to walk to the '67 Chevelle, I looked around and saw an owl flying overhead. Weird. I didn't normally see them here.

A few minutes later, I passed the Metropolitan club— a two-story warehouse—looking for parking. It pulsed with the latest dance tunes. As I circled the block for the third time in search of parking, I noticed Cricket waving from the line. And there's a dude with her wearing a military jacket over a flannel shirt and a pair of torn jeans.

Oh, well that's just great. It's fucking Barnabé. And ahead of him leaning coolly against the building, vaping was Jeremiah.

I gripped the steering wheel tighter. *Clearly, the goddess is testing me.*

Part of me wanted to say forget it. I could just head home. It's been one long ass day. *I'll just text and claim there's no parking… but then that smug little shit will win.*

I glanced at my cell. It'd been fifteen minutes since I'd first seen them in line. They were definitely inside by now. I'd text her as I walked and see. I could still change my mind.

I fixed my hair in my rearview mirror and as I stepped out of my vehicle, I could have sworn I heard growls or were those screams. A bad feeling tickled my skin, raising goose bumps. Playing it off as my imagination, I headed for the club.

No sooner had I crossed the road then glass shattered. *Okay, those were definitely screams coming from inside the club.*

All at once the owl I'd seen earlier landed beside me, shrieking and I almost tripped over a curb. *A great horned owl... what the fuck?*

I stared at it. Somehow, I just knew those eyes belonged to Grimm.

"Go back to the car!" I ordered. "No feet, no hands, no service!" I shouted.

Instead, Grimm flew into my shoulder, throwing me off balance. He dragged at my shirt, careful not to slice me with those razor-sharp talons and yet clearly, he was trying to stop me from going forward.

I tried to brush him off as I charged toward the front door—toward what used to be the front door. My friends were in there!

Ignoring the owl–at least he'd stopped hooting, I slowed, walked along the edge of the building quietly, and peered in.

The line was gone. Inside there was blood everywhere, with furniture knocked awry, body parts and a strange shuffling sound, like feet on a carpet.

A bullet whizzed by my head.

I dropped to my knees and rolled hard for the wall.

And that's when I had the displeasure of seeing the cause of the mass chaos: people with stringy hair, eyes of an unnatural milky white, and skin the color of a dead fish. As if that weren't creepy enough, they walked as if they had four feet, like a bear. Then some of them stood and I wondered if they'd suddenly noticed me. They didn't react which made me wonder if they were blind.

Adrenaline hit hard at that moment.

Under the strobing club lights, I saw that one of the zombies had mauled a body. As I stared at it, I realized the body was that of my high school crush, Zephyr Milano.

For all that is holy, why!

My self-preservation kicked in. It's selfish I know, but what chance did I stand if a vampire—a freaking member of the Monster Squad—couldn't fight these things off. Eleutian had his hands full but he must have noticed too because I heard him gasp. Then he twisted his torso, and hurled magic at the thing's chest. It dropped, but just as quickly stumbled to its feet.

Fuck me! It hadn't even phased it. The dude must be hurtin' if his magic was that weak. Next, he dove behind the bar and when he popped up, it was to fire a shotgun shell point-blank into the zombie's face. He barely had time before another zombie rushed him. He needed help, and there was no one else here.

Before I had time to talk myself out of it, I crept up on a zombie that was getting to its feet. With a quick glance down at the symbols painted on my knuckles, I went on the attack. *Pow pow!* It faltered and looked over its shoulder at me in confusion as I punched it in the back with my spell. For a breathless moment I realized I was looking into the face of a blood splattered woman, skeletal in appearance with large cheekbones and hollow sockets where the eyes should have been. This had been somebody's daughter, wife, or possibly mother. She started jumping in a circle, and kept jumping. Her fierce growl now sounded more like a bewildered wail. Even the flies that had hitched a ride on her body seemed confused, they shifted away and buzzed around me.

Zephyr was bleeding and shaking, but he managed to speak, "W-what is w-wrong with i-it?"

"Hey there hunk! Don't you worry about it. It can't hurt us anymore," I replied, giving the flies a cursory swat. "We need to get you fixed up. What happened?"

"W-we were taken by surprise." He was speaking slowly and having trouble getting the words out. Blood bubbled at his mouth. "M-my c-crossbow's outside." He closed his eyes as he said it, and he didn't open them again.

Panic whirled inside me and I wanted to vomit. "Don't die on me!" *My goddess, this was so cruel. I finally got to know my crush and now he's bleeding out.*

I needed to save him, but what could I do? I placed my hand over his chest where the zombie had pierced his heart with a piece of a broken chair leg, and attempted the words Julep had taught me for a voodoo-based healing spell. Nothing happened and I almost gave up… but then when I was right on the brink, magic thrummed to life inside me—so hard I almost got sick. This had never happened before. The feeling was unnatural—like an inky darkness was filling me. I panicked and pulled back but then the guilt took over. *How could I let Zephyr die?*

"What's happenin'?" Eleutian shouted.

"What do you mean? He's dying," I stated.

"He's a vampire," Eleutian shot back. "He's already undead!"

"I know that! But they must still be able to die because that's what happening here… I have to tether him to his body or mine," I shouted. "Throw me some salt."

"Salt? For what?"

"A margarita. I'm feeling a little parched!"

I felt a rush of air. The owl had flown over to me and in his claw was the salt. Eleutian jerked the rifle up to his shoulder and fired just behind me. Whirling, I saw the first zombie had climbed to its feet.

I was getting low on energy but before the zombie could scramble to its feet, I punched it with the second

165

insanity spell.

Then I went back to work on Zephyr. His pulse was back.

At that instant a howl burst through the club, carrying with it a familiar earthy smell, one I recognized from the séance—dirt. Every light flickered and winked out. Screams erupted—high-pitched and terrified—and I realized that, for the first time, I wasn't the only one who could hear them. But what did that mean?

"It's the new Hell Hounds." Grimm whispered from my side, now in his devastatingly handsome human form. "You've broken the natural law of death. You've got to hide him."

"How does one hide a full-grown man?" *Should I just shove him in my purse?* I thought, rather sarcastically to myself.

"Hurry up! You've only got seconds." My breath came in short gasps as I opened my purse and took out my knife and nail polish. It held drops of my blood. "I'm sorry. This will hurt." As fast as I could I cut a sigil into him that I thought would work. Swiping the coating over it so our blood would mix and seal. It would have to do until I could get to my tattoo machine.

"It's not working." I strained to keep my heart from battering my lungs. I wasn't ready to die—to have my soul obliterated! But the howls were racing closer, back on my trail. Nothing would protect us from the Hounds' supernatural jaws.

Grimm glanced desperately between Zephyr and me. His glowing white eyes locking at last on mine.

"It will. You need to do a binding spell now." The hell hounds were coming—with roars so intense they consumed my every thought.

"Say it!" he pulled me close.

The Hounds were growing near, I could hear the growls reverberating in their phantom throats. "I don't know what that is—" I shrieked over the gnashing of their teeth. "I'm only eighteen for fuck's sake. Help me!" I grabbed Grimm's sleeve and yanked him to me.

He started whispering words I didn't recognize and could barely hear. Then he leaned in until our foreheads touched. "Say *curabit nos. Impero.*"

I hesitated. The hell hounds' growls shattered through my skull.

"*Curabit nos. Impero!*" I screamed.

Bursts of kaleidoscopic color flashed in Grimm's eyes, and he placed his hand over Zephyr's chest. The air around us crackled with electric energy.

Abruptly, the room went silent and for a moment I assumed Cerberus—the guardian of the spirit realm had vanished, but when I turned... there it was—the five headed beast just as I'd drawn it. Only much scarier in real life.

I swallowed hard, almost choking on my own saliva. We hadn't fooled it. We'd fooled ourselves.

"Patience," Grimm whispered, sitting so utterly still he might have been a statue.

After what felt like hours of holding my breath, the beastly dog finally stopped sniffing the air. It let out one final howl and then dissipated in a twirling fog of black smoke. I darted forward to watch it go.

Over the dance floor they bounded, their feet barely skimming the ground, before they winked out of existence completely.

Grimm leaned onto his knees and rested his fingers at his temples.

"That was a close call. I don't understand though. If Zephyr is a hell hound, why was he in any danger from them?"

"Zephyr was a part of the hell hound. He's not anymore. He's still susceptible to the same laws as everyone else. When this unit was disbanded, they would have chosen five new protectors to become the beast."

"So, these guys aren't actually hell hounds anymore?"

"No, they were demoted. They are now known as the Monster Squad. They send the monsters—the ones the Hell Hound can't sense, back to Hell, but… if one of them dies, they die. They're not immortal."

More screams and then another gunshot split the night.

I winced. "I guess no one told them."

"Colt needs back up," Zephyr said, his voice shaking. He was recuperating but he was nowhere near well enough to fight.

"Find Bodhi," I screamed at Grimm, then I raced up the stairs.

Pausing as I entered the next level, I took in the details of the room at a glance—it was apocalyptic. Were those body parts? Oh fuck! The room had been painted in blood. Colten was holding his own, a lean-mean ginger-haired fighting machine. He was staving off a pack of zombies in the corner, but one of the zombies was in the process of tearing apart a closet door while someone screamed from inside it. He looked over at me and grinned, "Hey Midnight! Lookin' good. Feel free to jump in anytime."

Oh man. If Eleutian's magic couldn't take these bastards down, would mine do much better?

In for a penny, in for a pound. I couldn't stand by and watch this poor girl get devoured like a steak at the Keg. Marching forward with more confidence than I felt, I brushed my arm against the zombie's shoulder, activating the acid and narrowly moving back in time before it chomped on me.

In a matter of seconds, the spell began to eat away at the zombie's shoulder. Nothing like a little chemical burn to make you forget you're hungry. It moved away from the door and tried to swipe at its shoulder. Then it changed its mind and fixed its hollow eyes on me, or it felt like it did—I don't think it could actually see. Even as the acidic spell consumed flesh and bone, it moved toward me.

As I backed up, it advanced. I moved left, it moved left. I went right, yep, you guessed it. It did too. Damn. *It's like we're locked in a dance to the death.*

I had one spell left and a small knife. No wait scratch that, I think I dropped the knife. *Shit, Midnight!* This was going to suck so bad.

I looked over at Colten, "I need to get within chomping distance. Remind me to create magical throwing stars."

He grinned, "You know what they say, babe, necessity is the mother of invention, or some shit like that."

Keeping my eyes on the advancing zombie, I edged toward the door. The zombie turned its ear as if were tracking the movement by sound. For a moment I thought it was going to go after another girl. Then its attention came back to fix on me. It gathered itself, and I tensed.

It was going to leap, and when it did, it wouldn't be

expecting me to dive forward, because that would be stupid. *Like running into a burning building.* But if I could get underneath it, I could punch it with the spell.

After that, I didn't know what I was going to do.

One colossal mistake at a time. That could be my motto.

The zombie leaped, and I dove forward. As you can imagine, the maneuver didn't go to plan. *C'est la vie.* I landed hard on the floor and despite my fish flopping technique, I didn't get over fast enough, nor did I get a punch in, so when it spun around to face me, there I was lying on my back looking up at it like romance situation gone bad. On the plus side, the acidic spell had eaten away one shoulder and part of its torso. How the fucker was still moving, was beyond me. If the government ever got their hands on these guys, they'd make for scary, super soldiers.

My only option was to use my last spell while I faced all those killer teeth head-on. Not a great option.

Speaking of which, it bared it's disgusting teeth and snaked its head down to me, and on the edge of death, all I could think was: I am the worst zombie killer in the world and you could use a mint. Pain blazed and my arms shook as I fought to keep that mangled decaying corpse face at a safe distance.

"Come on stupid, don't you know you're dying." I

hissed.

Of course, it probably thought the same of me. Or it would if it could think.

Just as my arms were about to give out, a pair of strong hands clamped around the zombie's head, twisting it sharply to the side with a sickening crack.

My stomach flipped as the zombie's body collapsed heavily over mine.

Shouts sounded outside, and sirens, but in the room, silence fell.

I peered out from underneath my arm. I was pinned. Bodhi stood over me, breathing heavily.

"Do you have a death wish? Why would you run toward the murder scene?"

I wiped what I could only imagine was zombie blood off my lips. "Why would you?"

"It's my job." Bodhi ground out the words.

"Really? I hope the medical benefits are worth it."

Colten laughed from his corner of the room which earned him a dirty look from Bodhi who was now on his way to help me.

As I struggled to get out from under the dead weight lying on top of me, something heavy creaked on the stairs. Before I had a chance to call out a warning, Bodhi was attacked from behind.

His grunt gave me the push I needed and I wriggled loose—like a fish on the line. The zombie that had him pinned against the wall was chomping his teeth barely inches from Bodhi's face.

"Stab him, Midnight! Right where I showed you," Colten yelled from his corner. "There's a knife right there!"

I saw the knife on the floor and picked it up, slamming it right into the back of his neck at the base of the skull. I angled the knife up and pushed with all my strength just the way Colten had trained me. The sensation of the knife gliding between his skin and grazing off the bone was enough to trigger my gag reflex. I fought the urge to vomit and swallowed the bile that rose in my throat. An instant later the man was no longer struggling.

Silence fell again. Outside, sirens approached, and I could hear people shouting.

Bodhi looked up at me with such intensity. "You still have time to leave the city, you know."

"My mother is missing," I muttered. "I'm not going anywhere until I find her. Besides I don't think I have much of a choice. My Aunt Aurora is kind of a big deal. She's assigned a protector to me. He's supposed to move in with me next week."

Watching me, Bodhi said, "Aurora? What was your last name was, again?"

173

"Midnight."

Bodhi had straightened to his full height when I had, and he was watching me sharply. He took a step closer until I could sense his body heat along one side of my body. "How could I not have put it together? You're Aurora Batavian's niece! Holy Shit. Why didn't you tell me? What are you even doing out on your own? Does Demas know?"

"You know Professor Batavian?"

"Of course, he's the Alpha. Shit! I better call him."

The Alpha they mentioned before? *Wow. Small world.* "It's fine. I'll go home. I live a few blocks from here," I said but it was too late to argue, he was already punching numbers into a cell.

Bodhi's expression creased as he explained the situation. I could just picture the grim looks the studious professor on the phone would be giving if he were here.

"Yes, Sir," Bodhi said. "I won't leave her alone."

I raised my eyebrows as I looked at him pointedly. He looked magnificently impervious to my speaking glance. Actually, truly magnificent.

He hung up the phone, "Colt's going to take my bike and I'm going to ride with you. We're going to swing by the campus to speak with Demas and pick up some things and then we'll head on to the guest house on the Midnight Estate."

"But I don't have anything with me."

"Text your guardian and ask her to pack you a bag. Let her know that Eleutian will swing by now for your things. She's welcome to come if she's worried."

I laughed at the thought. "Fat chance. She's got Grand-mère to worry about, and Grand-mère would never leave the house. Good luck to any zombie that tried to make her."

"Well… all right, I guess it will just be you, me, Zephyr, Eleutian and Colten."

With an effort, I had to restrain myself from making a face at him.

"Are you sure there's no one else you'd like to invite to my place?" I said, in an icy tone.

"Now that you mention it. I might know a few others interested in your bodyguard/nursing services."

I smiled. "You'd better be joking."

18

MIDNIGHT WITCH

s I pulled onto the campus property, Bodhi turned to me. "Now wait here. I'll just be a moment."

Before I could argue, and argue was what I was about to do, he was off and running. I sat for only a moment before deciding that staying put like a trained dog was not for me. Part of me wanted to just ditch his bossy ass but then again, I really didn't want to face off against those zombies alone.

I turned to the owl in the back seat—who could thankfully dull his talons upon will. "Grimm! Let's follow Bodhi."

Before I knew it, we were out of the car and on our way into the hall. Thank you, Bodhi, for leaving the door open.

With a click of his talons, Grimm marched in the opposite direction from the one I had been heading until we came to a janitor's closet.

"What's this?"

Grimm scratched at the door.

"You want me to open it—it's just a closet."

Grimm looked up at me and I got the feeling he was distinctly unimpressed with my lack of trust in him. So, I pulled the door open and much like before—with Professor Batavian—a sparkling portal appeared.

"Very good," I said, and stepped through the shimmering wall of light. We walked some more until we came to a familiar place. "That's Professor Batavian's classroom," I said, pointing to the darkened room.

The light was on in the room next to his. That must be where Bodhi is. An obnoxious sign informing people to knock covered the glass portion so I couldn't see in, but he had to be in there. I knocked. As the moments ticked by and no one answered the door, my determination faded and frustration wormed in.

I pressed at the handle to check if the door was locked. It flew open and promptly hit something— presumably glass, judging by its spectacular crash.

"Didn't you see the sign?" shouted a frazzled man with shaggy hair the color of mud. It was the same man who'd flashed his fangs at me that day in the hall outside Demas' classroom.

What was his name again?

He still wore the same clothes although he looked much more disheveled, not to mention he wore oversized yellow rubber gloves and goggles that covered half his face.

177

"Didn't you see the sign?" he snapped.

I glanced behind. "I knocked," I said sheepishly, "but no one answered."

"Well, then take the hint." He stomped toward me, and I shrank back, ready to retreat through the open door should his fangs sharpen. I flicked my eyes down where broken glass and debris covered the ground.

I opened my mouth to apologize but clamped it back shut when he declared me reckless, thoughtless, and I even think I heard rude mentioned.

I took his foulmouthed moment to examine the classroom. It was crammed with books, beakers, and equipment one might find in more of an inventor's lair than a science lab.

He folded his arms over his chest. "You've ruined my experiment. What in the hell are you doing here, and how did you even get in?"

I took a weary breath, "I came with Bodhi."

He wrinkled his nose. "Well, where is he?"

"I don't know. He left me in the car but I decided not to wait."

"Of course, you didn't wait. Impertinent child. Well, he's not here," he snapped.

"I can see that," I replied, turning to go.

"Wait! Is that a fucking owl," he suddenly squeaked.

"What the hell is that thing doing in here?"

Glancing over my shoulder, I looked at Grimm.

"He's tame... mostly." I teased.

Squinting, the vampire studied me. "Hold up one minute. That's not just an owl." His eyes lit up. "Is this the psychompomp they've been chasing down?"

He stepped closer to me. I had to roll my head back to see his face—he was at least half a foot taller than I—and he gazed down with barely concealed distaste.

I didn't answer.

He harrumphed. "I have a mess to clean up thanks to you, so if you're planning to hang around, could you at least stand somewhere else?" he gripped me by both wrists, trailing his fingers strangely over my veins and pushed me backward out the door. I was so shocked to be touched I couldn't even protest. All I could do was skitter back where he directed.

With his hands still planted on my arms and with his lips curved in a satisfied grin, he drawled, "I'm William Van Rogue, by the way," he said it so casually, as if all introductions were preceded by manhandling. "Pleasure to meet you, Miss..."

I twisted free and gave him my haughtiest stare. "We've met before. Do you really not remember me? I'm Evangeline Midnight."

He bowed low and doffed an imaginary hat. "That's

179

right. We met in the hall. A Midnight, huh? Why then, you're practically royalty, of course I don't know what you're doing here. The Midnights always attend the New York campus." He whirled around and strode back into the lab. The door slammed shut behind him.

I stood outside the lab. My shoulders and neck were locked with fiery rage, and I felt as if flames might spew from my fingertips and eyeballs.

"I thought I told you to wait in the car," said a rich, baritone voice behind me.

"Oh great," I mumbled. "More assholes to deal with."

Surprisingly, Bodhi laughed. "Sorry about Van Rogue. He's in a bit of a mood tonight."

"I can tell. Who is he anyway? Is he another member of the Monster Squad?"

"Naw, he's part of the support unit assigned by the supernatural council. We're front line and they're behind the scenes. He gets bossed around by Aurora a lot, so he's not a huge fan of the Midnights."

"That explains it. Apparently, I belong in New York, whatever that means. So, he was never a hell hound? He's definitely got the demeanor."

Bodhi laughed, "I'll have to tell him you said so. He'll get a kick out of that but no. He's not a hell hound, just a vampire. Come on. Let's go. I met with Demas and got what

I needed."

I was about to question him further when I realized that we both stank like the Dead. "Yes, let's find some soap and water. The professor just sniffed me, like actually sniffed me, so I'm going to take that as a hint."

Bodhi laughed, "Well he is a vampire, and you are covered in blood."

"Oh, right. That also makes sense."

19

MIDNIGHT WITCH

"Here we are," I said as we turned down the tree-lined drive. The same place Aunt Aurora had taken me to not that long ago. I flicked a glance back over my shoulder to wear Grimm was leaning forward all willy-nilly in the back. "Hold on!" the words had barely left my mouth when we hit one of the many brutal potholes.

"Holy, did you miss any?" Bodhi snarked from the passenger seat after three more.

"In fact, I did." I snapped back.

Bodhi smirked at me. "Hey, eyes on the road."

I inhaled deeply widening my nostrils in frustration. I think he liked getting under my skin.

"Look at this place," he mumbled as the mansion came into view. "I can just picture the dames in their antebellum gowns sipping tea on the porch."

I snorted at the image. "Yeah, well, all I can see is the ghosts, spiders and animal infestations. Let's hope nothing crawled out of the water and made a home."

"Touché," Bodhi agreed. "As comfy as a crypt."

"What's wrong with a crypt?" Grimm asked, his voice testy as he rolled down the window. "Some people like crypts."

"Oh, you've decided to speak again," Bodhi said, ever the agitator. "Too bad. I was enjoying the silent treatment."

I cleared my throat. "Seriously, you two. Do you have to do this right now? I have a headache."

Grimm transformed back into one of his furry forms with a *poof* and flew out the window.

"Good riddance," Bodhi hollered after him. "I'd chase you but my wings are quite a bit bigger."

I rolled my eyes. *Men and their obsession with size.*

"So, my aunt said she'd have the guest house prepared," I said, changing the subject. "Fingers crossed it's clean, dry, and has somewhere we can get horizontal."

"I like the sound of that," he growled out.

I looked over at him and furrowed my brow. "Perv! You know what I mean. Somewhere we can put our feet up... separately."

Bodhi laughed, "Yeah, I get it, doll face. I'm teasing."

"Dollface? What are you like a hundred?"

Bodhi looked up like he was counting in his head.

"Whatever. Forget I asked." I tilted my head, staring up at the spooky, old house. The balcony's had changed position. I rubbed my eyes. I must be tired. "Does anything look funny to you?"

Bodhi crossed his arms again and stared hard in the same direction.

"No. What do you mean? He tilted, as though studying it. "You think we're being ambushed. You see something. Tell me," he said, his voice growing more hyper.

"No, sorry, nothing like that."

He relaxed back.

"I just mean, does it ever change in appearance to you?"

His attention sharpened. "I don't think so."

I gave the house a second, more thoughtful look. "It changes back and forth for me, but I think I'm the only one who can see it."

"That must be quite the mind fuck."

"It is," I agreed.

"Any hypothesis?"

"Huh?" I glanced over at him.

"Idea? Any idea why you're seeing things that other people aren't."

"Oh, right. No, I don't know why. My aunt said something strange though.

"Oh yeah? Care to share…"

"She said the house won't let just anyone in. My grandparents died a year ago, and now the key turns in the lock but the door doesn't open. It's weird, right?"

"Not really. It sounds like she needs a locksmith."

He didn't get it. I bit back my annoyance. "No, it's bigger than that. She said they even tried to break a window." I turned to face him and reached out my hand, turning down the music down. "This is going to sound 'out there' but I think it's because the house isn't fully here. It's mostly here, but it's like it's not in sync with out realm."

"Wow. You know about realms and you're only eighteen."

"Yeah, sort of had no choice given what's happening lately."

He frowned. "Do you think it changes for you because of your magic? Like maybe it's something to do with the fact that you're part-witch? If so, Lou might know something."

"Lou?"

"Eleutian, I mean."

"Yeah, maybe." Looking back at the house, I chewed on a thumbnail. "Aurora said it's 'cause I'm blood related."

"I'm confused. Your aunt wasn't blood related?"

"No, my grandmother had an affair. This house comes from my grandfather's side."

He rubbed his chin thoughtfully.

"She showed me a photo when she brought me here.

185

That's where I first noticed the house itself, looked different in person that it did in the photo. Like, really different. I've been thinking about it ever since."

"You think it was maybe in a different position when the photo was taken. Like the way the stars and planet move?"

I nodded, growing excited at his explanation. "Exactly. I hope I can get in tomorrow. I'm new to magic, but I want to experiment. Julep, the witch who's training me thinks I could have a talent for manipulating time and space. I know it sounds like I'm on a bad LSD trip, doesn't it? Well, I guess we should find that cottage, or guest house—whatever it's called. I clearly need sleep." I took my foot off the break as we pulled up to the guest house.

Bodhi grabbed his duffle bag out of the trunk and we headed inside. Once he'd opened and closed all the doors and looked under the beds like some sort of paranoid lunatic, he started a fire then walked to the door, cracking it open.

"Hey! Where are you going?" I asked.

"Perimeter check," he replied.

"But we just…" he'd already slammed the door so I swallowed the words and began making beds.

A moment after Bodhi returned, I heard the sound of a motorcycle arrive and shut off.

"Your guests, I presume?"

Bodhi headed for the window, standing off to the side as he glanced out. "Let's hope it's just Lou and Z," he said, opening the door and waving. "And not the undead."

"I don't think they're permitted to have a motorcycle license." I snorted at my own joke. "Holy shit! I'm giddy. Healing Zephyr zapped my magic."

"You healed Z?" Bodhi asked just as Eleutian stepped inside, "And some. Boy, oh, boy, that zombie made a meal out of him, I tell ya. She brought that vamp back to life, or unlife I guess should say." Eleutian chuckled at his own joke.

"Where is he?"

"He's outside. He mentioned something about getting some fresh air."

Bodhi nodded, "Can you go set some wards around the area. If we're lucky, the rest of the night will be quiet."

Eleutian nodded. "Quiet would be good. Unlikely but nice." He laughed to himself.

I could feel worry creeping in. What would happen. They couldn't stay with me indefinitely. "Are you going to leave me here once you know I'm safe?" My voice cracked on the last word and immediately I felt stupid.

"What?! Like we're going to let one of those things hunt you down Aurora Batavian's niece."

I faked a laugh. His comment hit a nerve. Was that all I was, Aurora Batavian's niece? "I guess I should get that

187

tattooed onto my forehead, huh?"

"It couldn't hurt and I know just the tattoo artist," he teased back.

Wow. What a doofus, I thought turning away. Could he really not see that he'd hurt me or maybe, more likely, he just didn't give a shit.

I shuffled my feet, moving onto another topic. "Those things, they hardly paused when you guys shot them."

Bodhi shifted his head like it was no big deal. "You have to hit them in the brain. End the connection…"

I stared at him.

"…with the necromancer," he explained when I motioned for him to continue. "It's sort of an exact spot. They're tough to kill, but if you put one between their eyes, it'll put them down or you can sever the spinal cord. Your choice."

"Which is why the knife worked." I clenched my hands. "I guess I'm gonna need some new designs for these guys. I'm thinking pulse bombs or guard dogs." I pictured the outlines in my brain, tracing the air with my finger as if I were sketching. "Anyway, I'm gonna go clean up. How are you so clean, anyway?" I muttered, eyeing his shirt with resentment.

"I don't know. I was on my feet a lot."

I tilted an eyebrow. "Liar."

He smirked. "I changed at the University."

"I take it your whole wardrobe is black?"

"I feel it best represents my happy soul."

I couldn't help but let out a huge belly laugh. Thankfully, I didn't snort. That had actually happened to me once in the cafeteria and I'd wanted to die for the rest of the day. "Oh, shit. I think I'm delirious cause, dude, you're not that funny."

As I turned away to head for the bathroom, he caught my arm. "Evangeline!" His eyes looked all big and soulful. He was pretty fucking hot when he wasn't pissing me off. "You went head-to-head with zombies that were over twice your size and weight, and you did it without hesitating. That was pretty fucking impressive."

I smiled, warring with myself for it. I didn't want to appear like one of those annoying girls from school who needed male approval. *Fuck the patriarchy!* That was my motto. Well, it was my mother's motto but I agreed.

"Seriously," he squeezed my wrist. "It was one of the bravest things I've ever seen. You were so badass. Are you really okay?"

"I don't know. Would you consider me a psycho if I said I was great. That I didn't feel bad at all about killing those things?"

"No. Of course not," he said without hesitation. "You did what you had to do."

"Right. But the law doesn't necessarily always see it that way. We can't just kill people because we feel threatened. Abused women everywhere are proof of that."

"Yeah, well, laws are sometimes about politics. You killed to protect others tonight." His lips spread into a soft smile. "Besides they were already dead. You know that right. The necromancer was just reanimating them like puppets."

He had a point. Though a little voice inside of me still told me I should feel bad. When I didn't answer, he prompted me. "So, you're okay then?"

"I will be," I nodded, "after a hot shower."

He grinned.

Whoa! "Stop right there, perv! Don't even bother picturing it. Trust me when I say, stripping off these blood-soaked clothes is not going to be sexy."

Bodhi shook his head, his smile wide. "I disagree."

***

THE FIERY TEMPERED BEAST

Bodhi watched Evangeline disappear behind the bathroom door. He hadn't been blowing smoke up her ass. She was a brave badass chick. She'd really surprised him tonight.

After speaking to her in the street, he'd texted his

men to let them know to set up a perimeter at the club where she was headed, then he'd followed her and she knocked his socks off when she'd race inside the club. What sort of eighteen year old girl raced head-first into a club that was under attack.

The sound of the water being switched on pulled him from his memory. He pictured her pulling back the curtain and stepping in.

Water dripping down the curves of her body.

He hardened.

Fuck! He felt like a teenage boy again?

He jerked away and hurried to the door, "I'll be outside helping Lou. Enjoy your shower."

Even the word caused a throbbing sensation.

Was it wrong that he wanted to share the warmth with her? It had been a long time since he was this intrigued by someone. Which was ridiculous because she was practically magical royalty. Aurora would surely have him skinned alive if he touched her. He had failed his duties and proved himself unfit. Besides, he had a job to do, he couldn't afford to think with his dick. At least not until Melinoe was back in the bowels of Hell where he deserved to be.

He got down to business and set a series of wards around the property. Whether or not they would work on zombies was anybody's guess, but at least if something triggered a ward, one of them would feel it, so they wouldn't be ambushed again.

After he doublechecked to make sure there were no direct scent trails leading to this location, he dialed the Alpha to give his update.

Once the conversation with Demas was finished, Bodhi pocketed his phone. He paused to consider the shadowed antebellum manor, and then strode back to the guest house. Inside, everything was quiet. When he walked into the living room, he saw Evangeline was wrapped in a blanket and curled up on the couch in front of the fire.

Gently he walked closer to her. Evangeline's weary voice asked, "All quiet on the home front?"

He stared at the gas fireplace for a moment, letting the flames mesmerize him. Slowly he said, "Z says he can feel that you're in pain," he nudged her thigh. As she shifted, he sat on the edge of the couch.

"Oww!" she said grumpily.

He angled his head. "Just be quiet and show me where you hurt."

She grimaced as she peeled back one corner of the blanket. Underneath, she wore a black Calvin Klein sports bra and boy-cut underwear. They showed off the long line of her slender, muscled legs. He saw large bruises and contusions. No doubt she had them on her back as well.

"Just assume if it's between the top of my head and the bottom of my feet, it hurts."

"You do know," he said, quietly stern. "Colt is going to need to increase your combat training if you're going to stay alive."

"Is that your professional opinion?"

"You're kind of a smartass," he said on a note of discovery.

She nodded. As tired as she looked, her eyes twinkled with mischief. "So, they tell me. Anyway, is everyone an instructor around here or is it just Demas and Colten?"

"Not everyone. Lou teaches light magic and science but Z was only a student up until recently although he's a major tech wiz so I don't know what his role will be at the academy yet. If we succeed in our mission then things may change."

"And you? What do you teach? Bedside manners?"

He smiled and traced a finger up her thigh. "The art of seduction."

She sat up and leaned toward him. "Really? Well, I don't want to show you how to do your job but...." Her fingers locked behind the back of his neck as she kissed him softly on the mouth.

And just like that, he was crazy with desire to feel her naked flesh. He reached down and cupped her breast; he could feel the jut of her nipple through the thin material of her sports bra. She had generous breasts and he imagined what they looked like. The curve fit beautifully into his hand. Her breath was coming faster, the more he caressed. Little sparks of painful need ran up and down his cock.

"I'm sorry." Her fingers closed around his wrist, and she turned her face away from his kiss. "Stop," she said, her voice strangled. Bodhi froze. "This–we–I shouldn't have kissed you like that. I'm sorry for starting something."

His cock pulsed even as he tried to make sense of what she was saying. Then her words sank in, and they leveraged a glimmer of sanity into his overheated, lust-filled brain. "Of course." He backed up worried his eyes and skin might change color and scare her.

"I don't mean to tease. I just forgot that I'm sort of outnumbered here and vulnerable. It was a stupid thing to do."

They were both breathing heavily, and he was sure that her heart was pounding as hard as his. There were six full-grown—very powerful—men here, or on their way here, and she was one eighteen year old girl. Of course, they would never hurt her but how was she to know that. "Don't apologize," he said, getting up, "I understand completely, but just so you know, so you can sleep easy tonight. We would never do anything to you without your complete approval."

She smiled and he was pleased to see that his words had comforted her. He, on the other hand was experiencing the most uncomfortable and painful hard-on he'd ever had. All he wanted to do was rip what remained of her clothing off and take her until she screamed with pleasure.

Instead he left her alone in the guesthouse, pulling the kitchen door closed behind him. He'd stretch his wings out and do a few laps to blow off steam. And if that didn't work, he'd jerk off.

20

MIDNIGHT WITCH

After Bodhi went outside, I got up to get a glass of water and stared out the window for a moment, listening to the sounds of the bayou as they seeped in—the guttural croaking of a hundred frogs, the splash of the gators. Perhaps, it was a good thing I'd put a stop to the romance, the fatigue of adrenaline was now setting in. Whatever the plan was, I hoped it would allow me to sleep-safely-for a few hours. I found a bed in one of the rooms and stretched out, immediately plunging into a dark pit. I slept like the dead—which was much better than fighting them— until I came alert with a jerk. I could sense the day had advanced well past early morning.

Pushing out of bed, I ran my hands through my hair and guzzled the water on the nightstand.

I felt dull and sore and, oh no, had I really kissed Bodhi last night? He was Hollywood sexy, like John Wick, damn it. Just the right amount of exotic good looks mixed with a macho personality and yet he'd been so open last night, I felt like I could just slide right inside his soul if I'd wanted to.

Evangeline Midnight, I chastised, *you have more to worry about than your libido right now.*

The guest house was warm enough, still the shivers hit me as I stood up in just my underwear. Thankfully, one of the boys had thoughtfully dropped off my black leather bag sometime throughout the night. Donning my robe, I shuffled my feet into slippers and went to see who was up.

I found Zephyr in the kitchen. He appeared to have recently showered. He wore a pair of black pants, but he hadn't put on a shirt yet, and his hair was wet and slicked back, outlining the strong, graceful bone structure of his head, neck, and shoulders. Great. More temptation.

He had positioned his chair so that he sat in a patch of sunlight streaming in through the window, and he was polishing a gun with slow, steady strokes.

I glared at him. His beauty was hard and uncompromising and completely, entirely masculine. Without a shirt, I could see his abs...drool... along with the scars on his torso where I'd healed him yesterday. The slanting sunlight sliced across his face, highlighting the sharp cheekbones, the bold, straight nose and lean jaw.

So, he was mouthwateringly handsome. Inhumanly handsome. He had that Vampire allure.

He glanced at me, a sharp, piercing look, then went back to polishing his gun. "No. Sunlight doesn't burn me."

"Huh?"

"Oh, you were staring," he said. "I assumed that's what you were thinking."

"I wasn't but that is a good question. Are all vampires like you?"

He shook his head. "No, it depends. Some are more sensitive to it. It's sort of like humans and food allergies."

I nodded. "Speaking of food…"

"Sorry. There's not much to eat besides toast."

"No coffee?"

He shook his head.

"That's a shame." I moved to fill the teakettle with water and set it on the stove. "Because coffee helps me do things…. like say words and not murder people. Like Aunt Aurora who is obviously a tea drinker."

"Shouldn't be long now. Bodhi went out for supplies."

Grimm appeared, still in his owl form. Most likely, he remembered how bitchy I was the other morning because he took off again. *Poor guy.* Looking through cupboards, I found a banana and an unopened jar of peanut butter.

While the water heated for tea, I bit off a hunk of banana and scooped out a spoonful, then turned to lean against the counter to watch Zephyr polish his gun. Good Lord, when was he going to put on a shirt?

"What's it like to shoot a real gun?" I asked, slowly licking the peanut butter from the spoon between bites.

"As opposed to a fake one?" he walked over to me leaning against the counter and licked the corner of my mouth. "I suppose the outcome."

"What'd you do that for?"

"You had a little peanut butter there. Thought I'd help you out there. Especially, since you didn't offer me any."

I smirked, "Stop watching me eat."

His pupils dilated and turned a golden amber hue, and he mouthed back, "How can I? Watching you eat that banana in your underwear is practically pornographic."

The air sucked out of my lungs. Pulling my robe closed, I whispered, "I should go."

He snaked an arm around my waist and hauled me against his torso, "Not just yet," then angling his head to swoop down and cover my mouth with his.

His kiss was just hot, but I'd just shared a kiss with Bodhi not twelve hours before. This felt shocking and blatantly sexual, and part of me was overcome with glee that I was crushed all up against that broad, muscled chest of his, while the other part melted down into wordless gibberish.

He took me by the back of the neck and ate at me like he was a starving man, pushing my back against the counter so that his hardened body was flush against mine. My arms lifted of their own accord and wound around his neck while I kissed him just as hungrily.

Heated images ran through my imagination. What I wanted to do to him. What I wanted him to do to me. I dug my nails into the back of his neck. He growled, thrusting the bulge of a long, hard erection against my pelvis, and his heart thudded, heavy and powerful, against my breasts.

Nothing else existed. Or maybe it did. The sound of a vehicle crunched over the gravel outside. He paused and lifted his head. His lips were wet from my mouth, while the look in his eyes was so heated, I knew the same images had run through his imagination too. We were connected.

"We barely know each other," I said. "But it doesn't feel like that."

"It feels like I'm already inside you," he growled.

Holding my gaze, he took hold of my hips, firmly enough so that I felt the pressure from each of his long fingers, and with slow deliberation, he pushed his hips against mine. It felt so good I let my head fall back as I watched him.

"I don't know what happened but I feel like an addict and you're my drug. I couldn't stop thinking about you all night. It took every ounce of strength not to walk into your bedroom."

I put my finger to his mouth. "I find you sexy as hell too."

I felt him smile against my fingers. His fangs had popped out and he bit at my forefinger lightly, then stepped back.

Outside, a vehicle's doors slammed shut and I pushed him away. I had no idea how Bodhi would react if he saw the two of us behaving this way.

Angling my jaw, I said, "I have to go."

As I stomped out of the room, the dark sound of his laughter followed me. It had almost the same effect as if he had licked down my naked back. Shivering from reaction, I slammed the bathroom door and stared at myself in the aged mirror over the sink.

"Who are you, Evangeline?" I whispered to the wide-eyed girl staring back at me. This will not work out. But what if they didn't mind sharing? What if it was all just sex?

How amazing would that be? I almost melted into a puddle at the thought. My body wanted sex, just sex, lots of exuberant pleasure.

I decided to get on with the business of washing up and brushing my teeth. Then I slipped into the bedroom to dress in jeans, combat boots, and a black scoop-neck T-shirt. A little warm for Louisiana weather but I didn't know what kind of condition the house was in and the less exposed skin, the better. I glanced at my makeup bag and laughed under my breath–like anybody cared what I looked like, least of all myself–and left it tucked in the open suitcase. Then I grabbed up my own cell phone and the heavy, old keys to the manor house and walked out.

Bodhi had just finished putting the groceries away.

"Hey!" he typed briefly on his phone then slipped it in his pocket. "Where you off to?"

"The main house." I was having trouble looking him in the eye so instead, I stalked out of the guest house and didn't stop walking until I stood a few feet in front of the white-columned plantation house.

21

MIDNIGHT WITCH

The day was gorgeous, a perfect hot summer day in Louisiana. Bees droned by. Lavish, untamed greenery spilled from underneath trees, barely held in check by the simple, crude mowing job that kept the wide lawn from turning into an overgrown pasture.

Bodhi caught up with me after a minute and forced something hot into my hand.

"Oow... What's this?"

"Cinnamon Dolce Latte?" he said between his teeth, "I didn't know what you liked. Is everything okay?"

"Yeah," I laughed, "it's better now. Thanks! I just needed to think." I bit my lip and turned my attention back to the house. "Zephyr tell you I was bitching about the lack of coffee?"

"He might have mentioned that if we wanted to see the more hospitable side of you, we should get some."

I laughed. Too true. "I'm worse than the zombies if you don't give me my morning shot of caffeine." I held my hands out like some cartoon cutout of a zombie, "Caffeine! Caffeine!"

"Oh no, zombie jokes."

"Too early?" I questioned with a grin.

"Never."

We strolled around the perimeter of the massive house as we talked and it wasn't long before my shirt was stuck to me. I almost wished I had put on a pair of shorts. Bodhi eyed the place with a curious gaze. At last he squatted, selected a stone—and before I could ask him what the hell he was doing—whirled it at the window.

Poof! The rock banged against the glass but it disappeared right when it hit.

"What the fuck?" I turned to him. "That's my property. You trying to break my window?'

"No. Well, yes, but I had a feeling after our talk last night that it wouldn't work."

"So, where did it go?"

"I haven't a clue. I mean, the stone hit the house. We heard it." I rubbed my face as I tried to formulate the right words. "Maybe it's like a zombie. You can shoot it all you want but if you don't hit the right spot, it doesn't go down."

"Like a glancing blow in a boxing match. Okay, I'm gonna try again," he said. "If that's okay with you?"

"Whatever," I said and rolled my eyes, "but you break it, you bought it."

"Deal." This time he took aim with his wrist mounted

crossbow and shot it. Like the stone, the bolt zoomed across the space to the window and impacted it with another crack but this time it shot back and hit him in the chest.

"Bodhi!" I screamed his name as sweat droplets immediately formed on my forehead. The arrow stuck out of his left side, right in the heart. He wasn't breathing or even bleeding. He simply had no pulse. The house had killed him. Hit me once and receive a warning. Hit me twice, you're dead, I thought to myself. It doesn't play around.

I pressed my lips to his. Definitely no breath. He was gone.

I was a good, competent magic user when it came to tattooing, decent with spells and healing, but he was dead.

So, what?

I wouldn't let him go.

I held my hands over his chest where the bolt had struck. I had no salt, no runes, nothing to protect myself. I just had to pray I wasn't opening myself up to some dark, unseen force.

I closed my eyes and focused on my heartbeat. I focused on tethering his still heart to mine. Its rhythmic thump was pleasant, like the gentle rock of a ship. I inhaled, filling myself with magic until it filled me up—

No! I snapped my eyelids open. Wait a minute. This hadn't happened last time. I'd done something wrong.

What had Grimm taught me. I needed to draw a sigil. I took out my pen and drew a pair of linked hearts then I squeezed Bodhi's fingers and tried again, *"Curabit nos."* I felt my body fill once again with magic.

No, no, no. I needed to use the magic on him. Why was it filling inside of me?

"Curabit nos," I repeated. Nothing happened. I tried again, panic rising in my throat.

But still nothing happened.

I frantically scanned the area for help—anyone—my vision was turning spotty. I couldn't breathe!

I slumped onto the ground as the trees spun around me. Grimm, help! Someone, please, help! Must save Bodhi . . .

And with that thought, power burst from my hands, and the landscape. I was once again staring at the waterfall between realms, and I could just make out the landscape of a jungle on the other side. A shadowy figure was there—he was walking toward me.

"Bodhi?" I reached for him. Suddenly I was there. I was on the other side of the waterfall surrounded by dense vegetation. Small monkeys cooed overhead, watching me. Vines and brush obstructed my path, and the heat... I'd never felt such humidity. "Bodhi, is that you? Come back."

"Evangeline! What are you doing?" Grimm was

running toward me. I blinked rapidly as the world around me dissolved back into reality.

Grimm appeared at my side. "For fuck sakes," he swore. "What have you done?" he slid an arm behind me. I glanced into a young man's face. He was no longer an animal. "You have a body again?"

His forehead wrinkled. "You already knew that. What's wrong with? Have you two been drinking or something?"

"No. What?" It's not even lunchtime," I slurred, and then tried hard to remember if what I said was actually true . . . cause to be honest I was feeling kind of blitzed. I remembered having a banana and tea and yep, nope, I definitely had not had alcohol. "I swear I haven't been drinking."

He glared at me accusingly. "Well then, what did you do?"

"I'm not entirely sure, but I visited the waterfall again, Grimm! It's the most beautiful place, and the jungle. The trees grow so tall and so tight that they form this beautiful canopy. It's like being inside Mother Nature's womb. I know I'm not supposed to go there but I just think it's just so peaceful. You should come with me."

His eyes grew huge. "Oh shit. What were you trying to do?"

"Save Bodhi. The house just killed him." I laughed hysterically. I couldn't help it. "That sounds ridiculous, doesn't it? How can a house kill somebody? Why am I slurring, Grimm?"

He took a moment and felt for Bodhi's pulse.

"You brought another one back. Damn it! You're lucky the hell hounds didn't notice you. You need training, girl. Well, you succeeded. He's alive," he muttered, "but you're drunk on your ass off magic. You clearly took in too much!"

"You can get drunk on magic? I didn't know that. You know, you are so nice… can you help me sober up, please?" I asked, pawing at his face.

"It's just gonna take some time, Evangeline."

"But I have things to do."

"Well, I'm sorry but there's only one way to get rid of a magical buzz fast."

"Okay, well, let's do it…" I waved vaguely in the air.

"Umm," he said, "I think not!"

I puffed out my lips. "Fine. It feels good, anyway! You know what else would feel good right now, kissing you!" I snorted, and then laughed hysterically at that. "Oh, what is wrong with me? Anyway, for a demon ferret, or owl or whatever you are, you are really good looking. Did you know that? You really got that bad boy thing working for you. Like

Bodhi, although he's more mysterious and sweeter and you kind of scare me a little." I pouted my lips together and leaned forward. "Kiss me, demon, or tell me how to get rid of this feeling."

Grimm looked around and then leaned in like he actually might do it. "Sex. Evie. That is the only way to get rid of the excess energy fast." His eyes smoldered and our lips were almost touching when he whispered, "I think now would not be a good time—" He suddenly pulled away and his mouth quirked up, the faintest sheen of triumph in his eyes. "Now have a little sleep and come back to the guest house when you and Bodhi wake up." He held out his hand.

"Bastard!" I mumbled as my eyes closed.

* * *

Like striking a match, sexuality flared through his limbs and shot along all his nerve endings. He was suddenly so aroused. He could barely think of anything else besides getting Evangeline naked. Then it dawned on him, she looked worried. Her plush, full lips were still trembling with emotion.

It was not an expression he was used to seeing on her face. Strangely, it made him want to pause long enough to pass his hand over the heavy, straight mass of her hair.

He sat up, "Wait. Why am I on the ground?"

Tears were streaked down her face and there were blackened soot marks on her palms.

"What happened to your hands?"

She turned them over and studied them as if she'd only just noticed, herself. "I guess that's what happens when I revive someone without my protective runes drawn on."

"Revive someone? What happened?"

"The house has some sort of defense system and that arrow you shot bounced off it and came back at you."

"I was hit by my own bolt?" he privately pondered how the hell the arrow had pierced his dragon scales but then he remembered he had armed up. He'd been afraid his shifter appearance might scare her. "That's embarrassing," he said at last.

She nodded. "It stopped your heart but my magic started it again. Only I used too much power and then I was drunk and Grimm came and lectured me and put me to sleep and now I'm hungover."

"You saved me." He grabbed her by the wrist, hauled her against his chest, and as she oofed at the impact and laughed, he snaked his other hand around the back of her neck and kissed her.

He ate it all down. He devoured her, greedily. He stiffened into a painful hard spike of desire, while she slipped her arms around his waist, molded her body to his, and kissed him back. She met him, greed for greed, ragged breath for breath. He had never felt so alive, so connected to someone.

So, perplexed by all of it. By her.

There was something vulnerable in her face, like fine, thin crystal. For a moment she looked blinded, lost, and her lower lip trembled before she sucked it between even, white teeth. The sight bothered him greatly. He wanted to tuck her face into his neck and shelter that fragile vulnerability from the rest of the world so no one else ever saw it.

As he stared, the expression vanished and she snapped back to alertness. The mischief came back slowly, but it did come back.

She laughed up at him. "I'm sorry but I'm not feeling the greatest. Grimm said there was only one cure but he wouldn't give it to me. I think he's punishing me."

Lightly, he touched the dark smudge of shadow underneath one of her eyes. All joking aside, she did need more rest.

"Thank you," he said seriously. "Now, let's get you back to the guest house. We'll try this again tomorrow."

22

MIDNIGHT WITCH

The walk back to the cottage was exhausting but I stayed quiet and trudged on. We were almost there now.

"You know, you look kind of wiped," Bodhi said, noticing at last. "Maybe I drained you of your energy."

"Maybe." Every step was getting harder. I'd slowed to almost a stop. Thank goodness the door was right in front of us.

"I'll whip us up some dinner," Bodhi said and scooped me up into his arms carrying me up the last three steps inside the cottage.

"Oh sure, be the hero now. Where were you five minutes ago." I tried to laugh as he set me gently on the couch but a smile was all I could manage.

Grimm appeared, now back in his ferret form and climbed up onto my chest. Nuzzling between my breasts—the little pervert. With a gentle hand, I stroked his back, lulling myself to sleep until the clatter of plates roused me.

Knuckling my eyes, I sat up. The light had changed, and the shadows in the guest house had lengthened. The ferret hurried toward the kitchen and the door. I forced myself upright to join him in the kitchen.

Hungrily, I bit into the cucumber he'd cut up. Oh yum. I said around my mouthful, "Thank you."

One corner of Bodhi's mouth lifted. "You're welcome. Are you feeling better?"

"Much."

"Good. I contacted Demas. He's going to come tomorrow morning."

He took a bottle of cabernet sauvignon and opened it. Pouring wine into a tumbler, he handed it to me.

I took a large swallow of the rich, ruby-red liquid and sighed.

He poured more wine into another tumbler, set it on the counter, and opened the stove. "I made a meat pie for supper."

"You made a meat pie?"

"Well, I mean I bought it and put it in the oven. Zephyr's usually the cook. I prepped a salad too."

"Was it a bagged salad?" I teased, inhaling the yummy, meaty scent as he cut into it and plated a piece for me. "You're a regular Bobby Flay. Should we call the others?"

"No, they'll eat once I'm done. We work in shifts so someone's always watching the grounds."

I picked up my fork and took a bite. "All teasing

aside, it's delicious." I moaned.

"Thanks."

"Why are you guys guarding the house like sentinels. I thought you put up those magic wards."

"We did, but you can never be too safe. The necromancer is very powerful."

I nodded and focused on eating the rest of my dinner.

When I finished, I strode quickly into the sitting room where I'd left my phone and opened my email account. Scrolling through the messages, I found a new message from my aunt.

"Everything okay?" Bodhi said from the doorway.

"Oh, yeah. Sorry. I just wanted to check in." I turned, frowning. "No word on my mother, still."

Strolling over to my side, he angled his head to study the small screen. "Don't worry, once we're in that house, we'll look for her."

His expression heated, and one corner of his mouth lifted in a smile. Turning me around and hooking his fingers over my shoulders, he dug his thumbs in and started to massage my neck. "Would you like me to pay you back now?"

Chills ran up and down my spine. The man was good with his hands. "For what saving you... from getting your ass kicked by a house?"

"Oh, very funny."

"What did you have in mind?" I asked.

"How about my specialty?" he turned me around and the intensity of his gaze made my insides tingle. Then he kissed me passionately on the mouth. Pulling back, I focused my eyes on the collar of his shirt. It was open at the throat, exposing the long-chorded lines of his neck.

Carefully, undoing a few more buttons, I slipping my hand inside and ran my palm over the bulge and hollow of his muscular chest. "I didn't want to embarrass you, but I hope your specialty isn't kissing."

Standing flush against him, I could feel his torso shake in a silent laugh. "That's cold."

"Sorry. Guess I'm feeling a little feisty lately or maybe just corrupted—not to mention drunk."

He cocked an eyebrow up, "On one glass of wine?"

"Well, that and the lifesaving magic. Also, I'm only eighteen, remember. I don't drink."

"Yes, I'm sure you follow the rules, Ms. Midnight. You do seem like the prudish type." He slid one large hand underneath my shirt, and the sensation of his callused fingers stroking over my sensitive skin sent a flash fire of sensation rippling over me.

"Do I?"

He cupped my breast.

"Tell me to stop," he whispered. "Tell me, and I'll walk away and say nothing more about it."

"But I don't want you to stop," I whispered back. "I want you. Every inch of you."

"This could cause a problem," he said. The line of his jaw had turned tight, and his fingers moved over my skin restlessly, as if he wanted to let go of me but couldn't. "You don't get it. I want to do so many things to you, I don't even know where to start," he muttered. "But I, I don't know that I have any gentleness in me tonight."

"That sounds fine to me. I like a good take no prisoners kind of lover." I twisted to whisper unsteadily in his ear just before I bit his lobe. Then reaching down between our bodies, I stroked the front of his pants.

Before I knew it, he'd picked me up, carried me to my loaner bedroom and practically stripped me on the bed. I rubbed my body against him while simultaneously working my fingers through his hair as he ravaged my mouth and neck. I could barely breathe, let alone keep up. Bringing the weight of his long lanky—now naked—torso over mine to pin me down, he ran a hand down my stomach pausing to tease my nipples, biting gently at the turgid peaks until I cried out.

His tongue lingered, and I bucked and arched underneath him, enjoying his response. I opened my legs and pushed up with my hips, rubbing myself against him.

When he moved back up. His thick, hard erection slipped in, just the tip, and as he broke through my entrance and felt my body grip his most sensitive place, a groan broke out of him and I felt for a moment by body temperature increase, like really, really increase. I felt like I was fucking on fire.

I flinched and he pulled back, looking into my eyes. His skin shimmered for a moment like he was something else and then flickered back to normal.

He pulled away and I whispered, "What is it?"

"You're a virgin!" he gritted between his teeth, resting his forehead on mine. "I told you I can't be gentle right now."

I laughed, and it was a completely joyous sound, as I threw my arms around his neck, my legs around his hips and hugged him with my whole body. Putting my lips to his ear, I gasped, "I'm not a virgin. Trust me."

"You flinched?" he questioned.

"Yeah, I just got really hot all the sudden."

His face changed and I wasn't sure what the problem was. He either had a secret or he was embarrassed about something.

"We can't do this." He spat.

"Why not?" I felt like a petulant child.

"Because I can't control myself right now." He broke away and left the room.

Seriously?! I closed my eyes. We had barely gotten started, damn it. What the fuck had gotten into him. Control himself? I didn't need him to control himself. I had things I wanted to do to him. Really cool, sexy, fun things. I had been hungry to try them, and I was still hungry. But apparently, he wasn't interested enough in exploring anything further with me because...I felt like a virgin?! Isn't that what most pervs want?

Pushing out of bed, I grabbed a nightshirt and went into the bathroom to take a shower. When I was through, I padded into the kitchen to drink the tumbler of wine still left on the counter.

Sipping it, I stood at the kitchen's farm sink, looked out the window, and then I felt his presence behind me. The moon still looked quite full, and the scene outside was almost as bright as day.

I turned. It wasn't Bodhi. It was Zephyr I could feel staring.

Staring at me like a starved animal. I blushed, he must have been able to hear Bodhi and me through the door.

Instinctively, I glanced around the guest house, but it was empty.

"Where'd Bodhi go?"

"He left in a huff. I take it you had a lover's spat."

"Not really." I shook my head, "Although I am annoyed with him. He thought I was a virgin."

Zephyr's eyes lit up.

"And he had a problem with that? Why?"

"Beats me, but I wish he'd get over himself. I was more than ready and willing."

Zephyr smiled, "Be careful what you wish for."

I smiled back at him. Was it just me or was Zephyr looking extra hot right now? "You know, I had a big crush on you. I was completely heart broken when you disappeared from school."

"Really?" Zephyr took a step closer maintaining his penetrating gaze. And by that, I meant, I felt like his gaze was penetrating my every orifice. "Did Bodhi happen to tell you about us?" Zephyr asked.

"About what?"

"About what it means to be a Hell Hound."

"He told me you guys took turns guarding the gate."

"Yes ma'am, we did. We're five people but we're also one unit. Literally, when we're in the underworld, we can join together."

"Like a transformer?"

Zephyr laughed. "Exactly. If we're under attack, we can shift into our Hell hound persona individually or join as one all-powerful beast."

"Wow. So, why don't you do that now so that you can beat Melinoe?"

"Because we're no longer the actual Hell Hound. There's a new unit as you know from the night you saved me. We're the *Monster Squad* now and with the portal closed, our power is limited. Only the Hell Hound can go between realms. Maybe you'll be able to figure out a tattoo to supercharge us," he said it as a joke but I could tell he was half-serious.

"I'll give it some thought."

"Do that. You should also think about something else if you want to stay with us."

"Oh, yeah? And what's that?"

"Sex."

"Oh, believe you me, I've been thinking about it. You guys don't leave me much choice."

"No, I mean you can't just have a relationship with one of us. That could be why Bodhi is being so stubborn. It would rip us apart and weaken us. That's one of the areas we're always connected ... so, if one of us is, you know, getting it on, then we all experience it."

I blushed, thinking of the last hour with Bodhi. "So, you, Demas, Eleutian and Colten could ... what?"

"We could feel, and sense exactly what Bodhi was

doing. Yes. The thing about a beast is, all of our senses are heightened. So, if you belong to us and we all have you then it's fine but if only one of us does, then the others will get jealous and the one will get possessive. Do you know what I'm saying?"

I nodded, my heart beating faster at his words.

"There's one other thing I noticed. I haven't talked to Bodhi about it yet, but I have confirmed it with the other guys, Demas, Colten and Eleutian. We think your magic did something to us when you reanimated me."

"What do you mean?"

"Well, we've always experienced the sex-by-proxy thing but the feelings are exponentially heightened with you, ever since the attack in the club. Immediately, after you brought me back to life, I had a raging hard-on for you. I still do." He undid my robe and reached a hand between my legs.

"Mmm," I said in throaty welcome as I reached for him with both hands. When I touched him, the bolt of pleasure was so sharp he nearly spurted into my palm.

"All of my thoughts, all of my dreams—they're about you, Evangeline Midnight." His voice hesitated as he ground out the words, "which is probably why Bodhi is acting like a horny teenager, since he's your handler and the one in direct contact with you the most. He's been feeling all of my feelings. It's like I'm a zombie now but instead of blood or brains, all I can think about eating is, well, you know. I'm fueling off your pheromones. It worsened a few hours ago when you brought back Bodhi. That's why he's worried that he won't be able to control himself."

"Control what? I'm not a virgin."

"We're not human, Evangeline. We don't want to hurt you."

"I don't care. It's my decision."

I stroked my thumb along the small, sensitive slit at the tip as he spoke, and in response a drop of moisture appeared. I rubbed it into his skin. At the same time, in his own exploration of my most sensitive flesh, he found the stiff, delicate little pearl hidden in my private folds, and as he rubbed it, I let out a strangled moan. Oh, he loved that. He loved my reaction and that seemed to be all the reassurance he needed. He kissed me hard.

I broke away from his lips to gasp, "But what if Bodhi comes back in?"

Zephyr smiled, "I thought you didn't care. I thought that wasn't going to be a problem for you?"

"Definitely not a problem for me," I started to laugh, euphorically, but my laughter was cut short as he lifted me effortlessly picked me up and spread me out on the table. Heat roared back to life inside of me as he bent to fill his mouth. Ravenously he nipped and suckled at my skin as he moved down my body, enticing every inch—the delicate spot at the juncture of my neck and shoulder, the round flesh of my breasts, oh damn, between my legs. I moaned at the feeling and that was it, and the tension in my body grew and grew until a fine sweat broke over my skin and I vibrated like the tattoo machine I so loved to hold.

Then my head fell back, and I cried out as I climaxed.

I touched his face, and I knew it was game on.

Barely waiting for my orgasm to subside, he rose up to unleash his own need. Kissing me, biting at my mouth, he took his cock and rubbed it against my entrance. Then he pressed into me, a little at a time. I was so ready. This was exactly what I needed. Unlike Bodhi, he didn't set me on fire but it was just as hot and I met him thrust for thrust, rocking up with my hips as he hammered down. So damned perfect, I wished he would never stop. Gripping me by the hip, by the breast, whispering in my ear, he let the fire smolder and build until it peaked.

My own climax roared up through my belly. I was helpless in the grip of it, while he thrust and thrust again with every new spasm. I ran my hands down his back, holding him to me, rocking with him until the rhythmic jerk began to subside.

Either he was shaking, or I was. I stroked his neck and he buried his face in the crook of my neck until we both caught our breath.

At last, he withdrew from me even though every muscle in my body wanted him to claim me again. He paused long enough to kiss me on the neck. "Thank you for bringing me back to life," he told me in a quiet voice. "I belong to you now, my Evangeline."

When I looked up, I saw Bodhi in the doorway, watching us. His erection stood out to me like a beacon demanding attention. I expected anger but instead I realized he was excited and pleased. I looked back to Zephyr and whispered. "I belong to all of you and all of you belong to me."

I smiled and kissed them each goodnight.

Climbing under the covers, I curled on my side and fell fast asleep.

23

MIDNIGHT WITCH

Cold, wet pressure touched the part of my leg that hung over the side of the bed. I blinked the sleep out of my eyes, my heart skipping when I saw Gran. Well, not the flesh and blood version—this was more of a white vapor. Before I could say anything to the ghost, she disappeared, leaving me questioning as to whether or not I dreamed her. Rolling over, I stuck my head under one of the pillows and tried to go back to sleep. The sound of clanging dishes and quiet chatter jarred me awake.

Who all was here now? I didn't recognize all the voices but one of them was definitely Bodhi and another, possibly Demas? And there was a female one at that.

I knew I would never get back to sleep now. Swearing under my breath, I got out of bed and dressed. The first light of dawn was already streaking the sky with pink and the palest of greens. What in the hell were they doing up so early? There were places all over my body, intimate places, that ached with a sensitized tenderness that hadn't been present yesterday.

I angrily thrust my arms into a red silk kimono, and

left the bedroom to go in search of coffee. I paused around the corner to listen.

"The council is getting antsy," I heard Demas state. "Aurora says there's been talk of complications."

"Complications?" Bodhi questioned.

"A virus. That's strictly confidential information right now but there have been rumors. The Fae are not happy that the humans know about us and neither are the packs. Hell, half the packs have either joined Melinoe or are fighting over every damn thing and bogging down the system. The Badeauxes are threatening to pull funding."

"Melinoe sure is doing a damn fine job of helping chaos reign." Colten thumped his fist on the table as he said it.

"Which I'm sure is all part of his plan," Bodhi agreed.

"I just wish we knew why. We still have no idea why he's doing all of this—" As I appeared, Demas stopped mid-sentence and gave me a smile. "Mornin' Evangeline."

"Oh, there you are, darlin'," Julep greeted me. "Sweet tea?"

"Julep, what are you doing here?"

"I missed ya, girlie. Thought I'd swing by and check on you today since I didn't have to work."

"Did you happen to bring coffee?"

"Why, I sure did. As a matter of fact, I brought a few

of your favorite things."

"Thank the heavens," I said, kissing her cheek.

"What about you, boys? You want a refill?" Julep posed the question with a hint of flirtation. Julep could gloss it up with the best of them.

"Oh, you know I can't turn down a refill of your sweet tea, Ms. Delphine." Colten offered his glass, and Julep filled it with one hand while adding some strawberries to his plate with the other.

Giving me space to wake up properly, the men resumed talking about people I didn't know, but I presumed I would probably meet at some point. Julep stood and worked at the stove, and within a few minutes the smell of frying bacon and eggs filled the air. Demas got to his feet to assist her and towered over everyone. God, I'd known he was tall but he was the tallest of the tall, most likely 6'3, and yet surprisingly athletic for that height. In my experience, tall guys were usually skinny.

When I'd drained the first mug of coffee, Bodhi took it from me without a word and set another full mug on the table near my elbow. His fingers brushed my neck like an electrical current and all at once all five men looked at me. Holy shit! They really were in tune. I smiled, and darted a look to Julep, who's back was to us, thank goodness. This time, Demas slid a plate filled with a hot, cooked breakfast in front of me. He placed his hands on my shoulders and rubbed away the tightness. Chills rang out through my body. I had a feeling if Julep hadn't been here this morning, I would have been breakfast.

I smirked at the thought and then stared at the plate. Bacon, grits, andouille sausages, scrambled eggs with sautéed onion, fried mushrooms, sliced tomatoes, and what looked like fried bread. It looked like enough food to feed someone twice my size. I could get used to being taken care of like this.

I fell on the food and practically inhaled it while Bodhi, Demas and Colten also ate.

Zephyr and Eleutian headed outside.

"Where are they going?" I asked.

"Guard duty, Midnight. We're rotating," Colten answered.

The talk fell away, and for a while all five of us existed in the quiet comfort of the sunny kitchen as we finished breakfast. To my own astonishment, I ate everything on my plate, and afterward I finished the second mug of coffee too.

Finally, I felt comfortably full and alert. I pushed the empty mug away and looked up to discover the men watching me, Demas with a slight smile, while Bodhi and Colten both wore a brooding expression I didn't know how to interpret.

I knew what two out of three of their mouths tasted like. I knew how Bodhi's hair felt, as the short, silken strands slipped through my fingers. Scowling, I averted my face and said to Julep, "Thank you for breakfast. That was amazing."

"You're welcome, dear." Julep stood. "I should probably clean up and get out of here. Go check on Grandmère."

"Oh, actually I think I'll come with you. I've been having the strangest dreams lately and I think they have something to do with—" I paused as the pouch of marbles she normally kept clipped to her belt tumbled and spilled onto the floor at our feet. They scattered, unnaturally. Moving like soldiers around me in a circle until they spelled out a pattern on the floor. I stared down in wonder as Julep appeared to be reading them—or was she casting?

I paused, suddenly confused in my intentions. What had I been saying?

Julep clapped her hands in front of my face.

"Evangeline," she barked. "Are you daydreaming?"

"No, ma'am," I said.

"Well, hurry on and finish your story then. I've got to get going."

"I-I can't remember, sorry. I'm a scatterbrain today."

"Alright, then. Well, I'll just mosey on out and check on our guards, then, won't I? See if they want seconds before we pack it all up."

After Julep walked out, Bodhi said, "You okay?"

"It's no big deal," I said. "Ever since Mama died, I can't sleep at night. I'm just more of a night owl now, which is why I'm so tired during the day." I rose to slap our dirty plates together in a stack and carried them to the sink. "I'm beginning to think I too am a bit of a zombie."

Bodhi and Demas both looked up sharply. "Were you bit or scratched?"

I shook my head. "No, this has been going on since before the undead rose."

Demas relaxed and set a silver suitcase on the table, opening it while I finished clearing. When I started to wash the dishes, Demas said, "Come sit down, Evie. I need your help with something." I glanced back and he rubbed the very spot on the table my ass had been on last night.

I blushed and looked away, remembering what Zephyr had told me. If one of them experienced it, all of them experienced it. Looks like we all got laid, I thought to myself with a laugh. You'd think there'd have been more smiles this morning.

"These'll just take a second," I pointed out.

By the stern look that passed over his face, I saw that he had grown serious.

"Yes, sir, Professor, sir," turning my back to the sink, I wiped my hands on a towel while I nodded my head. "Whatcha doin' with a portable tattoo machine, anyway?"

"That's sort of what we need your help with. Can you tattoo one of your defensive sigils on us? We need something that's going to work against the undead army."

I raised my eyebrows. "You want one of my sigils?"

"Yeah, like the ones you're always sketching."

Looking from Bodhi to Demas, I added, "Zephyr told me about how you guys can transform into one powerful beast in the Underworld, but I don't have the first clue how to make that happen. I was barely an apprentice. I can draw something for you but don't you know anyone else, like an ink mage, who does magical tattooing?"

Bodhi walked over and took the dish towel out of my hands. "We trust you." He hooked an arm around my shoulders and sat me down. "Besides, we think there's something special about you. There's a reason Grimm was drawn to you. We want you to mix your blood into the ink. That's how ink magic works and, if you are who we think you are, then it should help us." Bodhi smiled. "Not to mention it might help us control our sexual cravings for you."

I mock-frowned, "Well, that doesn't sound at all ideal to me."

Boom.

"What was that? Did something just breach the property." I ran into the living room. "Julep?"

"Evangeline," Bodhi snapped. "Get back here."

231

Before he could catch me, I bolted out onto the front porch.

A furious growl rose behind me, and I didn't have to turn to know it was Bodhi and that he was pissed.

"Get back in the house now."

"I agree," Eleutian murmured from the corner of the porch.

Hating that they had ganged up on me, and that they were right, I stomped back inside. "But where's Julep?"

Bodhi, right behind me, no doubt to make certain I followed orders, blanched. "Why didn't she come running too?"

"Z saw her drive away," Demas said returning inside. He rubbed my shoulder. "She's fine."

Lightning lit up the sky.

"We're getting a storm," he said. "You're just on edge. Everything's okay."

24

MIDNIGHT WITCH

With everything settled back down, we got down to business. In short order, we had the table completely cleared and sterilized. I brought my pen and stencil paper out to the kitchen, along with my sketch book and a fresh pad of paper.

"Okay, guys, now that you got me all geared up. What did you have in mind?"

Demas flipped open my sketchbook to the defensive drawings I'd done with him at the University. "I'm thinking of an anchor point for Vengeance."

"Who's Vengeance?"

"My guard dog from the Underworld."

"I didn't know you had a pet?"

"Well, it's not a pet—it's me, but different. It's like an extension of my hellhound. What's left of it anyway."

"So, you can shift into this hellhound like Grimm shifts to a ferret?"

"No," Demas seemed to pause as if we were unsure of what to tell me.

"What is it? I feel like you guys keep holding

something back from me."

Demas shook his head and smiled. "No. It's as Zephyr explained, hellhounds don't shift in this realm. That's why I need an anchor point—so that I can bring him here. He's like a familiar that I could send out to watch over you when I'm not around."

Bodhi pointed to my sketchbook. "Are those Egyptian symbols in there?" he angled his head to study the rune.

"Yes." I paused uncertainly. "That's not an issue, is it?"

He shook his head. "No. I like them."

"Thank you." I smiled. "I use the Eye of Horus for this particular spell," I said, pointing to the one Bodhi favored. "It's for protection."

Demas patted my shoulder, "You are ingenious."

Surprised by the compliment, I felt my cheeks turn warm. "That's a generous thing to say, but I can't take the credit. I learned much of this from being in Julep's shop."

By the time both men had decided and I'd transferred the ink from the stencil to the skin, it was almost noon.

I pressed down on the foot pedal and the buzzing of the needle started up. Creativity surged through my whole body —or maybe it was just adrenaline.

"Ahh, I missed this sound." The only sad part was

that it reminded me of my mother. Bodhi brushed a hair back from my face as if he'd just read my mind, which he probably had. I shook it off. This tattoo was going to be gorgeous, magical or not, so I didn't see any reasons why we shouldn't give it a try. Even if it was only for their peace of mind.

I picked the tattoo machine back up and started on Bodhi's forearm.

Three hours later, I straightened my shoulders from bending over the table. "You both owe me back rubs later."

Demas laughed, while Bodhi winked at me from across the room. He was admiring his ink in the mirror. After that he gave me a fierce, approving smile. "You are the bomb, girl."

"Hmm, I certainly am. Maybe I should get one of you to tattoo that on my ass."

"I heard ass. I'll do it," Eleutian said, walking in the door. "I am the only one who hasn't even been kissed yet."

"That's not true, I said glancing at Demas." But his comment caused the corner of my mouth to lift just a bit.

At that point, I held up my hands, stood up from the table, and said, "I'm done. I'm all done today. I haven't even showered or gotten dressed properly yet—and I need to go into town to check on Julep. It's still weird to me that she took off so fast."

Bodhi stood as well. "Do you think you could ask her

mother if she'd do a reading?"

"Sure. Can it wait until this evening?"

"Of course." He looked at Demas. "Do you think you could let us into the manor house?"

"Sure," I said. "Let's do that now."

Together we walked across the lawn to the front doors of the house "Shit! I don't have the key, guys. I'll have to grab it from home while I'm out."

I cupped his chin in one hand and looked into his eyes. "Did you just put contacts in?" I finally asked. "Your eyes are darker all of a sudden."

They had changed from a bright indigo blue to an almost midnight blue.

His brow furrowed. "I'm surprised you noticed my eye color at all. You're always so busy staring at Baudoin." He smiled as he said it.

"What?" I cracked a grin. "Are you jealous, Demas."

"Perhaps a smidge." He grinned. "The darkening of my eyes is probably from the anchor tattoo you just gave me. I tested it when you were working on Bodhi and it worked." Demas studied the blades of grass stuck to the tops of my feet with dew. "Does it bother you?"

"Your eyes?" I glanced between them. "No. I was just curious."

"I meant the hell hound," came his answer.

The hell hound? Oh. "Umm, no. Should it bother me? Will it attack me?"

"Actually, quite the opposite. I want to call him fourth to protect you. You said you wanted to go into town."

"Yeah, I do, but I really don't want to take a hell hound with me. It's hard enough fitting in."

"No one will see him unless they're supernatural too," Demas retorted.

Bodhi took hold of my arm. "Come on, Evie, be reasonable. You must understand why we're not comfortable with you going to town by yourself," he said.

Raising my eyebrows, I pulled away. "I do, but you must understand why I don't want a babysitter... Dad."

"Evangeline," he said in an abrupt, clipped voice. "The zombies could attack at any time."

I squared my shoulders at the reminder, and after a moment, I nodded. "Point taken," I muttered. "I'll go armed, and I'll be careful."

He angled his jaw. "I still don't like it."

"Fine. I hear you," I snapped. "Back off." I turned my back and stalked away.

Back in the guest house, I tattooed both offensive and defensive spells on my arms. Then I dug out a cream-colored baby doll dress with sleeves that flared at the wrists so that I could get at my tattoos if need be. I paired it with

237

maroon tights, a mustard vest and a pair of combat boots. I even took a few minutes to stroke on some makeup, enhancing my eyes, while brushing a matte black cherry lipstick on my lips. *Who was I trying to impress?* Bodhi's dark, intense gaze came to mind, so did Colten's broad shoulders, Zephyr's rock-hard abs, Eleutian's hairy chest and Demas' kissable lips... "holy crow, Evangeline...who are you?" I whispered to the girl in the mirror.

So. It appeared I was very much into the Monster Squad—all five of them. Sighing, I dug out my messenger bag and loaded it up.

With a bounce in my step, I tucked my cell phone into the front zipper pocket and hit the driveway. The muscle car's tuxedo-black paint job and red pinstriping gleamed in the sunlight. I chucked my bag and leather jacket into the passenger seat and basked in that aged leather smell as she purred to life. Hey! My tank was full. One of the boys must have topped her off. Man, they were handy to have around.

"Ready?" I called out to Vengeance—a bull mastiff as black as my last name with spikes along his spine, who materialized beside the car. "I'll take that as a yes."

My spirits lifted as I drove away from the property and flew down the roads of southern Louisiana, the hell hound racing at my side in a billowing fog. Strands of hair from my thick ponytail whipped my face, but considering the heat, the wind's attack felt great.

The familiar bucolic countryside made me feel practically normal—which I was anything but.

As I crossed the Mississippi, and neared the French Quarter, I thought of Mama. What would she say if she saw my living arrangement?

I honestly had no clue. These days it felt like I hadn't even known her.

First things first, I stopped by the house to grab some more clothes and the key. I was already at the front door with my bag packed, stepping out onto the front porch when I felt the certainty that something terrible was about to happen.

The street was deserted. The gingerbread-encrusted Victorian Italianate shotgun homes looked strange and silent, as if they might all be empty inside, like the houses on an abandoned movie set. They looked as if they were empty of people, and yet somehow full of eyes. I half-expected a tumble weed to roll down the street.

Maybe we really were living apocalyptic times. Something dark in the branches of the old oak tree in front of the house drew my gaze. A crow, sitting as still as the leaves around it. Somehow, I knew it wasn't Grimm... this time.

I tried to tell myself that this was ridiculous, but its greedy dark claws, sharp beak, and glittering black eyes reminded me of a predator. The way Barnabe looked when one of the girls wore a sheer blouse or crop top. Not a good omen.

Before I realized what I was doing, I had dropped my leather duffel bag and picked up a stone. "Scat!"

There was an explosion of leaves, but the crow soared up unharmed. Its wings were huge, and they made enough racket for a whole flock of crows.

Down the street a door opened and a family poured out, laughing.

I smiled at them, and took another breath, relief sweeping through me like sunlight. How could I have been so silly? This was a beautiful day, full of promise, and nothing bad was going to happen.

Nothing bad was going to happen. As I reached the Chevelle, I found Lézare Ludovic leaning against it. His bodyguard, I dubbed him Scarface lingered just steps away.

"Ms. Midnight. How do you do?"

"Mr. Ludovic?"

"Lézare, please. We're friends, remember?"

"What are you doing here?"

"I was worried about you. You weren't here when I came to pick you up for our lunch date."

"Oh," I felt my cheeks turn red, "I'm so sorry. I stood you up. How awful. Life got really crazy and it was just impossible for me to meet. I apologize."

"That's alright. Shall we go out now, then? I hear the House of Hecate serves up a life-changing meal."

"Actually, I can't. Listen, I know what you want Lézare, and as I told you before, I'm not interested in marrying you."

"How did you know I wanted to propose a union?"

"It doesn't take a genius to figure out why you're holding that ring box. Besides, I've seen my mother wooed and I'm not interested in having my heart broken."

"I know you think I would have a s-side chick, as you so eloquently put it at the ball, but our vows are sacred." He shifted to look at me head-on. "I would never betray your heart." His gaze skittered to the window. "I will admit when I first came to you I was prepared to sacrifice myself for my clan, but I see now I was a fool to doubt my master's wisdom. You make me feel things that I've never felt before."

"Whoa! Back that ass up. Your master sent you to seduce me?"

"Seduce you? Oh, no, believe me, this is hardly seduction, Mistress Midnight. I can seduce you if you'd prefer. But no, my master asked me to align with you and originally I thought I would propose it as a business arrangement."

"Who is your master?"

Ludovic smiled but remained silent.

"You won't tell me?"

"Of course, I will. Marry me and I'll tell you everything you wish to know."

"Aww… so it's proposal by blackmail. How romantic?"

"It's simply incentive."

"Whatever you want to call it. The answer is still no. Not now… or ever."

"Have I offended you in some way, Ms. Midnight?"

"Not at all," How was I supposed to explain that I was dating a small harem of men? I cleared my throat, "I'm involved."

"Ah…with the Monster Squad," he suggested.

"Yes. How did you—"

"I know many things about you, Evangeline. Many things. They don't know you like I do. They think you need protectors because you're weak and easily led. But I feel your strength, like the desert sun. You do know that, that you have a unique strength, Evangeline, but you could be so much stronger…"

I stared at him, not understanding, not liking the change of subject. "I don't know what you're talking about."

"I'm talking about power, sweet girl." Suddenly, he stepped close, his eyes fixed on me, his voice soft and urgent. "There's always something just out of your reach, something you need desperately and can't have. That's what I'm offering you. Power. Eternal life. And feelings you've never felt before."

I did understand then, and bile rose in my throat. I choked on horror and repudiation. "No."

"Why not?" he whispered. "Why not try it, Evangeline? Be honest. Isn't there a part of you that wants to?" His dark eyes were full of a heat and intensity that held me transfixed, unable to look away.

"I can waken things inside you that have been sleeping all your life. Admit it, you prefer the night. You're strong enough to live in the dark, to glory in it. You are already a queen of the shadows. Why, your very name is Midnight. Why not take that power? Let me help you take it." His voice was as caressing as the fingertips that touched my throat. "You'll be happy as never before."

"No," I said, wrenching my eyes away from his. I wouldn't look at him, wouldn't let him do this to me. I wouldn't let him make me forget… make me forget…

There was something terribly important I must remember. He was using compulsion to make me forget it, but I wouldn't let him …

"And we'll be together, you and I." The cool fingertips stroked the side of my neck, slipping under the collar of my dress. "Just the two of us, forever."

There was a sudden twinge of pain as his fingers dug into the flesh of my neck, and my mind cleared.

Make me forget... The Monster Squad.

That was what he wanted to drive out of my mind. The memory of Demas, Bodhi, Zephyr, Colten and Eleutian and Grimm. But nothing could force them from my thoughts now, not after what we shared. I pulled away from Ludovic, knocking those cool fingertips aside. I looked straight at him.

"I've already found what I want," I said brutally. "And who I want to be with forever."

Blackness welled up in his eyes, a cold rage that swept through the air between us. Looking into those eyes, I thought of a cobra about to strike, but before he could do or say anything Vengeance went crazy. He growled fiercely and positioned himself between me and Ludovic. Inching the vampire away from me and allowing me to get into my car without further molestation.

With Ludovic in my rearview and Vengeance at my side, I headed for Julep's Occult Shop, stopping on impulse at the grocery store instead. Perhaps, I'd bake the boys a treat.

Once inside, I pushed the cart to the baking section, scanning the bags of flour, and frowned. If I were being honest with myself, I didn't really bake. I was more a spectator of the sport. Julep was the baker in our home. I was the prize-winning spoon licker. *Yes! That's a thing.* Now, should I buy all-purpose flour? Self-rising? Was wheat flour healthier? And what about brown sugar, why the hell did it come in two choices. Carts and people pushed past me as I contemplated light or dark. Deciding to embrace my true nature and stay in my own lane as Mama always said, I headed for the other aisle and bought a ready-made cherry cheesecake instead. I also grabbed a bouquet of fresh flowers at the check-out. *Nothing wrong with prettying up the place.*

I was about to leave when Vengeance growled once again to stop me.

A prickle of unease raised the hairs down my arms, but it wasn't like I could stay inside the store forever. Was it Ludovic again? Jeeze, that man—no, not a man—that vampire was persistent.

"No one's going to assault me in public," I assured the hound.

Vengeance growled a warning again, but backed off.

As I pushed open the door to leave, my cell buzzed and I juggled my grocery bag. Dark boots came into view, and a man's strong, tanned hand took the door and held it wide for me.

"Please, allow me."

"Thank you," I said, passing through.

I took in the details of his appearance. He was mid-forties, tall and large, although not quite as tall as Demas or

Bodhi, and he was deeply tanned. He wore gray slacks and a collared blue shirt that was open at the neck, with the sleeves rolled up to reveal muscular forearms and a tattoo of an ancient necromancy symbol—a goat within a star set in a circle.

I took in other details. He had dark hair that silvered at the temples, a strong face with a good bone structure, and, while he appeared to be a man, when I looked into his brilliant whisky gaze, I felt such a roar of power coming from him that I staggered back a step.

Frowning, he held a hand out to me. "Are you ill?"

"I'm fine," I said tightly, staring.

I hadn't sensed his power until I had looked into his eyes, which meant he must have a titanic amount of control over himself in order to keep it so tightly contained. How could one person hold that much power and still remain sane?

Vengeance growled another warning.

Giving me a pleasant smile, the man said, "Would it be all right if I carried your bag for you to your car?"

"W-why would you do that?" I stuttered.

His voice was still controlled – but barely. I could hear the effort it cost him to keep it steady.

"Because," he said, "You... remind me of someone." He looked away and then at me once again, meeting my eyes directly.

"I remind you of someone you know?"

"Of someone I knew," he said quietly. "But," he added slowly, as if puzzling something out for himself, "you're not like her, really. She was much more fragile, delicate. At least she was when I knew her."

"And I'm not."

He made a sound that would have been a laugh if there had been any humor in it. "No. You're certainly no wallflower, Ms. Midnight. You are... unique."

I was silent for a moment.

"What happened to her?"

There was a long pause, so long that I thought he wasn't going to answer. But at last he said, "She had to let me go."

"I'm sorry."

He said nothing. His face had closed again, and he seemed to be looking far away at something terrible and heartbreaking that only he could see. But there was not just grief in his expression. Through the walls, through all his trembling control, I could see the tortured look of unbearable guilt and loneliness.

"You called me Ms. Midnight. How do you know my name?"

"Give me a few moments of your time, and I'll

explain," the man said. His quiet voice remained as nonthreatening as his body language. "Just a quick conversation, I promise. You are Evangeline Midnight, aren't you?"

"Tell me how you learned that name," I countered, taking another step back.

"The people here speak highly of you," the man said. "They say you're a damn fine woman, saved some people during that last zombie attack."

"You still haven't told me who you are," I said, eyeing him narrowly. I was going to have to drop my grocery bag to ensure access to my defensive tattoo, but I didn't like what that would signal.

If it came to that.

If he was going to try to do anything to me, I would make him do it right here on the street, in front of everybody, not tucked away in a side parking lot.

His body language remained open, easy. He had pearly white teeth and there were slight lines fanning out from the corners of his eyes. If he hadn't set off all the alarm bells in my head, I would have found him really quite charming.

His smile never wavered. "Mel."

Melinoe.

The sound of his name was like a punch to the

kidneys. The town wavered around me. Oh shit, no wonder he held such power. If he chose to do anything to me, I was toast.

My options ran through my mind at supersonic speed. I really needed to get one of those vampire hunter styled gun contraptions like Eleutian's, one that held all types of bullets—wood, silver and regular.

"Why are you talking to people about me?" I asked through numb lips. "What do you really want?"

"I just want to talk and to ask you a few questions, that's all. I mean you no harm for the moment, you are safe."

"For the moment?" I echoed. Then, because he had frightened me so badly, a wave of anger hit. I shifted my grocery bag as if I might throw it at him. "What the fuck do you mean by that?"

Out of the corner of my eye, I could see people on the street watching worriedly. Melinoe noticed too, and as he waved the fingers of one hand in a subtle gesture, the gawkers appeared to lose interest and dispersed.

Melinoe turned his attention back to me. The smile in his eyes had disappeared. He said in a quiet, courteous voice, "Like I said, I wish you no harm. I'm just trying to locate a missing pet," Melinoe said. "One of the local waitresses told me that she saw you with a stray ferret. If I might ask, what happened to him?"

The question fanned my anger into outright fury, and I jettisoned straight into stupid.

Advancing, I said between clenched teeth, "That ferret was hurt. Did you do that?"

His expression changed and a muscle flexed in his lean jaw. Still, he kept his composure and, still with that terrible, even polite tone said, "You didn't answer my question. Do you still have the ferret?"

"No, I do not still have the ferret. I have a dog, as you can plainly see," I snapped, throwing the weight of all my fury into a perfect blend of truth and misdirection, and I knew instinctively that I had hit the exact right note. "The ferret disappeared at the time of the club attack, and I haven't seen it since." Looking him up and down, I added contemptuously, "But if I did see it again, you can be sure as fuck I wouldn't tell you anything about it."

"No, I can see, dear, that you would not," Melinoe said, holding his body still, his expression calm and stony. "At any rate, not by choice." In an archaic-seeming bow, Melinoe inclined his head to me, then strode away. "I wish you well, Evangeline Midnight. Until we meet again."

Breathing hard, I waited a moment.

"Wait!" I shouted. "Tell me, what was so special about that ferret? Why do you want him back when you obviously mistreated him?"

He turned, "That animal belonged to someone I once loved. I know she'll want him back."

I stood staring until he disappeared around a corner. Only then was I able to get my feet unglued from the pavement. I made it back to the car, tucked my purchases in the back, then sat in the driver's seat and shook. Vengeance nosed at my hand and I patted his head. "I know you were right, bud. I promise I'll listen next time." When I felt I was capable of driving safely, I started the Chevelle and pulled out onto the road. I didn't even bother going to the shop, instead I sent Julep a text.

My mind was leaping around like a scalded cat. The ferret had belonged to my mother. Did that mean Melinoe wanted to use him against my mother? Maybe I shouldn't drive back to the property in case I led him to Grimm, and in turn, my mother. But everybody in town knew I was staying there. Maybe it would look worse if I didn't go back.

Help, help, help! Someone was screaming. I slowed to look around and when I did, a familiar gray-haired woman in a black maid's uniform dashed out in front of my car. I practically had to step on the breaks to avoid hitting her. She shrieked bloody murder. "The monsters!" she cried. "They've trapped her." I climbed out of the Chevelle only to realize I was in front of the Badeaux mansion. It was typical in style to New Orleans, and yet it was at least three times the size of any other home on the street.

"Ms. Midnight! Evangeline!"

Shit! It was Katherine. She worked for the Badeauxes. I remembered her from the séance. She certainly had a flair for the dramatics.

"You're here to help—thank the heavens."

The woman babbled some more, mostly incoherently, something about the lady of the house and the undead running loose. I thought about driving off but how could I when she recognized me.

"I just called the Delphines but no one answered so I left a message. I can't believe you got here so fast."

"You called Julep?" A red flush ignited on my cheeks. I couldn't very well say no now, could I?

"Come on." She guided me up the stairs to the mansion's front door.

Vengeance growled and I knew I was going to catch hell from the boys for this.

"Katherine. Calm down. Tell me what's happened?" I said, gripping her shoulders once we got inside.

"Jilaiya is trapped by a corpse. We have to get her out. As capable a woman as Jilaiya is, no one lives long with one of the monsters nearby." Then, with a grimace, she added, "It was my fault," she added. "I shut the corpse in the lady's dressing room, but I didn't realize the lady was in there."

"How long has she been in the same room with it?"

"No, she's in the bathroom. She's just trapped there."

I followed her through the red front door, and up the winding staircase remembering the trouble the zombies had experienced when attempting the stairs at the nightclub. They'd been treacherous for the clumsy corpses.

"I have an idea.," I started, "but I'll need you to lure the dead downstairs? It's not a werewolf, right? It's an actual human corpse?"

She nodded.

"Okay. I'm going to go back downstairs. Just open the door and run back down here to me. I'll be waiting with Vengeance." I wasn't sure if she could see the ghostly beast but she didn't question me.

I took out my pen and sketched a rope sigil. Then forced myself to inhale, to focus, and the magic flared to life in my belly.

It was then that the noises from upstairs ceased.

One breath passed. Then two, and the only sound was the whir of the glass.

Then the calm was broken.

"Here we go!" Katherine roared. "Be ready!" Heavy, sure footsteps banged through the hallway.

I looked at Vengeance, "You ready for this. I'll need your help."

Then a new pounding came in an awkward counter beat to Katherine's. A split second later, Katherine hit the stairs and came flying into view. "Oh God! I think my heart is going to give out."

Katherine hit the main floor, her eyes white and bulging, and dove into a crouch behind a piece of furniture. Behind her came the hollow punch of limbs against tight walls, the snap of bones on steep, crooked stairs, and the chomping of jaws in search of prey.

Mine stayed glued to the stairs—each step was slowing the zombified butler, but was it enough?

I could see the man's face: empty, bloody holes where his eyes had once been and crusted, brown blood all over his wrinkled skin.

Without thinking, I acted. I threw one hand over my telekinesis spell, latching onto my spiritual energy, and drawing in a warm, buzzing well of power. Then, like cracking a whip, I flung it at the body.

The instant my magic hit the zombie; a leash formed between us—but not a leash I could control.

I had no idea how to blast its magic back to the spirit realm. Yet I found I could affect the corpse. I could pump my will into it.

"Stay!" My voice ripped out, high and desperate. "Stay back!"

The zombie hesitated, then it slogged forward as if in waist-deep mud.

"Stay!" I yelled again.

Sweat dripped down my face. Despite the pleasant heat licking through me, holding this corpse was exhausting me.

"Stay, stay, stay!" I shouted. The zombie's teeth clacked in spurts now, but with less time between each bite. And no matter how hard I strained; the corpse was gaining ground. Faster with each passing breath . . . until it was almost to the bottom step. Until it was only feet from reaching us. From reaching me.

"Stay!" I shrieked. "Stay, stay!" I couldn't maintain this much longer. I looked at Vengeance. "Help me! Attack it! *Impero!*"

At that moment, Vengeance made his move. He flew at the dead man and tore him apart.

For half a ragged heartbeat, the zombie kept moving. Then at last, it collapsed in a heap on the floor.

And we stared at it for several long, shaking breaths. The air was heavy with magic and humming with nerves. And when no twitch came, Katherine let out a great whoop.

25

THE FIERY TEMPERED BEAST

After listening to Evangeline's harrowing experience, Bodhi crushed her body against him. She coughed. "Yo, dude! Not so hard."

"Sorry," he growled.

Relaxing, she gave in and rested her head on his shoulder. "You can't bubble wrap me, Bodhi. I'm not a child."

"Evangeline, for fuck sake," he snapped while he stroked her hair. He couldn't seem to help himself. His hands needed to confirm she was here and safe.

At that, she seemed to get how genuinely upset he was. Lifting her head, she met his gaze. "I'm fine. Seriously, everything is okay."

He took in her appearance for the first time, and his eyes narrowed. Her dark hair was glossy and pulled back, but it still fell down her back in an extravagantly feminine mane. And she had done something to her eyes and mouth, making them more dramatic and sensual than usual.

"You look very pretty especially after fighting the dead," he said.

"Thank you."

He touched a forefinger to her dark, ripe mouth. A soft smear of color stained his fingertip, and he licked at it. It tasted of her. His mood went from zero to sixty in a single second, rock hard and straining against the seam of his jeans. "You look good enough to eat."

Her pupils dilated in a quick, involuntary reaction just as the guest house door opened and Eleutian appeared.

"Evangeline, you're back," he drawled. "How'd it go?"

"She ran into Melinoe," Bodhi bit out.

She glanced at him. The flush of pink color had fled, leaving her looking pale and strained.

"Come inside, sugar," Eleutian said while looking around sharply at their surroundings. He put a protective arm around her. "Tell us all about it."

Rooted to the spot, Bodhi watched them step into the guest house together. Just before Demas stepped inside behind them, he speared Bodhi with a look that clearly said Vengeance had updated him on the situation.

"Tell us what happened with Melinoe."

"Okay, but I need a drink." She pulled out a chair, sat, and put her head in her hands while Demas broke open the bottle and poured some of the amber liquid into a glass for her. She took a deep, bracing swallow, coughed and then told them everything.

Just listening to how she had confronted Melinoe over his cruelty had Bodhi heading for the whisky bottle himself. This girl had no idea who she was dealing with. He poured a hefty amount into a glass and knocked it back. It burned all the way down. Then he pivoted to glare at her.

"Are you nuts?"

Her beautiful, luscious mouth dropped open, and she glared back. "No, I'm not. Mostly I think I'm just fed up with oversized neanderthals bossing me about."

"Neanderthals who have your best interests at heart." Bodhi advanced on her, rage blinding him. "You could have been kidnapped and tortured every bit as badly as Grimm or worse. Do you even get that, or are you to stubborn to recognize reality?"

Out of the corner of his eye, he saw Demas shift away from leaning against the counter, but Evangeline beat the other man to it as she stood and advanced quickly to Bodhi.

"Hey," Evangeline said in a soft voice. She spread her fingers over his chest, and he clamped his hands around her wrists. "Melinoe's a douchebag, and he triggers you. I get it. Me too. But nothing happened. I'm here and I'm unharmed."

"You're right." Touching her felt too good, and he didn't want to stop. Releasing her wrists, he stepped away, back to the counter to pour himself another whisky.

Evangeline felt her way back to her seat and sank into it, while Demas rubbed his face hard with one massive hand.

"Melinoe may be a great many things, but he's also a man of his word," Eleutian said. "He said he meant you no harm for the moment, but he also gave you plenty of warning that will change. Are you sure he believed you when you said the ferret disappeared?"

"Yeah," Evangeline said. She ran her fingers through her hair, turning it into even more of a wild, unruly mane. "I'm confident of that."

"Good," Demas murmured.

She looked at the both of them. "But all he has to do is start considering what Grimm is capable of, and I'm sure he'll put two and two together." She sighed. "I think we need to prepare for the worst."

As she spoke, Grimm appeared from behind her as a man, and she put her arms around him, hugging him tight. "I'm glad you weren't with me."

Grimm looked angry. Not with Evangeline but with the situation, much like the rest of them.

Bodhi's blood boiled ever so slightly watching Grimm touch her, and he had to work hard to keep his wings in check. He couldn't blame him–or Evangeline. He had lost his damn mind. Glancing around one last time, he clamped down on his self-control. Zephyr was right, she had to be with all of them or it was going to tear them apart.

"We need to consider our choices," Bodhi said, looking at Demas.

Demas blew out a breath. "One choice is, we go after him. Grimm comes with us, and Evangeline goes to headquarters for protection."

Evangeline shook her head. "Unacceptable. I'm not going into hiding while you guys get yourselves killed."

"Not to mention, she wouldn't necessarily be any safer at headquarters. What about the antebellum mansion? It's basically a magical fortress," Bodhi said.

"I like that option," Demas said. "We barricade ourselves in while we come with a plan of attack."

"What if he finds a way in. We're cornered like rats," Colten said coming around the corner, "I say we call in Van Rogue and the back-up team. That way, if we do have to fight our way out, we have the numbers. They'd need to get here as quickly as possible, of course."

"Oh, a sausagefest, great!" Grimm exclaimed sarcastically with a lopsided grin.

"Yes." Bodhi turned to face Colten. "Where's Zephyr?"

"Patrolling the property," Colten answered. "I'm going back out. I just came in to get a drink."

Demas dug out his phone. "I'll contact the others and

tell them to get here as soon as possible."

"Tell them to swing by headquarters and pick up more of an assortment of weapons. We don't know what kind of creatures Melinoe will bring with him," Bodhi said.

"Of course," Demas said.

"And camping gear, food and fuel. We need as many supplies as they can lay their hands on." Bodhi moved to kneel by Evangeline's side. "Lou, can you go all X-Men on us and cover our scents?"

Eleutian nodded and headed for the door, "One order of deodorant, coming up."

"There's a shed behind the guest house with an axe," Demas told them. "I'm going to start tackling that firewood issue."

"I'll help," Grimm mumbled.

That left Bodhi and Evangeline alone. He still knelt by her side, and instead of rising to his feet, he took one of her hands in his.

She shifted to face him. "You wanted Grand-mère to do a reading. I'm sorry, I was so frazzled that I forgot to ask her. What is it you want to find out? Maybe I could try the mirror."

"I don't know that it's relevant any longer." Absently he rubbed her fingers. "I wanted to find out more about the zombies that attacked the nightclub. Someone told Melinoe where we were headed that night." He looked at her broodingly.

She gave him a lopsided smile. "You think you may have a leak?"

He nodded and rubbed the back of his neck. "Yes, or maybe they have another new way of tracking us that we don't know about."

"I'll get my stuff." Squeezing his fingers, she let go of his hand and stood.

Bodhi rose as well and watched her leave. Then he walked back to his glass of whisky to take another hefty swallow. He held it in his mouth for a moment, focusing on the subtle, warming flavor.

As she stepped back into the kitchen, he turned. She carried two candles, incense and a small silk pouch, which she set on the table as she took a seat. He sat opposite her and watched with fascination as she pulled out a black obsidian mirror. Magic unfurled in the air.

"All right. Now I need for you to be quiet while I say a protection spell. Don't ask questions until I'm done."

As he watched, she held the mirror her features settled into an expression of concentration. Then she closed her eyes.

He watched her closely, fascinated by every small, minute shift in her expression. Her attention focused on things he couldn't see.

As he watched, her skin darkened. Her mouth opened as if she would speak, but no sound came out. She placed a hand to her throat, and then she hit the floor. The mirror smashed alongside of her.

"Evangeline," he said. His heart pounded and panic fired along all his nerve endings.

She'd gone completely white and just passed out. He felt along her throat for a pulse.

Suddenly she gasped for air, and her eyes flared wide. She stared at him, then rolled onto her side, sucking air and rubbing at her skull.

"Easy, take it easy," he said hoarsely while he rubbed her back. "You're okay."

As she pushed herself into a sitting position, he slid an arm underneath her to help. She didn't appear to mind. Either she was shaking or he was. Damn, this day had been hell on his nerves. At this point, combat would be a relief.

Putting his face in her hair, he forced himself to say calmly, "You passed out."

"Yes, thank you, Captain Obvious," she croaked. She was still sucking in great lungfuls of air. "I need a drink."

Immediately, he rose and got her water. He knelt on one knee while she drank. She drained the glass, and he took it from her to set it aside.

As her color returned to normal, he said, again in a too-calm voice, "What happened? Why didn't you tell me gazing into that black mirror was so dangerous?" she tucked her face into the crook of his neck and leaned against him, and it was so unlike her that it actually panicked him. He growled, "What did you see in the vision?"

When she didn't respond, he slipped a hand underneath her chin and forced her to look up. Her eyes had filled with tears, and she looked at him with such... such compassion? ... it started an entirely different alarm going off inside him.

"What?" he said.

Her face tightened. "I think you're right about the squad. One of your men wants to kill me."

26

MIDNIGHT WITCH

"Kill you?" Bodhi questioned. "That makes no sense."

A gentle buzz suddenly twirled in my gut, and I knew without looking that Grimm was near.

He leaned against the doorframe taking it all in, his cheeks bright and his eyes glossy. "Oh, Evie, just tell him everything!"

Bodhi whirled around, staring daggers at him. "What are you talking about, demon boy? Did you put her up to this?"

Grimm looked past him giving me a reinforcing look. "I can feel you holding back the truth. Just be honest."

Bodhi turned his gaze on me now looking wounded as if I were the one about to betray him. Then his dark eyes snapped with anger. "What are you playing at, Grimm?" he growled, looking around with fresh rage. "Are you using her to turn me against the squad?"

His expression was frightening. "You sound jaded, Bodhi. There's obviously a history between you two but this has nothing to do with him."

Bodhi didn't glance up.

"Bodhi." I took hold of his wrists.

"What do you expect me to say?" he confronted me fiercely. "The Squad is my family, and you want me to trust a demon over them.

"No, I expect you to trust me. It was my vision."

"Which could have been planted by a demon. A demon who may very well be behind the sacrifices."

A second surge of panic flooded my brain. A demon behind the sacrifices? What are you talking about? I sputtered a cough. "Wh-why would you think that?"

Bodhi looked up at me. "Because Evangeline the number of sacrificed victims suggests more than a single necromancer at work."

"Well… so… then maybe it's several necromancers? And not a demon?" My words sounded pleading.

"Doubtful. According to this"—Bodhi pulled a book from out of a bag and rapped the page—" most magical partnerships are made with demons. Demas thinks we're dealing with either a necromancer-demon pair or a free demon."

"A free demon?" I bit my lip as I glanced from Bodhi to Grimm. "What the hell is that?"

"A free demon can exist in this world as long as it is hidden. Masked." He ran a hand in front of his face. "The mask is created by the necromancer to hide the demon from the guardians. Which means a free demon is not bound to a necromancer but in an agreement with one."

"Okay," I said in a gentle voice, my fingers tightening on him. "Fine. Maybe Melinoe is working with a demon. That doesn't mean it's Grimm. This was all a big mistake." I turned to Grimm who still leaned against the doorframe. "Right?"

As if in reply, Grimm stepped into the kitchen. Giving Bodhi a wide berth, he strode toward me and pulled me into his arms.

Glaring at Grimm, Bodhi started to pace like a caged, wild creature. "Grimm, just tell me this, did you help Melinoe's zombies find us at the club that day?" Bodhi's fury seemed to reach its peak. "Did you?"

Grimm turned to Bodhi, matching his rage, "Fuck you, Remoussin. Stick your head in the sand if you want but I won't go down with you."

"No, of course not. You'll run away like you always do."

Neither of these assholes was going to back down.

Just as Bodhi strode forward to try to grab at Grimm, the psychopomp disappeared.

"Stop," I yelled before he could chase Grimm down the hall. "Bodhi, leave him! Grimm isn't Melinoe's demon and he didn't have anything to do with how the zombies found us."

"What do you know? You're just a naïve little school girl who didn't even know we existed until this year. It's demon nature to lie and manipulate."

"First of all, fuck you! I'll remember that. Secondly, it's human nature to lie too, Bodhi. You may not believe Grimm. That's your choice, but why are ignoring your own gut?" As he shrugged off my hold angrily, I caught at him again. "Somewhere inside you suspected something."

For a moment I thought I hadn't broken through to him. Then the tension pulled back, and he stopped straining against my hold. In a low voice filled with reluctance, he muttered, "I need some air." Not looking at me, he turned and walked out.

My nerves were shot. I gathered my stones and headed for the bedroom. Fuck him. I didn't need his bad attitude. I'd barely had time to call him every name in the book when I heard a whispered apology. I turned to see his large frame filling the doorway. "You're not a naïve little school girl. I'm just a dick who can accept when I'm wrong."

I nodded. "Sounds accurate to me."

"But I'm ready to listen now. Tell me, who is it? Who can't I trust? Who wants to kill you?"

I looked into his eyes and shook my head. "That's the thing. I don't know. It was a vision and they can be vague—like a dream."

"Tell me what you do know, then."

I nodded. "We were all in the antebellum mansion. I was alone and then someone came up from behind. He grabbed me. I fought, but he was really strong."

"And then what happened?"

"And then I opened my eyes to you, remember? That was all I saw—maybe I pass out?"

"Damn. That's not a lot to go on."

"I know. I'm sorry. Oh, he was tall, maybe as tall as you, or even taller. A big man, with big hands."

He walked forward, put his arms around me from behind, and buried his face in my hair.

"Demas?" he whispered. "He's tall."

My chest squeezed tight with compassion.

Leaning against him, I reached to cup the back of his head. "No," I whispered back as gently as I knew how. "This may sound weird, but Demas smells of ink and herbs to me, and the man from the vision did not."

He lifted up his head to pull the long, straight length of my hair aside, then he put his face into the warmth of my neck, skin to skin. "Good. Because I think my mind would splinter if it were Demas. Anyway, from here on out, you stick with either him or with me, got it? And don't give me any of that snark. You don't go anywhere by yourself, not even to the bathroom."

This was no time to take a stand over free will. He needed reassurance, so I gave it to him. "Yes, Sir. Captain, Sir."

"I said, no snark."

"Sorry. That was the toned-down version."

He held me so tightly I felt the pressure of it in my bones, but I didn't protest or try to pull away. After a moment, he muttered, "Thinking that any of them could do this is wrong, but if I set a trap, will you play along?"

"I love to play," I said instantly. "I'll do anything you need."

As my words hung in the air, I listened to what I had just said and inwardly winced.

We both laughed and the tension lifted.

"You know what I mean."

He nodded, sullenly. Caressing my lips with both thumbs, he whispered. "I'm sorry you're stuck here with us…" He bent his head to cover my lips with his.

I wound my arms around his neck to kiss him. "I'm not." Tugging his shirt up, I ran greedy hands over his long torso as he angled his head to kiss me back. "You're not going to break me," I whispered between kisses. "Just let go."

Then he did. His palms connected with my shoulder as he shoved me back. My ass hit the dresser as he pounced, shocking me and exciting me all at once.

"You're a primitive beast," I whispered.

"You're right. I am. I'm a dragon. It doesn't get more primitive," he retorted and I moaned against his mouth as he wrapped my hair around his fists.

I was feeling pretty primitive, myself. I groped at the button of his jeans, trying unsuccessfully to unleash the beast. The buttons kept slipping out of my grasp. Partially because I wasn't super experienced at this and partly because his humongous bulge didn't leave much room.

With a muttered curse, he brushed my fingers aside while still assaulting my mouth, and ripped his pants own off. I laughed and took the cue to wiggle out of my tights.

There was no delicate seduction to what we were doing. Just animal instinct. He tugged my dress and sports bra up, and I raised my arms over my head so that he could pull them off. As my breasts leapt free, he made a hungry noise at the back of his throat and cupped them.

I wrapped my legs around his hips. His thick erection brushed against my sensitive parts.

Twisting to reach for him, I gasped, "This isn't just another one of your teasing games, is it?"

"Hell, no." As my fingers wrapped around him, his eyes closed in an expression that looked almost like anguish. He picked me up and pinned me against the wall. Our eyes met as I rubbed him against my opening, then positioned him just right and with a slow, relentless thrust up, he dove deep. In this position, at this angle, he felt massive, and I heard myself gasp as my inner muscles stretched to accommodate him.

"So wet for me already."

I tightened my legs around him, drawing him farther in. "Fuck, yes," I breathed in his ear.

He angled his head to look at me. With one hand braced against the wall by my head, the other arm wrapped low around my hips, he began to pump into me.

The connection was savage. I couldn't look away. I couldn't take him in deep enough. Flexing, straining, I squeezed tight around him.

A groan broke out of him. "Stop that! You're going to push me over the edge."

But I didn't stop. I couldn't. It was so powerful to know I was the one in control, besides if I was being honest, I was already there.

I whimpered with pleasure.

His strokes were hard and powerful as our bodies pounded together.

As he pounded into me, I was clawing at his back. Bound by him. To him. He snapped his hips, withdrawing just enough that I felt the loss of him before filling me again, thrust after thrust.

"Go for it, Evangeline." As he hissed in my ear, he gave my hips an insistent yank while he ground himself against me. "Cum all over me."

What a naughty thing to say, and yet, he'd asked so nicely. I felt euphoria rise up from deep inside. Arching off the wall, I gripped him by the back of the neck as I slammed into an orgasm.

Still inside me, he sank to his knees with me sitting on his muscular thighs, I wrapped my arms around his neck while he began to rock me back and forth again. Nibbling at his lip, I egged him on until I felt him spasm and then he was spurting inside me. Rocking gently, I helped him as he had helped me, drawing out every last moment of pleasure.

I ran my fingernails through his hair in complete satisfaction, enjoying how hard he still felt inside of me. Even though it was over, I couldn't stop touching him.

Was this love?

No, just lust. I laughed at myself. I hadn't understood it before but it was easy to see now how my girlfriends from school had gotten clingy after sex. I'd clearly screwed all the wrong dudes.

Almost as if he had heard my thoughts, his arms tightened around me. "I don't want to let you go," he ran his finger down my cheek, tracing my jawline and sending chills down my spine. "but we have to get into that mansion."

"I know." I sighed. I paused for a moment, "But…could you try not dying on me this time?"

He leaned back and looked me in the eyes, smirking as he did. "Let's make that the goal."

27

MIDNIGHT WITCH

This mansion truly was a ghost house, and like a ghost—for some reason or another—it was not held to the same laws of physics as our dimension, or some shit like that. I would need to see it for what it truly was, if I were going to get inside. Easy peasy, right? That's what I thought, but after crossing to the front porch and climbing the steps to the heavy oak door, I rose on my tiptoes, stuck the key into the mouth of the lock and failed to open the door.

"Damn!"

"What's the problem?" Bodhi asked, coming to join me—looking all sexy in his black jeans. *Focus Evangeline!*

I turned back to the mansion and tugged the skeleton key back out of the lock. "You're testing me, aren't you, girl?"

"Is it stuck?" he asked, "I could try pushing it open?"

"No. It's not about manpower. I don't think it can be forced. This house is like a ghost, if that makes any sense at all."

"How so?"

"Well, you know how ghosts appear out of sync with

275

our physical surroundings."

"Like how they float or walk through walls, you mean?"

I nodded, turning to face him and his gorgeous puppy dog eyes. "It's because when we see ghosts, we are seeing through a thin spot of the membrane that separates realms or parallel universes, or wherever they're from.

"I get that. Ghosts are not perfectly aligned with our world. What does that have to do with the Midnight Mansion?"

"It has everything to do with it. So, for a ghost, the floor is in a different position. I think that this house is in some ways like a ghost. It's actually from a different dimension or realm or maybe time—I don't know. My point is, the key lock that we see is not really there. It's a hologram. I need to find where the actual key lock would be in the mansion's own dimension. I just don't know how." I smoothed my fingers over the warn metal of the door knocker attempting to connect with the house. Apparently, it didn't like that. The metal nipped and cut me.

I pulled away and centered myself. This was the second time I'd been bitten by an inanimate object.

"Try again." Bodhi encouraged. "We have to do this."

I nodded. *Easy for you to say.*

I position the key between my fingers once more, my

blood transferred onto it, but that couldn't very well be helped.

This time when I extended it, I felt a tug, and just like that, I could see another lock—two inches higher than its earthly counterpart. Like double exposure on a photograph. I placed the key in the higher lock this time, tensing when the teeth sunk perfectly in. I looked back at Bodhi and gave a nervous smile. When I twisted, the latch sprang free.

"It worked!" Bodhi shouted.

"I think so," I replied. For a brief, heartrending moment, nothing happened.

Then with a gigantic, rusty creak, the door sprang open. A large, open room stretched out before us, the space two stories high, its ceiling and walls encrusted with ornate crown molding. I turned around and threw my arms around Bodhi's neck. He scooped me up and laughed with me, then he kissed me.

I kissed him back, meeting his every shift and caress fiercely, tenderly, sensually, only breaking away from his mouth to suck in another gulp of air.

"I'm sorry," he muttered. Finally, setting set me down.

As I swiveled to take in the room, the sight made me catch my breath. I entered hesitantly, feeling out of place in all the grandeur, and treading lightly on the dusty but smooth wooden floor. Pistachio-colored curtains lay over ceiling-high windows, and there was a glittering chandelier suspended from the soaring ceiling, large corinthian columns, and a grand staircase at the far end of the open space. I tilted my head, looking for any potential weaknesses, signs of rot, or water stains that might indicate a possible collapse.

"This place is beautiful," I murmured, half to myself, half to Bodhi who stood behind me, hands in his pockets.

"It feels a bit chilly though, doesn't it?"

Now that he mentioned it, I became aware of a deep chill creeping over me. It wasn't the normal cool of a shaded and well-ventilated summer home. It was the biting chill of a cold, empty house.

"This is a large space. I don't know where to go from here."

Doors opened to our left and right, and through them was parlor furniture covered in old sheets. At the far end of the great hall, another set of doors led to a dining room. A massive table filled the space, surrounded by over a dozen chairs, all draped in dust-covered sheets.

"It feels funny to be in the place where my mother grew up."

Strange warmth spooled up my leg from the floor grate.

"What are you thinking about?" Bodhi asked, "you

look surprised."

"I think Gran' just said hello. My aunt said she controlled the house. When I mentioned my mother, I felt warm air as if she was remembering with me."

"She could be."

"No, that's crazy." Suddenly, a blast of arctic air blew up the leg of my shorts. "Okay, yep. I definitely felt that. She's here and she can hear us."

The lights blinked on and off.

Bodhi looked at me in shock and I shrugged. *Who was I to argue with a bewitched structure?* We walked to the fireplace where two hurricane lamps and a giant candelabra decorated the mantel next to a photo of my mother and her family.

I studied the graceful curve of her lips, tilted into the sweetest smile. It was like peering into a looking glass showing me in the future; even our expressions were similar. Tearing my gaze away, I dialed my aunt's number and held the phone to my ear. Distantly, I knew, Bodhi could hear it ringing.

"Aunt Aurora," I said, when she answered, "It's Evangeline. I got inside the house." I laughed gleefully. "It took some realigning but I did it."

"Congratulations! I just knew you were the Midnight for the job!? Is Demas with you? That house is dangerous."

"No, Bodhi helped me but Demas isn't too far away.

I wanted to contact you first." I turned slightly away, "So, you still think it's possible that I might find Mama somewhere in here, right?"

"It's possible. I'll be there to help as soon as I can get away from this damn council. This city is experiencing a supernatural clusterfuck—pardon my language—at the moment."

I looked over my shoulder at Bodhi. "Well, don't worry about me. I'm well taken care of."

"Good. I'll be there as soon as I can get away."

I laughed as I hung up, ready to explore. The prospect of finding Mama had me exhilarated.

28

MIDNIGHT WITCH

An evening mist settled over the area. Somewhere on the far bank, a gator splashed into the water, looking for dinner. I, personally, hoped it favored zombies. The cricket song was swinging into full chorus while clouds amassed on the horizon, and the air grew damp and electric with the energy of impending rain.

Eleutian had disappeared to cloak the plantation using his magic while the rest of us ate supper. I'd quickly tattooed him beforehand to mask his magical signature since we were about to spread it all over us. After dinner we got down to work chopping wood and transporting things we would need from the guest house to the manor. I helped too but mostly I drooled. I couldn't decide which of the men looked more appealing—all sweaty and manly—lifting and shifting heavy things. I know. My libido had its own heartbeat lately. I felt like it had something to do with my use of magic but without my mom or Julep around to ask, I couldn't be sure.

I glanced from Colten's broad shoulders to Bodhi's dark hair that had fallen onto his brow. They looked handsome, dangerous, and kissable all at once. Being with two of them had only made me fall harder for all of them.

The crunch of boots on gravel nearby snapped me back to the present. When I turned around, I found Demas approaching with a load of firewood. From the intense look and the weight of his step, I could tell that Bodhi had finally talked to him.

He put an arm around me and squeezed me against his side tightly enough to make me grunt. "You're going to be safe with us," he told me. "I swear it."

Sighing, I let my head fall onto his shoulder as I slipped an arm around his waist. "I already knew that," I told him.

"Good." Unexpectedly, he turned his head to press a kiss against my forehead. "You matter a great deal, not just to me—because of your aunt—but to this whole unit. You've managed to integrate and you're one of us. I hope you can feel that."

At his words, my heart turned to mush. I barreled into him to give him a full-bodied hug. "Thank you for saying that, Demas."

He returned the hug and stroked my back. "Stick with us, Evie. We'll do right by you." As he let me go, he smiled and brushed a strand of hair back from my face with his knuckles.

We jogged over to the manor house as the first few

raindrops turned into a steady rain; it quickly became a downpour.

"You gonna get some heat circulating?" Demas called out.

"Yep," Bodhi shouted back. "You got the wood?"

"Got it right here. Come on, Evie," He reached for my hand. "Help a bookworm out."

Within moments, we'd tossed the wood inside the massive front door and Bodhi had stacked it beside the fireplace.

"Holy, Evie," he exclaimed. "You got some pipes on you, girl."

I felt his eyes drift over my biceps before moving to my nipples which were now promptly on display thanks to the rain.

"Hey!" I pointed my two fingers at my eyes and then motioned to his. "You keep staring like that and I'm going to charge you."

"Well worth the price I'm sure."

"Perfect. The price is an old-fashioned doughnut. I'm hungry after all that lifting."

He motioned toward the house. "I know just where we can get one of those."

Suddenly lights appeared off in the distance, shining through the woods. Breathing hard, I paused to stare, and then jerked my eyes up to meet his. "Is that Melinoe?" I asked, noticing a large vehicle, approaching the front gates.

Demas dug in his pocket to check the screen of his phone. "No. That's the backup unit. I think you may have to find that snack without me."

Between the distance and the deep shadows, I couldn't make out many details of the newcomers. They conversed quickly and then backed the truck up to the house as close as they could. Then, while it sat idling, they unloaded the contents from the back, carrying heavy armloads of weapons and supplies into the front foyer at a dead run. A couple of them gave me a nod in greeting as they came close, but nobody paused to talk. Talking could happen later.

While they worked, I pulled a blanket around my shoulders and sat by the hearth, munching on carrot sticks. Sadly, I couldn't find the treats. A chill had set in the house with the storm, and fine tremors ran through my muscles.

Lightning flashed overhead, showing through the thick, archaic glass in the windows and briefly lighting the interior. More quickly than I would have thought possible, they finished unloading the truck.

Bodhi jutted his chin toward the open door. "We need to hide the truck. We don't want Melinoe knowing your here."

"Already on it," one of the men said, holding up the

keys to jingle them. "I'll go drop it in the woods and walk back."

Demas turned to him. "I've got a better place for it. Come on, I'll take the bike and we'll get back here faster that way."

As I watched the exchange, the angst in my gut grew. Something wasn't right but I couldn't pinpoint what. Maybe it was Eleutian's absence. What if he had collapsed outside? Pushing out of the armchair, I approached the group of men still standing on the doorstep just as one of them lit an oil lantern and held it high. As one, they turned to look at me.

Bodhi introduced them quickly and, one by one, they stepped forward to shake my hand. I'd already met the brutish vampire, Professor William Van Rogue, but there were three new names to learn: Jude, Ryder, and Zagan.

"Has anyone checked on Eleutian?" I asked.

"I'll find him," Bodhi said and strode out into the storm. Almost immediately, my angst heightened. Something was very wrong. I took a couple of steps and saw the trees move.

"Hey, Bodhi," I yelled. "Come on—"

I stopped, mid-sentence as I saw what had been bothering me.

My blood ran cold. A hairy, fanged creature not twelve feet away appeared behind him, emerging from the nearby tree line.

The zombies had arrived, and they weren't human.

29

THE FIERY TEMPERED BEAST

Chest heaving, Bodhi stared at the undead army pouring out of the woods, namely the lead one that was racing straight for him. Time to shift. He lifted his shoulders to pop his wings out but nothing happened. What was going on? They were stuck. He tried again. This time he attempted to change his skin—the dragon scales were like an impenetrable coat of armor. Nothing. That damned necromancer. He must be doing something to screw with them.

Ten feet… nine feet…

Bodhi was running out of options. He reached for his beloved Heckler & Koch. Shit! What had he been thinking, removing his semi-automatic pistol? He was a sitting duck out here.

Eight feet… seven feet…

Shit! He couldn't outrun it.

Just then, he heard the erratic percussion of a gun. Only it wasn't a gun, it was Evangeline's magic firing as she took down the lead wolf, the one not six feet from Bodhi.

Suddenly remembering his own new tattoo, he

gathered his power and fired at the second closest wolf. Like a bolt of horizontal lightning, the energy ball split the darkness and exploded in the thing's broad, furry chest. The force slammed it to the ground, and it didn't rise again.

Bodhi might not be able to shift but he still had his super speed and super strength, and he was a sure shot with any weapon. Still, he'd never cast magic like that before. These were a product of Evangeline's tattooing skills, but they were an energy suck. Whirling back around, he raced toward Evangeline.

Sighting down the length of her arm, she'd held her hand out and fired magical bullets repeatedly at the approaching zombies. He cast a quick look around while he ran. There were four bodies lying on the lawn, but there were at least fifteen more still coming.

Evie was doing magnificently but what if she ran out of magical bullets. Was there such a thing as an infinity rune? He longed to thank her for saving his ass, to tell her he was sorry for getting her into this shitstorm. As he battled one of the werewolf corpses. One of the zombies then grabbed her. A regular undead creeper, not a werewolf, thank fuck for small miracles! He tried to keep his eye on her while fighting his own battle but it was hard. He was nearly hyperventilating, unable to control his airflow when he saw her bring her knee up hard into its groin, the thing's glowing white eyes had bulged. Bodhi almost laughed. It might be a monster, but clearly not all of their nerve endings had died off. The zombie loosened his grip on one her wrists, and she wrenched it free, bringing the full force of her palm into his Adam's apple. Bodhi heard the crunch from where he fought.

"Remoussin!" The shout came from behind him. As he looked over his shoulder, Colten tossed his gun holster at him and then took aim with his wrist mounted mini-crossbow to cover him.

Bodhi kicked the werewolf away and snatched it out of the air. "Get behind me," he snapped at Evangeline.

Behind him and low to the ground, her magic spat multiple times. She must be getting tired. Magical weapons were hell on the body but it wasn't slowing her down one bit. Around him, Jude, Colten, and Van Rogue were armed with guns, knives and repeater crossbows too. The rest of his men slammed into combat with the zombies, so he drew his pistol and dropped the holster to the ground.

Not ten yards away, Colten was facing off against two zombies. Moving forward rapidly, Bodhi engaged the closest wolf.

The battle turned into images he saw in microsecond snapshots. The wolf turned its slavering jaws toward him, and they circled each other, the driving rain making every step a hazard.

It was a sloppy, ugly battle. Naturally, Evangeline had stayed in the thick of it and was now holding one hostage with one of her spells so that they could question it once it turned back—if it turned back. That woman was a force to be reckoned with.

Bodhi was able to amass two more energy balls before he tapped out. Aiming the last one strategically, he was able to take down two zombies at once, and then he had to rely upon his guns and knives.

Within a half hour, the battle was over. As Bodhi drew his knife from the throat of his last kill, he surveyed the field. Bodies littered the ground.

The sound of Evangeline's shouting had him spinning on his heel. "What the hell is the matter with you? Don't shove me!"

Van Rogue advanced, his fangs out and on full display. He shoved her in the chest, pushing her back as he shouted hoarsely over her, "Then get inside, little girl!"

"Fuck you, you sexist piece of shit."

Bodhi lunged and slammed into Van Rogue so violently the other man skidded on the wet grass and went down on his ass. Breathing hard, Bodhi brought the muzzle of his gun to Van Rogue's temple.

Van Rogue's face distorted with rage. "What are you doing? She's going to get herself killed."

He pressed forward until the muzzle pressed against the skin at Van Rogue's temple. "You touch her again like that, and I will stake you in the fucking heart."

"You've just accepted her into the team now, have you?"

"Yes." Bodhi bared his teeth in savage, naked aggression and his voice turned stone cold.

"Well, you're an idiot. Females don't belong in battle. She'll get one of us killed."

"The only one in danger right now is you." Bodhi could feel his temper rising. His inner beast wanted to emerge. He tamped it down. "If Evangeline hadn't acted so quickly and been such a good shot, and if she'd never tattooed me with those magical weapons, this would have been a bloodbath. We are guests in her house, and you will respect her expertise. Is that clear?"

Zagan stepped forward to put his hand on Bodhi's taut forearm. "You're right, Bodhi," he said, his voice clear and calm. "That's not who we are, right William?"

Van Rogue huffed but nodded. He looked at Evangeline. "I apologize. I don't know why I'm acting so crazy and protective. It must have been the heat of the battle."

Bodhi glanced at Evangeline to see if she was buying it?

291

She nodded easily and smiled. "Battle fever can make the best of us do crazy things. No harm done this time. Just don't do it again, or you can forget about being staked. I'll send you spinning into next week, myself."

Expectedly, Colten started to chuckle. "That a girl! Have you seen her spells?"

Others started to laugh, and the tension eased. Zagan's grip tightened on Bodhi's arm until he forced his rigid muscles to relax. Taking a step back, he bent to retrieve his holster from the grass, then secured his gun in place.

He asked, "Did we get them all?"

"No way to tell," Zephyr replied. "There could have been others holding back, in the woods, but they would have charged too, unless they had other orders."

Out of the corner of his eye, he saw Evangeline offer a hand to Van Rogue to help him up. After a second's hesitation, Van Rogue accepted it. He watched closely to make sure nothing else happened. Then he said, "I guess it doesn't matter. None of these zombies will be returning, which is a message in itself."

Evangeline's shoulders sagged. "This is my fault for going into town. Damn! I can be so stubborn. Melinoe must have known I was lying about Grimm after all?"

Colten gave her a light tap in the shoulder, "Nah. Forget about it, Midnight. If Melinoe suspected that you were lying, you'd be his mindless, walking sex toy by now."

She heaved a sigh. "How cheery a thought. Thanks, Colten, for making me feel better."

Colten laughed. "What? You wanted it sugarcoated."

Evangeline shook her head. "It must have been Eleutian's storm, then. Maybe the magic attracted the zombies."

Although Bodhi didn't say so, he disagreed. Eleutian knew what he was doing. But he also agreed with Colten. Melinoe wouldn't have let her go if he thought she was hiding Grimm.

He watched Van Rogue closely for the next several minutes as they stacked the bodies of the zombies together close to the tree line. Why had Van Rogue tried to get Evie inside? Was he the man from her vision?

"That's it," Bodhi said, wiping his hands on his sodden pants, just as a single headlight of a motorcycle appeared. Demas and Ashe had returned. "We're done. Let's get inside."

The others didn't hesitate. They jogged to the mansion, and as soon as everybody was inside, Bodhi and Demas closed the iron-bound oak doors while everyone else watched in the dim glow thrown from the fire across the foyer.

While Demas issued orders, Bodhi turned his

attention to Evangeline. Damp, like the rest of them, she was visibly shivering and her face was completely colorless. Searching the immediate area, he found the blanket she had left crumpled on the doorstep and enveloped both her and the ferret in it.

His hands were reluctant to leave her. He clamped his fists in the blanket and drew her close. She didn't resist him. Neither did Grimm, as the psychopomp turned his face away and laid it on her shoulder.

"You looked spent hours ago, and a lot has happened since then," Bodhi muttered. "Let's get you out of these wet clothes. Then will you please sit by the fire and warm up?"

Her teeth chattered. "I would l-love nothing more than to fall asleep by the fire, but I need the bathroom first."

Heaving a sigh, he conceded. "All right, but only after we change into dry clothes."

They changed quickly. First Bodhi held up a blanket in one of the two corners closest to the fire so that she could strip out of her wet clothes in relative privacy. When she was freshly dressed in jeans, a sweater, and her black boots, he changed too.

"Follow me."

As tired as she looked, her expression was alive with interest. She fell into step beside him as he led her toward the huge fireplace. "Why are we going into the corner–oh!"

Her exclamation came as he took her hand and led her into the deep shadow at the side of the huge hearth. Only when they came close did the light from the oil lantern reveal a dark, narrow hall, craftily designed to remain hidden by the massive bulk of the fireplace.

He grinned at the look in her wide eyes. "I found it when I was clearing the chimney. It's not quite a hidden passageway, but it's close. Servants would have used this, probably to carry food and drink to the high table and important guests, so it should lead back to the kitchen, buttery, and pantry."

The sounds of the men working faded as they went down the dark, narrow hallway until black silence pressed at them on all sides. They could walk abreast of each other, but Bodhi's sleeve brushed the wall on his side, and he could see that Evangeline didn't have much room on hers either.

She whispered gleefully, "This is creepy as hell."

"It is, a bit." Smiling slightly, he laced his fingers through hers. "Are you sensing any magical pieces?"

She shook her head. "Not at the moment. I'll be sure to tell you when I do." Her eyes gleamed as she glanced behind them. "You suspect Van Rogue, don't you?"

His brief amusement faded. "He has pressed me for details at suspicious times. He knew about Grimm and the nightclub. And tonight, not an hour after the men arrived, we got attacked by a large pack of zombies. He killed our only chance at information. None of it is definitive, but yes, I do suspect him."

As they talked, they came to a heavy door. "There's your bathroom."

"This is fantastic." Her eyes shone.

She returned a few minutes later, but as they headed back a flash of light snared their attention as a ghostly woman popped into existence beside them. She wore a long blue dress and had a mass of white curls.

Evangeline affixed a smile on her mouth. "You must be Gran'. Nice to meet you."

The black voids of her eyes sparkled like polished coals then she darted away.

The magic that had swelled in the space momentarily, easy to sense, now vanished.

"Hey! There's a piece over there." Evangeline pointed down to the floor where Gran had just disappeared. "I think that's what Gran' was trying to show us."

He looked in that direction. "Where? What does it look like?"

"A rainbow or a kaleidoscope. It's hard to describe unless you've seen Grimm's eyes when he uses magic. It's almost as if someone has sliced the canvas of a painting and a patterned rainbow is peeking through." She shuddered.

"How very 1970s."

Evangeline smiled. "I wouldn't know. So, did you see her? Did you see Gran'?"

"Yeah, it's part of the Monster Squad charm," Bodhi replied. "We can see spirits. You saw her too, though? It must be your connection, or do you always see ghosts?"

"No, thank goodness. This would be my first. Aside from the séance, of course, and those zombie creatures... and your ghostly dog. Well, actually, it would seem, I can see quite a few things now." She held her hand out in front of her and waved it back and forth, "I wonder why you can't see the piece?"

"Hey! Don't touch it. The last thing we need is for you to disappear into some sort of portal." Setting aside the lantern, he drew her into his arms. She leaned into his embrace and tucked her face into his neck.

"Relax, Mr. Worrypants. The piece is much lower. Anyway, I was feeling for the magical energy to see if there was more nearby.

Rubbing his cheek against her damp hair, he muttered, "Good. You make me crazy with worry sometimes."

Crazy with worry and a tangled mess of so many other emotions. Interacting with Evangeline was like trying to herd cats through a pond.

"I make you crazy?" Dropping the blanket, she slipped her arms around his waist. She whispered, "I almost threw up when I saw those zombies racing after you, Bodhi." As she spoke, she rubbed his back, the touch soothing and arousing at once.

He slid the tips of his fingers underneath the edges of her sweater, connecting with the warm skin at her torso. The need to kiss her, to feel her full mouth pliant and moving under his, was pounding in his head. He tilted her face up. "Evangeline," he whispered. "We're no good for you. Our life is desperate and violent all the time, not just tonight, and now you've gotten trapped in a conflict you can't leave."

"Oh, Bodhi," she murmured, stroking his hair. "It really is impossible for you to grasp that I love it. I am where I need to be. Well... almost... I need to be in bed."

30

MIDNIGHT WITCH

The smell of sautéed onions wafted in from the kitchen tempting me but I remained curled up in the room adjacent—still within earshot—reading one of Demas' books on defensive magic. Bodhi and Demas had disappeared to do something secretive and made me promise not to move. I needed to sharpen my spell casting anyway, if I were going to be of more help. I was busily reading a page on blocking outside magic when I heard Colten call my name from the other room. I sniffed the air. Was that bacon and ham too? My stomach growled. "Okay, fine," I mumbled relenting and closing the large tome.

A sizzling sound greeted me as I entered the kitchen where I was met with friendly looks and a few smiles. "Mmm. What smells so good?"

"Supper," Colten replied. His spoon hovered close to his mouth. "Split peas and ham. There's sandwiches too," he said as he bit, chewed, and swallowed.

Soup and sandwiches sounded more like lunch to me, but beggars couldn't be choosers, or at least that's what Mama said when she made me eat her dry-ass meatloaf.

Colten shifted over to make room for me at the long table, but I shook my head, "Thanks but I feel like one of those walkers—dead on my feet." The reading had made me tired, not to mention the magic usage. "Can I just get a sandwich to go? I'm gonna crash in t-minus sixty seconds."

"Course. No shame in being tired, Midnight," Colten said, with a light smack to my bum. "You were the MVP today. Good job."

"Gee, thanks Coach."

"Wait," he said as he stood. He dug out a large mug, filled it with steaming soup, and offered it to me. "Take this."

I accepted it, along with a sandwich, and retired to a chorus of good nights.

Before I could plop down onto the closest sleeping bag, Demas nudged my shoulder and pointed to a tent in the adjoining room. "Over there, Evie. We thought you might want a bit more privacy."

He lifted the flap, and, with one hand, urged me to step through. I complied and discovered a cozy double bed, and someone had even made it. The bedside table held an oil lantern, and my luggage was stacked neatly at the foot of the bed. "Baudoin and I will be sleeping right outside. Nobody will get past us, and tomorrow I'll help you look for your mother."

"Ooh la la." Setting my food on the bedside table, I

gave him a hug. "Why didn't you just set me up in one of the bedrooms upstairs if you didn't want me breaking up the sausage party?"

Demas laughed. "We need to be able to keep an eye on you while also keeping an eye on the men."

"Gotcha." I winked back. "You never know what I may do to them in the night. Anyway, you've moved me further away from the fire so I think it's only fair that you climb on and warm it up for me."

Smiling at my suggestion, he took a seat and whispered, "With pleasure."

I stripped out of my clothes and crawled, shivering, between the blankets. Looking momentarily surprised and yet also pleased, Demas wrapped his arms around me and while I waited for the bed to warm up, I sipped at the split pea soup, savoring the warmth.

Thanks to the professor's body heat the worst of the chill had split like the soup, so I stretched out horizontally, and as I listened to the men's quiet conversation, I fell into a black pit.

I plunged awake to long, hair-sprinkled legs touching mine. The men must have all gone to bed, and the indirect light from the fire had died down, leaving the space in near total darkness.

Bodhi whispered, "Shh, you okay? It's just us, love."

The comfort was immediate and staggering. I turned into Bodhi, burying my face in his chest while Demas stroked my hair.

"You were having a nightmare and whimpering."

Unsurprised, I nodded. "Sorry, that's sort of my trademark move. I woke you guys?"

Bodhi exhaled. "It's okay."

"Better?" Demas asked, as he ran his fingers through my hair. My scalp tingled at the release of endorphins. He was longer, broader, but Bodhi was more muscular, and the sensation of their bare skin against mine caused a tension that was coiled tight inside of me to ease.

I nodded. I felt enclosed, surrounded. Instead of feeling trapped, it felt comforting and good. The rightness of it hurt more than almost anything else I had ever experienced.

The rhythmic caress soothed me like nothing else ever had. My muscles went pliable and boneless. "You called out for your mother," Demas said. "You know you can talk to us if you need to, right? It's okay to be vulnerable."

"I'm fine. As a matter of fact, this feels pretty damn nice."

"Good. We've lost people, too," Bodhi breathed against my lips. "You don't need to suffer alone, Evangeline," Bodhi said, and he kissed me.

I lost myself in the sensation of his mouth moving on

mine, the weight of his body, the warmth radiating off his skin. Desire hit me low and hard. My body felt empty and aching and, as I wiggled, I felt Demas stiffen into a hard, thick length that pressed against my bum.

While Bodhi slanted his mouth over mine, kissing me with such wild heat, Demas kissed the back of my neck. A moan trembled on my lips. Bodhi swallowed it down, thrusting deep with his tongue while he ran his fingertips along the edge of my Calvin Klein's. The light touch left a trail of fiery sensation in its wake.

We kissed and touched together like that for the next hour, joined in the great room's chill silence. The only sound I could hear was the quiet seesaw of our ragged breathing.

Afterward, we slept long and hard, and when I woke up, I was alone in the bed.

A percussive blast rattled the foundation beneath my feet. We must be getting another storm, I thought. Sighing, I dragged on the same jeans and sweater from before, tugged on my combat boots and ventured out into the common area. Several of the men sat at the table, drinking coffee and talking. The smell of bacon hung in the air.

As I appeared, they turned to look at me. There was a moment of silence.

Then Zephyr said, "Morning Evie. You look sexy— crazy hair and all."

Warmth washed over my cheeks. Bodhi stood whispering to Demas and Ashe, looking intensely out the windows. He didn't turn at the exchange and I wondered what was going on.

I slipped into the washroom to wash up, and when I returned, Demas slipped a plate of bacon and eggs in front of me, along with a cup of black coffee.

"Mmmm…. coffee. The most magical potion of all."

"Told you she's an addict," Zephyr said.

Demas smiled, "Well enjoy it, and enjoy the eggs. They won't last too long, especially with this kid around." He pointed his thumb at Zephyr who grinned sheepishly.

"What? I'm a growing boy."

"You're a vampire."

"Sort of. I can't be defined by your terms." Zephyr winked at me.

"Thank you so much." I glanced again at Bodhi by the window, then turned my attention to the hot meal.

As I ate, Colten slipped a couple of pieces of toast on my plate. At first, there was a lull in the conversation but then, as the men grew used to my presence, the talk resumed. Only Eleutian was quiet. He looked exhausted and I felt for him. I pulled out my pen, while the other men were busy and reached for his arm.

He looked up in surprise when I caressed the spot I

planned to sketch. "It's okay," I whispered. "I'm just gonna share some energy with you," I sketched out a battery like rune with a power symbol on both he and I, then I made tiny cuts in both and rubbed them together. Afterward I sealed them with polish. "There," I said. "You should get your second wind soon."

He reached over and cupped the back of my neck, pulling me in for a kiss. "Thanks, darlin'." His lips were soft and his hands were gentle. I had a feeling Eleutian would be a really great lover—he oozed romance.

"You're welcome," I whispered when he let me go.

As I finished the last of my breakfast, Bodhi stalked over. He was dressed in black again–I didn't think he wore any other color. He looked leaner, darker, and harder than ever, and his dark eyes glittered with an expression I didn't want to try to interpret.

He said, "Ready to get to work?"

My jaw tightened. "Good morning to you too," I said, sarcastically. "How are you today, Evangeline? I'm fine, thank you very much. I got a good night's sleep."

Someone across the table made a strangled noise. I thought it might have been Colten. Other than that, dead silence washed over the group.

Bodhi shot me a wicked smile, and my insides clenched. "Glad we have the pleasantries out of the way," he said in a silken voice. "So, ready?"

I straightened, crossing my arms across my chest. "Ready for what?"

"A little puzzle solving. Didn't you say you wanted to crack that portal code?"

I drained my coffee and nodded. "Right? Reality. Got it."

He told me grimly, "Melinoe is here."

My stomach clenched. "That's what you were up to?" I went over to the windows, murmuring, "Pardon me," to Ashe, who moved to let me look out.

Melinoe, the familiar silver-haired giant had his arms crossed, looking fierce in his leather jacket. A dark, dank nocturnal power crackled in the air around him, old as time itself. He studied the house with his chin tucked down while shadows whispered around him. A pit opened in the hollow of my stomach. He knows what I did, and he's here for revenge. On either side of him, rows of corpses lurched to a start. Feet scuffed and bones creaked, and in seconds the zombie militia was shambling forward. Toward the house— toward us like creepy marionettes.

My panic bubbled to the surface. "Holy fuck! What if they can get in?"

"They can't! It's a power play," Bodhi said, placing his hand on my shoulder. "You know this." He took my hand.

"Come on. We have work to do. Where do you want to start?"

Immediately I turned to walk down the hallway where I'd found the first piece. "We know this one is here." As soon as we were far enough away, I dropped my voice, "Why did you and Demas leave me in bed?"

"We took turns keeping watch."

I frowned. "You're worried someone... Van Rogue will let them in?" I was so focused on him I almost forgot to watch for the place where I had felt the piece. I looked down at the last minute and saw the prism of color.

"Wait!" I said, grabbing his arm. "We're here."

The corridor looked the same in both directions. Bodhi frowned. "I can't sense it."

"Maybe this one is a smaller piece, and you'll be able to sense a bigger one," I said. *Boom! Boom! Boom!* I frowned. "Did you invite a marching band into my mansion as well?"

"Yes, Melinoe and the fucknuts," Bodhi snarled. "I heard his vibe is deadly."

I smiled. "He's attacking the house, isn't he?"

We raced back to the great foyer and the front window, where the rest of the men had gathered, their expressions grim.

The low rumble began and rose in intensity. Rubbing a clear spot on the dirty window to peer through, I saw

Melinoe head and shoulders were bowed, and even from that distance, I could see the strain in his body. Behind him, a tree toppled over and crashed into the roof of the guest house.

Rage and fear hit in equal measures. "He's destroying my property! Gran! Get him!"

A death rattle of sadness shook the darkened chandelier.

I looked at Bodhi, "Gran is unnerved."

Bodhi said harshly, "Maybe she doesn't know to fight him off. He's using magic."

"You used magic and she kicked your ass."

"True, but I wasn't expecting retaliation at the time so I didn't have my defenses up. I would imagine Melinoe's more prepared, considering he has us to contend with. Also, he's been using some pretty dark magic."

Brightness exploded in the room, and my retinas ached like they had been stabbed. It seemed Gran was worried. I had to agree.

I could feel the blood rushing to my head. I squeezed my eyes shut and thought it through. The house was like a mirage in the desert. It sat partly in other realms, always moving in and out. So, it would be hard to make a direct hit. Then again, if Melinoe was as powerful as they said. He could maybe find a way to attack the other realms too. If he was blocking Gran's retaliation then he might eventually wear her down. *Did ghostly buildings get tired?*

"Can he do it?" Zephyr asked.

"Only a witch would know," Bodhi replied.

Opening my eyes again, I realized they were staring. "Well, don't just look at my warts? Ask Eleutian?"

Reluctantly Eleutian said, "I'm a mage but to answer your question, the house isn't entirely in his realm. It moves in and out of multiple places so, without witch or Fae magic I don't think he can get inside the house, otherwise he would have done it by now. But I don't see him giving up either which leaves us with two problems. He could wear down our defenses, or he could collapse the portal, taking us with it."

31

MIDNIGHT WITCH

An image of Melinoe bringing down the mansion with us inside flashed in my brain. He was so powerful. Colten pulled out a flask and handed it to me. "Here. This will help with your nerves." I took a sip of the pungent liquid.

"Better?" he lowered his eyes.

I handed him the flask again. "Yuck no, that tastes awful. And unless you're trying to cloud my judgement, I'm not sure what getting me tipsy is going to do."

Colten grinned. "It's never hurt before."

So naughty. I shifted my eyes from him, "As far as I can tell, the house is like a picture that's been torn up or maybe it's more like a combination lock. I'm not sure yet. I've got to line up the pieces of magic. I've got to get them in the right order."

"So, first things first. You need to know where all the pieces are, correct?" Bodhi pointed out.

I nodded.

"Alright, let's help her find them, boys!" Colten shouted. "And let's get this supernatural safe cracked."

Brightness exploded in the room, again. "Chill Gran'!
My retinas can't take your excitement. We get it. You're on
board." As she dimmed back down to a normal level, I
prayed, please let us find all of the pieces of the portal.

I couldn't imagine what kind of power it took to
cause that quake repeatedly. Melinoe couldn't keep it up
indefinitely—I hoped.

We went down the hall, and I quickly noticed a
pattern. Gran was playing hot potato with the lights. She
flicked a path on and led us to a library that spanned two
entire floors. Eleutian and Ryder headed in the same direction
as us, while the rest of the group followed her in another
direction. Books and manuscripts lined the library's wooden
shelves. A twisting, dark wooden staircase sat in the corner,
while tables with stained-glass lamps flaked upholstered,
overstuffed chairs.

"Right there," I said, squatting to draw a quick line
with chalk near one corner. Each time we came upon another
piece, we marked it with chalk. It wasn't long before we
realized that I was the only one who could see the broken
magic so each time I drew a line, Bodhi and I kept moving,
while the others stayed behind to add it to the manor's floor
plan that Demas has roughly sketched out. The floor plan
was going to help me visualize at the end.

There was an interior corridor from the kitchen

leading back to the foyer.

"There's magic nearby, I can feel it," I murmured, turning around in confusion near the end of the corridor. We had been combing the house for hours but there was still a piece missing and it was the largest piece. The energy hummed and vibrated throughout the house, calling me to it and yet there was a wall. An invisible barricade that I just couldn't get through. I was tired, thirsty, and hungry, and even Gran seemed stumped. As I turned around again, clenching my hands in frustration, Bodhi thrust a water bottle into my hands. "Take a minute. I'll go grab you a snack from the kitchen. Just stay in here and keep your back to the wall so no one can get the jump on you."

I nodded, accepting the need for at least a brief break, I moved to the railing. Perhaps a birdseye view of the floor below would help. I could see Bodhi headed for the kitchen. Something about the kitchen struck a chord inside of me. That room had felt different to me—like an illusion. That's it! That was why I couldn't find the last piece. There was an illusion in place, meant to confuse—like a vampire's glamour.

"I've got it. I know where the last piece is!" I screamed, hurrying back to the wall so Bodhi didn't catch me disobeying his orders.

Quick footsteps came up from behind me. I turned around to see who it was but all I saw was stars, and all I felt was pain.

**

I touched my forehead. There was something wet running past my eyes. Slightly disoriented, I pulled my hand back, and looked at it.

Blood.

What was going on? My neck was hurting and someone was gripping me from behind.

In an instant, I recalled hearing footsteps behind me.

"Move, bitch. Quickly and quietly. Got it. You're my ticket out of me," The familiar male voice growled in my ear.

"Bitch?" I uttered. "I've been nothing but nice to you."

"Not as nice as you've been to the other guys. Didn't see you in my pants? Not that it's too late."

Oh really. What a slimy bastard, I thought. *I'm going to kick you in the balls one extra time for that.* "Naturally. Unfortunately, I forgot my tweezers at home."

He pressed the knife a little deeper. "One more comment like that and I'll bury my blade, got it? And I don't mean that as sexual innuendo."

"Eww." I was about to take another jab when I realized I was on the wrong side of the pointy object.

"Ashe! What are you doing?" Demas yelled.

Several feet away, I caught a glimpse of the others flanking him—Jude, Van Rogue, and Bodhi.

The men had come up the stairs and were now stalking toward us. Bodhi's expression turned savage.

"Get back," Ashe barked. "Get back, or I'll slit her throat! I mean it—back the fuck up!"

The men stopped and glared.

"I'm going to murder you and I'm going to enjoy it," Bodhi whispered. His eyes blazed.

"Not if you want your bitch to live. She's coming outside with me. Melinoe's waiting for us."

"Why, Ashe?" Bodhi asked. "You were one of us and you sold us down the—" Bodhi stopped, clearly unable to continue without taking a breath. Evangeline could see that he wanted to end this traitor's miserable life right here, right now, but she could tell that he also didn't want to cause her pain. His hands shook with the burden of restraint.

"You already know why?" Ashe's voice was strained.

Bodhi cocked his head sideways. "I want to hear what you have to say, you sack of—"

Suddenly Ashe flared his nostrils and roared, "Because you fucked up and took us—the backup unit—down with you. You were exiled, and we were assigned to support you. We weren't even at the gates the night that necromancer escaped."

"Don't lump us in with you!" Jude yelled. "You coward! We don't blame them. It could have happened to any one of us."

I knew the boys couldn't make a move with the knife at my throat. It was up to me to save myself. Bracing myself back against his chest, I pushed as hard as I could against his forearm, lifting the tip of the knife momentarily from my throat—just an inch, but hopefully it would be enough. With my forearm, I reached back and did my best to make contact with my fire rune.

The sound of his skin sizzling like bacon on a grill made him jump and I took the opportunity to hook my leg around him and we both fell. As we did, the heat traveled up my neck and into my collarbone where the edge of his knife had pressed.

Kicking free of him, I scurried back like a crab and readied myself to fight back.

"Easy, *chère*," Demas muttered in my ear as he grabbed me from behind. "I've got you."

Bodhi had drawn his blade and was slashing with vicious, brutal accuracy at Ashe, who gave way down the corridor and parried as well as he could with his knife.

"Wait!" Ashe backed down the hallway cursing. "Let me explain."

Colten lunged so fast he turned into a blur. He began

punching the traitor. I'd never seen such violence, but everyone just stood back and let it happen. "You're going to pay, you rat!" Colten huffed between punches. "You told Melinoe about the psychopomp? About us at the club? Innocent people died."

"Let's put down the weapons and talk." Ashe exclaimed, through a blood-filled mouth. "I can help get us out of this. There's a secret tunnel. I saw it on the floor plan."

"What floor plan?"

"This one. How do you think I knew about that bookshelf?"

I glanced over only now realizing that was how Ashe had come from behind. One of the bookshelves opened.

Pressing relentlessly forward, Colten lunged again and pierced Ashe high in one shoulder. "Liar! You're just trying to lure us into a trap. You should have run away with your tail tucked between your legs."

"I tried to go." He spat blood to the side and winced.

"Oh, you mean after you fucked us... when you went to drop the truck off. Demas ruined your little plan, didn't he? I guess we weren't completely oblivious."

Ashe reeled back, then in a twist, advanced to slash at Colten's abdomen. With a ninja-like stealth, Colten leaped back, and the attempted blow went wide.

"You fed the enemy information so you could deliver

us to him."

Zephyr's fangs grew longer and sharper than I'd ever seen them and his eyes glowed with madness.

The nearest window exploded in a fit of pique. I could tell you one thing, Gran' was not happy.

Down the corridor, the other men had appeared. They encircled the traitor forcing him down the stairs. They walked forward, staring, their expressions stricken and shocked: Bodhi, Colten, Zephyr, Eleutian, Zagan, Ryder, Jude, Van Rogue. Even Demas joined in. The pain and rage emanating from every one of the men was so raw and palpable I could hardly bear it.

I covered my head with a hand, but I still heard the body as it fell to the floor with an audible thump. Fresh tears snaked down my cheeks.

Grimm stood over me in his human form, hands shoved into his pockets. "Why are you crying, Evie? You don't care about that asshole, do you?"

I shook my head, "Hell no," I uttered, catching the smell of something strange—foreign magic. Then I remembered what I'd discovered before Ashe had tried to kill me. The kitchen! Goose bumps prickled on my skin and Gran's consciousness stirred and she appeared beside Grimm. She reached out a hand, and enveloped my wrist in magic before tugging me to my feet. She then led me across the kitchen and slapped her hand on the wall. Strange vibrations ran all through me.

"Is it Mama?" I asked Gran's ghost. Is she in there?"

She shook her head no, and as if that small effort had been too much, she winked out and left us alone again.

Magic lingered around the door, pulling me closer. The magic rippled off the wall in waves, skimming over my skin. Frowning, I concentrated. Was she trying to tell me that the massive broken piece in magic was behind this wall? This close, it felt bigger than ever.

For the first time, I focused on the wall. Part of it was wooden. I ran my fingers along one side while I studied the square. There were hinges like the passage beside the fireplace. Or was this a broom closet?

It called to me now, sucking me in like the gravitational pull of a black hole. As I pulled open the door, it let out a loud creaking noise that echoed off a high, peaked ceiling. Empty. What the hell? I could still smell the magic and see the lingering glow.

Another boom sounded from outside.

"He's throwing fireballs," Zephyr shouted.

Colten shot to his feet and Bodhi's face tightened.

Honestly. Such an attention seeker. "Ignore him," I said, and patted the closet. "We need to go in here."

Demas and Zagan shouldered their way in. Opening

the door, Demas said, "Evie, this is just a broom closet. There's nothing in it but cleaning supplies."

I twisted to look at Grimm, who now stood at my elbow.

I had never seen him look so serious.

"She's right. There's something in there," he said. "I'm going in."

He stepped inside and when he did the floor pushed down and he disappeared.

"Grimm!" I flung myself forward, hand outstretched, but I was too late to stop him.

Zagan rubbed his face and swore. Bodhi said, "Get one of the lanterns."

The group had two lanterns with them. Ryder lit one of them, tore the edge of his T-shirt into a strip to tie around the handle, and passed it forward. Accepting it, Bodhi lowered it into the blackness.

As he did, Grimm flew out in the form of a bat this time and the floor rocketed back into place.

"Holy fuck!" Colten swore. "You just took ten years off my life, asshole."

Grimm shifted back to his human form, laughing as he did. "Did I? You'd make an ugly old man, anyway."

"Screw you!" Colten gave the demon a playful shove.

"Well?" Bodhi asked.

"It's a crawlspace hidden by a false floor that operates using weight." Grimm replied.

"Very clever," Demas said, coming into the room with a giant length of rope on his shoulder.

"Aww, were you about to come rescue me?" Grimm dusted off his shoulder. "I couldn't see it, but it feels like there's a massive piece down there."

"I need to go down to confirm that we've found it," I said, elbowing my way in.

Bodhi knelt beside me. Then his eyes blazed, and he grabbed hold of me with tense care. "Goddamn it, Evangeline! Can't you feel the blood?"

"Huh?" My gaze followed the direction of his, down to my shirtfront. "Why are you always overreacting?" *Okay, so maybe he had a point. That looked pretty bad.* Blood had soaked into my sweater, and it had run down my side.

"Let me see," Eleutian said, coming to kneel by me. His touch was much more gentle than Bodhi's tone, as he eased the collar of my sweater aside so he could inspect the wound. He pressed lightly against my skin near the long cut.

"Ouch! Stop that!" I tried to shrink away from him.

"Dammit," Bodhi growled. "Cooperate, please, for once in your life, Evangeline."

I squirmed to glare at him.

"Hold still, darlin!" Eleutian eased out. Something

about the way he said that told me he was barely holding on to his self-control, and that said a lot, considering the man could charm honey from a bee. I forced myself to sit still, although I couldn't help bitching about it.

Setting my hand gently to the side of Eleutian's furious, dangerous face, I said in a soft voice, "It happened when I burned him, but I wasn't gonna wait around for rescue."

"And why the hell not, Midnight?" Colten exclaimed.

"Because Coach Ryu, you taught me to fight, remember? If you want me to be some sort of princess sitting in a tower braiding my hair, don't train me to kick the shit out of people."

Colten tilted his head, "Fair enough."

"Hush now." Eleutian placed the flat of his palm over my injury, gathered his power, and spoke in witch tongue. Vibrations tickled the area, and I could feel the wound weaving together. It was a slightly itchy feeling, but one I was totally willing to endure for the healing.

When he'd finished, he kissed my hand and whispered, "Good as new, my sweets." The sensation of his skin pressed against mine lingered. They were all so different but I loved each one of them so much it twisted me up inside. Stroking his lips with my thumb, I leaned my forehead against his. "You are a true gentleman, Eleutian, thank you.

Now if you're all through babying me. I need to go down there."

Bodhi looked conflicted but Demas nodded his agreement.

"I'll go with her," Grimm offered.

"Just get the floor out of the way and we'll lower her down enough to see." Bodhi instructed.

Grimm stepped inside and disappeared once again.

They tied the rope around me and as promised they slowly lowered me into the cave like area.

The light touched rough-hewn rock along the sides and what looked like it might be the bottom. I leaned farther to get a better look. At the very edge of the light, I caught sight of Grimm. He'd placed a boulder on the moveable floor and he now appeared to be exploring.

"Do you see it yet, Evangeline?" Bodhi called.

I shouted back, "Yes, it's massive."

They pulled me back up and Demas took me aside, handing me the floor plan, "Can you align the magic so the portal opens back up, Evangeline?"

I nodded. "Now that I've found all the spots, I can picture in my mind which way I need to twist the house. The thing is I'm going to need a lot more power to do it. It's going to take all of my strength and maybe even some help from you and Eleutian." I turned to the other man, "You'll both need to act as my batteries. I'll have to drain your power to recharge my own. Which means, I'll need to tattoo the three of us but the answer is yes, I'm sure together we can do it."

Bodhi smiled, "That's great news but we're not in the clear yet. Now that we know where the passage is, we need to capture Melinoe to take him back through. And in order to capture him, we need to take out his magic."

"Capture him?" Colten questioned. "Let's just kill him and take his body back."

32

THE FIERY TEMPERED BEAST

"We can't kill him." Eleutian clarified, faint lines appearing in his forehead. "We can't even incapacitate him unless and until we have a plan for those zombies."

What? Why?" Colten scoffed.

"That militia of decayed corpses is tethered to him which means he controls them. If he loses control then they go rabid and spread a virus infecting the human population, not to mention the carnage. Get it?"

"I might be able to help with the zombies," Grimm said. "If you and Evangeline will agree to tap into my magic, we can tether to them and slow them down while the rest of you attack Melinoe. It won't stop the corpses but it will feel as if they're slogging through quicksand to move. And if anything happens to Melinoe, then control will revert to us."

"That sounds good to me." Evangeline agreed. "We also need to find out what he knows about my mom."

Demas nodded, "Of course, Evie. You two work on the tethering. Now, how do we capture him? He's got some sort of magical ward around him. Our bullets just bounce off him."

"Can you bind him?" Evie asked. "Then he won't be able to use his magic."

Eleutian shook his head, "I don't think so. He's not a witch. Besides we don't have what we'd need to do a binding spell."

Evie's eyes widened and she ran away.

"Where are you going?"

"To get the book I was reading on defensive magic," she shouted back. A moment later she returned, licking and thumbing through the pages.

"Here it is. What about muting his magic long enough to get a bullet through?"

"With what?" Demas asked, taking the book from her hands. "It's not like you can tattoo the bullets." He took a minute to read over the page then cleared his throat. "I can see what you're thinking Evie. How much of that nail polish do you have?" Demas asked.

Evangeline turned away from her conversation with Grimm, "Not enough to spell all their bullets."

"That's okay. We don't need to spell them all. We just need one to hit him. Bodhi, can you get to him?"

Bodhi closed his eyes and attempted to release his scales. His wings were much too large to release inside but if he could form armor then he'd know he could shift.

A bead of sweat formed but that was it.

"Sorry. Melinoe's got me on some sort of magical lockdown. You?"

Demas shook his head.

"Alright then, choose your best sharpshooters, and Evangeline and I will see what we can come up with." Demas ordered.

While Bodhi located the bullets, Evangeline retrieved her nail polish. "Demas? What's your plan?"

Demas shouldered through to her. "We'll need to use our blood?"

"Our blood."

"Yes. Use Eleutian's too. Mix it with the polish so that it will go further. This doesn't have to be pretty. Then dip the tips of the bullets in the mage blood and polish solution, and cast the spell."

Nodding, Bodhi strode to Demas and Evangeline, where they bent over a knife set on the dining table. Another low rumble started. This time it rose and rose, and a sharp crack sounded overhead. Immediately Bodhi lunged forward to cover Evangeline's head and shoulders with his, while the other men swore and crowded as close as they could to the walls.

For a long moment everyone in the manor held still as they waited, but nothing fell. Then Evangeline said in a cranky, muffled voice from underneath Bodhi, "We'll get you ten spelled bullets as soon as you get off me."

With a growl, he expelled a sharp breath and rubbed his face in her hair.

Crazy. She made him crazy. Somehow in spite of that, he was more in love with her than ever.

Straightening, he said to everybody, "Get back to work."

Activity resumed. Eleutian made a slice to his palm, "This old place can't take much more." He added his blood to the bowl and within five minutes they had spelled and handed over two fistfuls of bullets.

"These are only to be used on Melinoe," Bodhi said as he gave the sharpshooters the strongest ones—two bullets each. "This is your only job."

"Understood," Jude and Colten both said, their expressions direct and clear.

As Evangeline joined them, Bodhi said, "Melinoe doesn't know we've located a portal."

They headed for the grand doors. Demas said to the men, "Get ready."

The men drew their guns and readied their knives, then silence fell.

When Bodhi, Demas, and Evangeline reached the front stoop, Eleutian cast a massive cloaking spell over them and the other two sharpshooters who took their places behind them. Then Bodhi fixed Evangeline with a stern look. "You'll do your part but you'll stay back."

She widened her eyes. "Oh, believe me, I'm more than happy to."

They pulled open the doors. Melinoe lifted his head, "Well, well, well, Evangeline Midnight? And so we meet again."

"And so we do, and might I suggest you be a gentleman and take your leave now," Evangeline said. She stepped to one side.

Bodhi whispered, "Now."

Three bullets flew through the air. Melinoe dodged, moving so fast he turned into a blur. Most of the bullets missed.

One didn't.

It struck him in the arm. The zombies to either side of Melinoe broke into a run, hurtling toward the house.

Evangeline, Eleutian and Grimm recited the words Grimm had taught them and the three of them focused on tethering to the dead.

Even as Melinoe reeled back, he flung his hand out in the direction of the open doors. Nothing happened. Behind Bodhi came the distinctive sound of the sharpshooters readying themselves. Raising his hand, he kept his eyes trained on Melinoe and the approaching zombies.

Melinoe took a knife and dug the bullet out of his arm. Bodhi gave the sign and the sharpshooters released their bullets, and he blurred again as he dodged. Another bullet hit, this time in his side. He stumbled and fell to his knees.

Bodhi dropped his hand and roared, "Go! Go! Go!"

The remaining men sprinted out the open doors and collided with zombies. Bodhi drew his favorite blade and lunged onto the field eagerly, looking to finish Melinoe off.

33

MIDNIGHT WITCH

The map of the mansion's floorplan stared back at me from the top of the granite surface, taunting me. Circles of highlighter signifying the magical bits dotted it. I leaned back against the counter, studying it. There was no rhyme or reason as to where the magical bits lay. I turned and looked out the window to the fighting outside—Monster Squad versus the monsters. Things had wound down now. Part of me, a very, very small part—was tempted to run outside and join in the fight. But the reality of the situation was that I was exhausted from tethering the walking dead, and more likely to be captured and turned into a brainless lemming at this point. Not that I'd admit any of that to anyone.

No, if I were going to help out, I was going to have to play to my strengths. So, I scooped up the map to inspect it once again for patterns. I took a pen and tried to connect the dots. I was missing something. There had to be a way to heal this house and its magic. Dejected, I folded it up and stuffed it into the back pocket of my jeans.

First things first, I'd need supplies—a light to cast by,

a pen to cast with and a way down to the portal. I headed for the living room, keeping an eye out for Grimm. He could help me down by transforming. A quick search of the main floor did not uncover his whereabouts—sneaky little demon—luckily, a Coleman camping lantern in the parlor caught my eye. And beside it was one giant ass length of rope.

Tying the rope off to the faucet in the kitchen—it was the best I could do—I entered the secret broom closet and lowered myself down like some sort of Indian Jane, into the magical cavern below. It was terrifying and yet freeing to do something all on my own. The boys had really been coddling me. The basement level was cold and damp which was strange for Louisiana but it was like this house was in another realm—or stuck between. So, I switched on the lantern and unfolded the map, once again inspecting it. Suddenly an idea struck me. I folded the map into this weird origami configuration making all of the pieces align. Then I pulled out my pen and sketched a healing sigil that covered the whole thing.

"Okay, here goes nothing," I said, aloud.

I carried the paper and placed it over the portal closed my eyes and waited for the healing to take place. Usually I felt the magic work. Hmm. I opened my eyes. Nothing was happening. I took the pen and tried sketching the healing rune on my own skin then I placed my hand once again over the portal. Seconds later, peeking one eye open first, and then the other, I saw that the magic still lay dormant. Well, that was anti-climactic. Perhaps, I needed to build my strength back up.

I climbed back out of the hole and watched from the doorway, waiting for the last of the zombies to die a horrible, awful death, again. The gunfire had mostly ceased and at last I saw Eleutian and Colten in the distance. I almost ran for them. Two seconds later, a fierce and magnificent looking Demas strode across the clearing—bloodied knives in hand or were those his nails. They seem to retract. Still no sign of Bodhi—no sign of Melinoe, either for that matter.

Bodies littered the area as far as I could see. The nearby clumps of forest had been all but leveled. After some time, Ryder walked out of the swamp. But I still couldn't see Bodhi.

Then something made me look up. A dark shadow circling over me. It had to be him—it was Bodhi, but he had large black leathery wings that spanned at least twenty-four feet. He landed next to the other men and the ground shook.

They looked in my direction and strode across the field to me. Bodhi's skin changed as he neared. They were all streaked in blood.

My hands clenched and I managed to ask without a quaver in my voice, "Is anyone hurt?"

"It's not our blood."

Relief made me lightheaded. I looked at Bodhi. "What was that? Are you a dragon?"

"A dragon shifter," he corrected me.

"Wh-why am I just seeing this now? Why the hell didn't you do that in the bar that night when the zombies first attacked us? Or earlier on the field."

Bodhi looks to Demas out of the corner of his eye.

"What are you looking at him for? Answer me!"

"Well, there were a couple of reasons. For one thing, that bar was small and I don't know if you noticed but I sort of need wide open spaces. Secondly, I don't technically have permission to shift right now."

"Permission from who?"

"The council. We're trying not to freak out the general public."

"I see. And Melinoe? Why not earlier when we were attacked or trying to kill him?

"He had somehow bound my shifting abilities, but when you and Eleutian muted his magic—great job by the way—it freed me."

"Good. So, did you get him? Where's my mom?"

"Sorry, Evie. He disappeared." Demas shook his head grimly. "We don't know how he did it. He must have had help from a demon. I'll have a couple of the men check the house over, and you can go to bed in one of the upstairs bedrooms."

"No thanks. I need a break from playing at this real-life night of the living dead. I'll go home to Julep and Grand-mere for a bit if that's all right."

At that, Bodhi turned his full attention onto me. "No, that's not all right. You need to stay right here where we can keep an eye on you. Did you not just hear us say that Melinoe got away."

I let an angry laugh slip. Was there any point in discussing this? I'd been held at knifepoint under his watch but it was like arguing with a dictator. Instead, I nodded, "Sure, Bodhi. Whatever you say."

"Are you being sarcastic?" he snapped. "We don't have time for this. The council's here. They want to see the portal." As he spoke, someone called out from the direction of the house, and he raised a hand in answer.

"I'm not arguing with you," I told him. I took a step back. "Go do what you need to do."

He frowned at me. "We'll talk about this later. Don't go to Julep's!"

I gave him a grim smile. "If you say so."

I watched him stalk back across the lawn with Demas. After a few moments, they both walked around to the back of the house.

No sooner did they disappear then I headed for the garage where we'd stashed my car. The Chevelle's engine purred to life. Screw him and his authoritarian attitude. Gah! I can't believe he's a dragon. That explained so much. Carefully, I drove between the gate pillars and pulled onto the road. I didn't slow down until I reached the French Quarter, checked into a hotel, and texted Julep the address along with a message: Will gossip for food.

Technically, it wasn't Julep's house so I wasn't outright disobeying Captain Bossypants' orders. *Smirk.*

I'd barely made it out of the shower and pulled on my yoga pants and t-shirt before I passed out on the bed. I was plum tuckered out. Next thing I knew there was shouting, a roar of zombies gnashing their teeth, and the ricochet of guns.

I plunged awake in a panic. A cold sweat settled at the base of my hairline. Disoriented, staring around the strange bedroom, I listened hard for any sound of battle, but there was none.

Dragging myself off the bed, I glanced out the window. It appeared I had slept quite a while. Then I thought about Mama. I hadn't realized how much I was hanging on this battle. I thought if we'd won then I'd get my mother back. Suddenly, tears poured down my cheeks. *Hormones… who needs 'em?* I grabbed a Kleenex—okay I grabbed five…

maybe seven and cried myself silly. Then I started the self-pep-talk. I'll get some food. I'll pull it together. Food and a hug from Julep, and we'll make a plan. It's not over—we're going to find her.

Speak of the devil, I'd no sooner thought of Julep than she'd texted that she was at my door. We sat for the next hour, eating delicious ginger snaps and chocolate peanut butter balls, and catching up, until I remembered that I should probably call Aunt Aurora. There'd be hell to pay when everyone noticed I was gone.

I used the suite phone to call while Julep used her cell to make us dinner reservations.

A knock on the door interrupted me before I could dial, and Julep and I exchanged wary glances.

"Sit tight," I told her. The door swung open under my fingers, and Ludovic smiled. "Hello, beautiful. You left in such a hurry the other day. I didn't get a chance to give you this." A white card with my name scrolled across it was clutched in his hand.

Despite his friendly tone, there was something intimidating about the way he was looking at me. He reminded me of someone who was being tempted by a succulent-looking steak, and I was in no mood to be lunch.

"That's my mother's handwriting," I said, reaching for it.

"Is it now?" His fingers wrapped themselves around my wrist like a snake coiling about its dinner and before I could pull away, he used the sharp edge of the card to slice my finger—a papercut. As soon as the bead of red welled, his fangs popped out.

"*Owww.*" I started to pull away but it was too late, my blood had released his pheromones.

A fever spread throughout my body beginning with my arm, running through my chest, past my jaw, until stars danced across my field of vision. Heat pulsed and throbbed low in my nether regions, and I smiled at him, tipsy, as the envelope landed on the hallway carpet.

Before I knew it, I was falling at his feet—quite literally. The thought momentarily occurred to me that he could be in league with the necromancer but then I realized how silly that was. Afterall, I was in love with this man. I wanted every inch of him. I'd follow him anywhere.

"Evangeline," Julep cried out from behind me. "Don't—"

"This should have happened long ago," the male guard sighed, his voice husky and deep.

His voice sounded so familiar… I angled my head for a peek at his face, but Ludovic cupped my jaw and turned me back to him. Try as I might, I couldn't look away.

"Come now, William, trust is important in a

marriage." His thumb kneaded my breast. "I wanted a willing partner."

William…I knew that name.

Thanks for reading **Book One**. Keep reading **Book Two** to find out what becomes of Evangeline and her Monster Trackers.

1

THE MIDNIGHT WITCH

I woke with the distinct notion that something bad had happened—you know the one? It's a prickling sensation that starts at the scalp and moves quickly to the chest, gripping your heart like a blood pressure cuff.

"Hello? My voice cracked and the sound echoed back to me hauntingly. "Anyone?"

My head throbbed and I closed my eyes, trying desperately to picture the dragon shifter and the howling wolf who'd just been comforting me in my dreams. I could barely feel their warmth now. It was slipping—being replaced by the hammering effect of fear.

"Anyone?" I called out again in a slightly stronger voice. "Julep?"

The room swam into slow focus around me—it was wallpapered. This was not the Delphine's dark wooden furniture. Shimmering metallic and red accents. A hard lump formed in my throat.

Where was I? I rubbed my pounding forehead in confusion and winced. It felt like I'd been beaned with a soft ball. Perhaps some old bruising from when Asher had hit me. It took a few stretched-out seconds for me to remember it all. Then my stomach plummeted. Asher! The traitor! The battle! Instantly, I returned to the events of earlier today, or yesterday – or however much time had passed and I'd been unconscious. Showering in the hotel, hugging Julep, answering the door, and then nothing.

Fucking hell! Bodhi was never going to let me live this down. What was I thinking going off on my own?

Groaning to myself in despair, I climbed from beneath the blankets. I was sure I'd seen a vampire before my world had gone dark, Lézare Ludovic.

"I'm awake, you blood sucking bastard! You may as well come out!" I screamed.

***

THE PROFESSOR

Demas Batavian walked to the bar cart and poured himself a glass of whisky. He rubbed his shoulders as the chill from the manor's ghost permeated his bones. A huge difference from the sultry heat that lingered outside. Not that Demas couldn't hack the cold, he'd lived in Ohio as a pup and moved to Chicago and New York from there. It was just that, the chill combined with Evangeline's disappearance had him on edge. He slugged back the whisky and watched Baudoin Remoussin enter. The tall, dark dragon warrior had already retracted his black leathery wings but his skin still shimmered with the outline of dragon scales.

"Well?"

"No sign of her, Sir," Bodhi answered.

"Damn it! Try her cell again." Demas was doing his best to remain calm, but his words came out like the crack of a whip. He was just so frustrated, they all were.

The Midnight Plantation was in shambles. The showdown against the necromancer had left the grounds a mess. It was going to take a hell of a lot of magic to heal it. Worst of all was Evangeline Midnight's absence.

Demas' heart hurt at the reminder.

"Her phone must be dead," Bodhi swore, slamming his fist against the door. "Where the hell could she be?"

Demas paced the room noting the look of worry on Zephyr's face. He rubbed his eyes assuming they'd turned yellow as they did when he went into wolf mode.

The young vamp was doing his best to keep busy, sweeping up shards of broken glass. Demas had rescued Zephyr from one of Chicago's downtown hives many, many moons ago. The young man who was just a boy at the time had moved in with Demas and his step-mother, Aurora Batavian and because of that, they shared a special bond. But Zephyr wasn't used to seeing Demas in a state of chaos. As a member of the Supernatural Council, Demas made a point of controlling his inner wolf... losing Evie tripped a nerve. It was like a live wire in his body and it reminded him of losing his real mother who'd died in childbirth when he was young.

He glanced out the window, noting the room was growing darker. Several dark clouds had covered the sun.

"I hear something!" Zephyr breathed suddenly, his dark eyes piercing under the shock of black hair. "Can anyone else hear her?" he asked on a rising note.

"I don't hear anything," Bodhi said tensely. "It must be a vamp thing. Is she on the property?"

Zephyr deflated and shook his head. "No. I've searched every inch three times over. I can't make out what she's saying. I just know she needs us."

Demas stood frozen in front of the parlor's fireplace staring at both men as if he'd lost his senses. Maybe he had—he heard something too but it wasn't Evangeline. His hell hound was calling to him via their connection. The beast was on his way back from its search mission and Demas could feel that the news wasn't good—although he had no details.

"Damn it!" The usually cool-headed professor let out his breath in a rush. His voice was raspy and thin and the men looked up at him in alarm. "Damn it all to hell! I bet it was a trick. Melinoe duped us into a false sense of safety. We annihilated his undead army and he let us think we'd won. But he never cared about this battle"—he waved around the grounds— "he came for Evangeline."

He took a seat and closed his eyes, attempting to get details from Vengeance.

Entering the parlor, Colten Ryu, their-tough-as-nails-gargoyle, stumbled through the doorway attempting to hold up the barely conscious mage. Zephyr lunged forward with his lightning-fast reflexes and helped to ease Eleutian Dupre III down onto a bedroll. Demas had liked both Colten and Lou—as they called Eleutian—the moment he'd met them. They were both hardworking and honest, two qualities Demas respected most. They always gave everything they had and clearly this time had been no different. From the looks of it, the battle against the necromancer and his zombified werewolves had drained Lou of his energy. Magical warfare was like that.

Colten straightened and looked to Demas. "What are you talking about, Sir?"

"Evangeline's in trouble. We think the necromancer may have lured her away under a false sense of security. This was all an elaborate setup."

"Evie would never be so stupid," Bodhi said. His eyes widened before he could even finish the thought. "Oh, for fuck' sake... she did mention going to the Delphine's." He paused to throw something. "I was busy with Councilman Badeaux and the rest of the Supernatural council, and Demas, you were with Mayor Perry. We were all busy... that damn hard-headed girl. I vehemently told her no!"

"Well, there's the problem right there." Zagan, one of Van Rogue's men from the back-up unit joked as he walked into the room. The men turned to glare, and Colten gave him a hard shove. "You think you're funny, asshole?" Usually they all loved a good laugh but the idea of Evie missing hit them more on the funny bone—as in there was nothing funny about it.

"Sorry." Zagan said, putting his hands up in the air. "Geeze. I was just trying to lighten the mood." The back-up unit that Zagan belonged to had betrayed them during the battle. As far as they knew, Zagan was clean but he and the rest of his team were on a short leash at the moment.

"Please go outside, Zagan. This is a team matter," Demas barked.

Zagan nodded and left the room.

"How can you be so sure it was a set up," Zephyr asked glancing sideways at Bodhi who was currently ripping the place apart in anger. Punching and kicking anything that stood in his way.

"Vengeance," Colten replied as he flicked his eyes to the window where they could see the dog racing toward the manor.

Zephyr rubbed his eyes and nodded wearily. "Where did he take her?"

"I don't know yet. He was too far away to fully connect," Demas choked out. "Wake Lou. I'll need his help to track her."

Zephyr's shoulders drooped. "But he's barely conscious."

Demas looked to Bodhi who finally stopped smashing things and shook his head. He now leaned against the wall, his eyes half closed. Demas could tell from his posture that guilt wracked the man.

"There's nothing more you could have done, boss," Zephyr said to Bodhi, attempting to assuage the situation. "Evie's a headstrong girl."

"I should have fucking chained her to the bed," Bodhi uttered the words, as if they were poisonous, burning as they released.

"She wasn't a prisoner, Baudoin. You couldn't have stopped her. Now, pull it together," Demas scolded. "We need to focus and you're the unit's leader. Is Grimm still here?"

Zephyr planted his hands on the worktable. "Yeah, I saw him near the portal a few minutes ago." He turned toward the door. "I'll go look for him."

"I'll come." Colten picked his way around the bedrolls and joined him.

Demas connected with Vengeance and his mind was filled with images. They had annihilated the zombies, but they had never even considered that the vampires might be involved. He could see from the hound's memory that it was Ludovic and Van Rogue who took her, but he was still no closer to finding her. He wanted to punch the shit out of something, to give in to the hysteria of the night like Bodhi did, but someone had to remain calm. Besides, he found himself too numb with exhaustion to punch walls. And to rush Ludovic's home would only mean certain death. They would be expecting that, and Melinoe was clearly an expert at laying traps.

"Fucking Van Rogue, how many other traitors do we have amongst us?"

"Bodhi, leave Eleutian with me and Grimm and take the rest of the team to do reconnaissance on Ludovic's house. We need to know if she's there. And for fuck's sake, don't you dare charge in. You know it's a trap and we need to be strategic."

Bodhi nodded and they stepped outside. "What are you gonna do?"

"I'm going to call Aurora."

"Your mother?"

"Step-mother, yes. I'll need to meet with the Supernatural Council. See if they can find out what this Lézare Ludovic has to do with Melinoe. If she's not at Ludovic's place then we'll need to figure out where they've taken her and why. Which is why I need Grimm—it's time he started talking and if I need to force it out of him then so be it. I'm done playing nice."

Bodhi growled. "I'd love to be there for that, but I'll see to Ludovic, Sir." He turned and walked back inside, leaving Demas alone outside to stew.

"Professor Batavian," said a woman's voice.

His heart heaved as a figure emerged from the shadows of the willow tree. For a moment he thought maybe it was Evangeline, but it was her mother's best friend, Julep striding toward him. He tugged Vengeance tightly to him and absorbed the dog into his tattoo. He knew from Evie that her guardian was a witch, but still Vengeance was a mind fuck and he preferred not to spook her.

"I know what happened." She called out. Then she lost it. She launched herself at him and pounded on his chest. "I wish I didn't, but I do, and you must get her back!"

Demas wrestled her off. She didn't resist. Somewhere in her pummeling, she had started to cry.

"Calm down," he said. "Miss Delphine. Please calm down. Or you'll have the whole bloody unit out here." He pushed her down onto a fallen tree and sat beside her.

"How can I?" she whimpered. "How can I be calm when sweet, sweet Evangeline has been taken and her mother is still missing—this whole thing is a mess… it's all my fault. I should have told her about Melinoe." She laid her face in her hands and sobbed.

Demas yanked her hands from her face and made her meet his gaze. "What do you mean you should have told her? What about Melinoe?"

"He's her father. The necromancer is her father."

"How do you know that?"

"Because I just do! Now let me go!" she wrenched free of his grasp. Demas reached for her, but she stepped away.

The muscles in his jaw twitched. "What you're saying makes no sense. Melinoe lived in the underworld. I know because we were the guards, he slipped by. Now explain."

She wiped at her eyelashes and damp cheeks. "Wh-where are the other men?"

"Around," Demas said. "Don't worry. You're safe. Even if you don't see them, they're lurking nearby."

She laughed, a breathy sound. "I'm not worried, but you need to go after her right now. You need to save her."

"Are you sure Melinoe is her father and if so, would he hurt his own daughter?"

"Absolutely," she snapped. "He went crazy with power. He just kept delving deeper and deeper into the magic until he was no longer human. Briar was nine months pregnant with Evangeline when Melinoe died—killed at last by a demon he'd attempted to summon and control using the Grand Grimoire."

"The Grand Grimoire, you mean the Red..."

"...Dragon. Yes."

"My mother and I found Briar, bent over his lifeless body. She was attempting to use blood magic to bring him back but the pregnancy had muted her powers. She was hysterical. My mother even felt her attempting to access the baby's powers but he'd been dead for too long and we made her stop."

Demas stared, suddenly tongue-tied. All this time... Melinoe was Evangeline's father. She really was the connection. And she was part-necromancer, no wonder she'd been able to revive Zephyr and Bodhi. With one hand he patted Julep's hand. "My familiar tells me she was taken by the vampire known as Lézare Ludovic. We'll need to uncover the connection. Do you know what that could be?"

She nodded though she seemed to be somewhere else. "Briar was never the same." She mumbled, "my girls...Briar and now Evangeline.... oh, I'll never see them again." She hefted up her skirts and turned to go, but Demas clasped her arm and whipped her around.

"Where are you going?" he cocked his head and gestured to the manor. "Come inside and help us plan. You know Melinoe in ways that we don't. We won't give up. We'll find a way to get your girls back. We'll find a way to get our Evangeline back."

Check out *Book Two* to find out what becomes of Evangeline and her Monster Trackers.

Interested in more RH books by Rae?

Check out Nancie Dru and her Harem of Scarem in the Haunted House Rehab series.

There's nothing I enjoy more than making magic in the bedroom but taking on this 'hotel of horrors' is driving me crazy. Quite literally, I'm having the strangest flashbacks of kidnappings and asylums. Are the ghostly girls of Wolfeboro trying to tell me something or am I losing my mind?

Do you also enjoy historical romance? Give my new time travel romance series a whirl: Bewitched in Time. It's the first book in a four-part series called Spelled Portals & Cursed Mortals.

AUTHORS NOTE:

Well, hello there! Thank you for reading my debut reverse harem novel! No dead bodies were raised in the writing of this book, although my browsers history is now sufficiently questionable. Many enormous liberties were taken with spells, landmarks and symbolism, making this book a hardcore fiction of the quirky, fun kind. Absolve me and I'll do it again for the second book in the series.

As per usual, a big thanks to my family, friends, reviewers and fans for their generosity and encouragement. Thanks to my awesome editor, Susan Croft. My beta readers, and of course, a big shout-out to my ARC readers, of which there are too many to name. If you find an error, feel free to drop me a line. No matter how many times we go over things, errors do slip through. Once again, thank you for reading my books.

If you want more, please be sure to review them on Amazon, Goodreads and BookBub.

Cheers!

Rae

Printed in Great Britain
by Amazon